THE
SILENCE
BEFORE
DAWN

AMANDA LEES

THE
SILENCE
BEFORE
DAWN

Bookouture

Published by Bookouture in 2022

An imprint of Storyfire Ltd.
Carmelite House
50 Victoria Embankment
London EC4Y 0DZ

www.bookouture.com

ISBN: 978-1-80314-687-4
eBook ISBN: 978-1-80314-686-7

This book is a work of fiction. Whilst some characters and circumstances portrayed by the author are based on real people and historical fact, references to real people, events, establishments, organizations or locales are intended only to provide a sense of authenticity and are used fictitiously. All other characters and all incidents and dialogue are drawn from the author's imagination and are not to be construed as real.

For John, who read it first.

PROLOGUE

Black. White. Black. White. Like a giant blinking eye, the searchlight swept the prison camp on the hour, bathing the watchtower in its dazzling glare. Watchtower 7. Still empty.

Jack counted round one more time. All the others were manned, the guards in their turrets just visible, the moon a mere sliver of a crescent that cast little light. It was a deliberate choice, to go on the new moon. And tonight was perfect, with a low cloud cover that provided a safety blanket. Perfect except for one thing. No signal. Looked like the bastard had pocketed their bribe and scarpered.

Soon the moon would set as the sun rose in the sky, taking with it their chance of escape. Jack glanced at his watch – 3.10 a.m. They had about an hour. He could feel the impatience rising all around him from the other men.

'I say we go now,' muttered one.

'Don't be a fool,' snapped Jack.

He fingered the key they had painstakingly fashioned from smuggled parts, going over the plan again in his head. Three hundred paces to the first fence. They had counted, over and over again as they played boules in its shadow, identifying the blind spot nearest Watchtower 7. One minute to cut it. Two to scramble under it and through the barbed wire to the outer perimeter. Another minute to jump the wall and make a break for it. All of it meticulously planned down to the last detail. Except for this.

'There.' Guy nudged him, pointing through the hut window.

Jack stared at the watchtower again. Guy must be mistaken. Still nothing. Then he saw it, the faint orange glow of a cigarette, glowing brighter now as someone took a drag on it. Their guard. He was there. Giving them the signal at last. He wanted to punch the air. Stopped himself. Took a breath, feeling his heart start to gallop.

'We're on.'

He inserted the key in the lock and turned it. Felt it stick. Tried again. No luck. Cursing under his breath, he jiggled it, exhaling as the lock finally clicked and the door swung open.

Jack stepped out first and swept the yard with his stare. All clear. He beckoned to his men to follow. 'With me.'

As one they sprinted for the fence, feet pounding against the dirt, arms thrusting them on. Jack fumbled for the wire cutters, snipping once, twice, tearing at the barbed wire, wrenching it back so the first man could crawl under and through.

'Come on – come on, lads,' he hissed.

Four more to go, including him and Guy.

The first man was already at the perimeter wall. Another one through. No. He was caught, the wire snagging his jacket. Jack reached forward, tearing it from his shoulders, tossing it after him once he was free.

He gestured to Guy. 'Go on.'

He saw him hesitate, gave him a shove in the small of his back. Then it was his turn, dropping to his belly to crawl under the wire as it pinged back, grabbing at him, Guy hauling him to his feet, hearing his own jacket ripping, reaching for the perimeter wall, scrabbling to get purchase.

A yell from behind. More shouts. Then the sound he'd dreaded – the death rattle of machine guns. They'd been spotted.

The first man fell without a sound, toppling backward just as he crested the wall, dead before he hit the ground. Bullets ricocheted off brick as the rest of them scrambled to get over, picked out now by the searchlight as the high-pitched wail of the alarm filled their ears.

Jack reached for the top of the wall, every muscle screaming as loud as that siren. Almost there. Legs kicking, hands clawing. A howl of agony bursting from his lips as pain seared through his side.

Through the red mist, he could hear Guy yelling at him to keep going. Then he was there, on top of the wall, one leg hitched over it, then the other, the man beside him letting out a grunt of what sounded like surprise before he, too, fell in a hail of bullets. Nothing for it but to jump, flinging himself into the darkness, hands helping him to his feet once more, the adrenaline coursing through him, heart pumping, legs pumping harder as they ran for their lives towards the trees and the road beyond.

Had to keep going. Had to reach her. *Stay alive, Jack.* It was the last thing she'd said to him. *Stay alive. Come back to me.*

'I'm coming, Marianne. Wait for me. I'm coming.'

A chant in his head, growing louder, drowning out the gunfire behind him. His throat burning, raw as he panted. Body burning too, wet with his own blood.

The trees seemed to be getting further away the more they ran.

He blinked and licked his lips, tasting sweat and more blood. His legs felt like lead, his feet moving through treacle.

'Come on, mate.'

Guy shouldering him, taking his weight, half-dragging him through the trees to the farm truck that waited, engine running, to spirit them to safety. The last thing Jack remembered was the smell of straw, sinking into its soft embrace, staring up at the stars as the engine rumbled beneath his back and his blood soaked into the pale golden strands that pillowed his head.

'Marianne?' he murmured.

But the cool hand that brushed his brow was no more than the dawn breeze stirring. Soon, now, he would see her. He would make it to that rendezvous if it killed him.

It had almost killed him. Almost but not quite. She'd be so angry with him. Furious that he had managed to get shot. He could picture her now, mahogany hair framing her heart-shaped face, incandescent even as her eyes shone, soft with concern. She never could hide her true feelings.

As his blood seeped into the straw, Jack smiled. Marianne. The very beat of his heart. The breath they took as one. And he had kept his promise. He was coming to find his girl.

ONE

The tips of the corn glowed amber, burnished not by the sun but by fire. I could hear the crack of beams breaking, smell the acrid smoke that billowed, a grey plume against the ink of the night sky. The wind that fanned the flames ran through the corn with a ripple and sigh. Or was that a human sound? Someone maybe only feet away, hidden by stalks taller than a man.

'Marianne.'

A whisper so soft I scarcely heard it above the shouts from across the field and the sounds of the farmhouse burning down.

Then a hand on my arm, a spider-soft touch.

I could smell him beside me now – that rancid reek of pork fat he carried with him everywhere.

'Henri. Thank God. Where are the others?'

'Over there.'

'All of them?'

'Yes.'

Another burst of machine-gun fire raking the field, throwing up the dust not twenty metres in front of me. In the brief silence that followed, I could hear more groans and cries. Then a whistling noise followed by a lightning flash that erupted into a roar, a tsunami of flame that rose like a wave, surging towards us.

'Run,' I shouted, but Henri was already on his feet, racing beside me towards the edge of the field, the thick smoke lending us cover.

Another blast and we fell to our knees. I flung my arms over my head, bracing myself for the next one... but it never came. I could feel my heart battering my ribs as I counted the seconds.

I risked a look. The farmhouse was fully ablaze now, an angry red furnace that lit up an otherwise cloudy night sky.

Only twenty minutes ago we had been gathered in there, awaiting our orders. If it hadn't been for Maggie pedalling like fury up the track to warn us, the Germans would have caught us all, trapped like rats in the farmhouse kitchen. It was thanks to her we had just enough time to flee into the relative safety of the cornfield. My last sight of her had been her copper curls flying, bright as those flames that now roared, slender legs pumping as she pedalled back towards the enemy. I could only hope she'd found her hiding place before they'd arrived.

I peered through the pall, trying to make out the forest that edged the western side of the field, its ancient oaks and pine offering dense cover and a route to safety. It was still a hundred or so metres away, too far to make it in one dash.

That was when I saw it, between me and the treeline – the glint of light hitting metal. I froze. There was someone not thirty metres away with a gun. A gun aimed at me.

Slowly, I raised my eyes, trying to make out who was holding it. A German? Surely not.

I blinked. Stared harder. Then watched as a face broke into a familiar smile. A smile that pierced my heart.

'Jack, it's you.'

I had no idea I had spoken aloud.

Jack. Over a year since I'd last seen him. A year of silence save for a snatched message here and there, whispered words and rumours that kept hope alive. And now here he was. I had to get to him. Had to reach him.

'No,' I thought I heard him shout.

Another roar and a wall of dust and dirt filled the air, choking up my throat, obliterating everything. The ground gave way beneath me. I was falling forward once more, dragging myself to my hands and knees, staggering, stumbling towards those trees, head ringing, heart numb.

We were almost there, the branches of the trees reaching out like helping hands. I glanced at Henri – his eyes were ringed with dust and soot, his face streaked with sweat and tears – then looked back over my shoulder, peering with smarting eyes through the smoke. Finally, the guns had fallen silent. The Boches had done what they'd come to do. I could see the farm-yard where the lights of German vehicles blared. Silhouetted against them, three objects were being hoisted from one of the joists that still stood while others crashed to the ground around it. Not objects. People. What looked to be two men and a woman.

I stifled the sob in my throat. So not everyone had escaped. Then the headlights began to turn, arcing until they pointed towards the lane that led back to the village. I stared at the receding tail lights, watching until they were nothing more than pinpricks, smaller than the stars that had started to reappear as the clouds of smoke dissipated.

'They're leaving,' I murmured. 'The Germans. They've gone.'

No doubt they had left men behind to guard their spoils. And they would be back. Which meant this was our best chance.

'Come on,' I said. 'Let's go.'

I stared again at the spot where Jack had been standing. Nothing there save a crater. Please God, let it not be his grave. It was too dangerous to run back. I had to get my men out of here.

I let out a long, low whistle. I could see the corn stalks stirring as the men responded, passing that whistle along. Without waiting another moment, I began to move stealthily towards the forest at a half-crouch, my thighs screaming.

In my head, I could hear a voice screaming too. *No, no, no. I can't leave him.* We needed Jack. But alive or dead, I had to leave him, to lead my men to safety.

As I reached the edge of the forest, I hesitated, half-turned and felt a hand wrap itself around my wrist, pulling me in. Antoine had beaten me to it.

'Where the hell have you been?' I hissed.

He shrugged in a half-hearted apology. 'I got held up.'

'Did you see him? Jack?'

'I saw him with two other men. At the far side of the cornfield. They looked as if they were heading for the road south.'

He was alive. Thank God. Of course he was. And then we were running, crashing through the trees, the drum of feet behind me, too far from the farmhouse now to be heard.

At the other side of the forest, we emerged into a clearing that bordered on neighbouring farmland. In the hollow a few hundred yards distant lay a barn that served as a safe house.

I could hear nothing now save the panting of my men all around me. Damn it to hell. Today's meeting had been vital. We needed the money Jack had brought. More than that, we needed information – dates, times, orders for Operation Dragoon. The final operation. The one that was going to finish this war in France once and for all. But the Germans had got there before him. Someone must have tipped them off. Why else would they descend on a remote farmhouse on this very night?

There was nothing for it but to hole up in the safety of the barn and plan our next move. Or rather, I had to plan it. This was my network. These men were my responsibility. We had to see this through. We were so close now.

I put my hand on the barn door and eased it open. Stopped dead as light seared my eyes. This was no ordinary lamplight. This was a beam directed straight at me, the kind of beam the Gestapo liked to use. I swallowed, not daring to call out, praying that the men behind me would see it and scatter.

Then a torch clattered to the floor and I heard a familiar voice say my name.

'Marianne.'

I blinked, my eyes adjusting to the gloom once more. A tall figure, almost too tall, I often said, emerged from the darkness.

'I nearly shot you.'

I looked at the gun in his hand and then down at the one I held in my own. 'Snap.'

A laugh I had known since I was a small girl rang out.

'Marcus.'

'Marianne.'

'What the hell are you doing here?'

He squeezed my arm. 'Later.'

I heard the warning note.

I beckoned my men to follow me from the doorway where they stood, weapons still raised.

'Gentlemen, this is Marcus. He's one of us.'

And my baby brother, although they didn't need to know that. Other networks had been blown or compromised through carelessness, and revealing true identities was a cardinal error. It helped that we looked absolutely nothing alike.

They dropped their guns and nodded their greetings, bone-weary as they shuffled towards the table where food lay waiting. I let them sit and eat first, the adrenaline still coursing through me, fizzing like a thousand Catherine wheels. First Jack and now Marcus. It was a night for the men I loved. Or rather a new dawn to celebrate being alive once more. To feast on my luck staying with me in spite of everything. To sit and eat with the brother I hadn't seen since the war began and hold in my heart the lover who had stolen away once more into the night.

TWO

A curl of smoke rose from the cigarette Marcus had cupped in his hand, swirling around our heads as we sat, hunched in the lee of the great oak that offered us a place to sit and talk. Above us, the night sky was scattered with a thousand stars, their diamond-bright beauty almost impossible to behold. A canopy of stars and a carpet of forest earth. It was all we had right now, aside from one another. But that was enough.

So many times we had sat like this in the orchard at home, drinking in the peace away from the house and our mother, with her unpredictable moods. It wasn't so much the shouting as the silence that shimmered in the air, daring us to break it. Marcus usually bore the brunt, his careless laughter quickly turning to tears as she unleashed her fury, lashing out with an anger that erupted from a place she would rather forget. Then, while Edward played big brother and calmed her down, I would take Marcus by the hand and tiptoe out to seek comfort from the trees, feeling their sturdy warmth against our backs as we told one another stories or counted the stars until the world felt safe once more.

Tonight, though, the world did not feel safe. A knot of dread was pulling ever tighter in my stomach. I could see Marcus's hand, rigid where he held his cigarette. As stiff as his jaw. He had something to tell me. Something I already knew I didn't want to hear. But I also knew Marcus. I would have to coax it out of him.

'So tell me,' I murmured. 'What are you doing here? It's marvellous to see you of course. I can't tell you how marvellous. But I had no idea you were coming to the meeting too.'

He shifted his weight from one buttock to the other. A typical Marcus move. Even when we were children bent over a game of whist or gin rummy, Marcus would play for time.

'Edward is dead,' he blurted out.

In the vacuum of silence that swallowed his words, I felt my whole world implode. I stared blindly at the stars, watching as they dissolved and washed over me, raindrops made of dust that mingled with the tears pouring down my face. I couldn't breathe. Couldn't think. The fist of fate had punched me in the gut and all I could do was reel from it. My big brother. Our big brother. Dead.

'How? When?' I managed to gasp.

'They arrested him the day before yesterday. Took him straight to Klaus Barbie. Barbie tortured him for hours, but Edward wouldn't talk. Barbie knew he was the leader of the Lyon network so he shot him in the back of the head.'

Klaus Barbie. The head of the Gestapo, better known as the Butcher of Lyon. For good reason. Edward would have had no chance. Damn him and his moral courage. Damn it all to hell. Edward was so thoroughly, bloody decent. It was one of the things I loved most about him. Had loved. Still loved. None of it made sense.

'But how did he know? Edward is... was always so careful.'

'Someone betrayed him. Possibly the same someone who betrayed you all here tonight.'

I stared at Marcus. Something chimed inside me. The ring of truth.

'There's a mole,' he said. 'A spy in the network. Only this spy has access to several networks, or at least their secrets. Too many things have gone wrong. The SS showing up at precisely the wrong moment. Local Resistance groups rounded up. Agents exposed and arrested. The Lyon network blown. You saw that tonight. Someone knew that you were all meeting here. That same someone tipped off the enemy. How else did the Germans know where and when to arrive at a farmhouse they had ignored until now?'

I could feel my heart drumming, frantic beneath my breast-bone like a trapped bird. He was only echoing my own suspicions.

'Do you have any idea who it might be?'

I felt rather than saw him nod in the dark.

'We know it's someone who goes by the codename of Claude to his German masters. Possibly one of Jack's network. A double agent.'

'We?'

'This goes all the way back to London. High-level stuff.'

'So who is this traitor?'

I could feel Marcus hesitate.

'We're not yet sure.'

'Does Jack know about Claude?'

'I can't say.'

'For God's sake, Marcus. Stop being so bloody obtuse. Edward is dead. Jack may be next, for all we know. Someone has to warn him. Before it's too late.'

'If we do that, we risk alerting Claude that we're on to him. We have to let this play out, Marianne. Until we are sure.'

I stared up at the night sky spinning above me, sucking in a gulp of air, feeling the tang of the trees hit the back of my throat.

'I saw him. Tonight. In the cornfield.'

I didn't mention the gun. Or the smile.

'Good. Then he's alive. And we need to keep him that way. Jack is crucial to Operation Dragoon. He's the only man on the ground who knows the landing sites and the exact times and dates of each stage. He also knows the names of every agent and Resistance leader on the south coast who are supporting the operation. London thought the safest place for all that information was inside his head so there were no leaks.'

A cold sense of dread settled in the pit of my stomach. If Jack was such a valuable source, it made him an even bigger target for the traitor in his ranks.

'We're sure the Germans don't know any of that?'

'Quite sure. Their communications indicate they know something is coming but they have no idea precisely what or when. They suspect we will land on the south coast because that's the obvious choice, as it was with Normandy. But as for the exact beaches or the land and air operations, they haven't a clue.'

'So what are our orders?'

'To do everything we can to ensure Dragoon succeeds. Which means focusing on that to the exclusion of all else.'

'What about Jack?'

'We have to keep him out of German hands. Whatever it takes. If communication with London and the Allies is cut off before or during Dragoon, Jack is the backup.'

'Fine. But once Dragoon is over, all bets are off. I'll find out who betrayed Edward and his people and I will make them pay. As for Klaus Barbie, I'll kill him with my bare hands if I have to.'

Marcus glanced at me. 'You won't get anywhere near Barbie.'

'Watch me.'

'Trust me, you don't even want to try it.'

'Trust me, I will.'

Marcus sighed, a sigh laden with so many memories. 'I do trust you. That's the problem.'

A final drag on his cigarette and then Marcus ground it into the earth. He held out his hand to me.

'We need to get back before your men come looking for me.'

'They're not that protective.'

'You could have fooled me. The skinny one looks like he'd happily slit my throat.'

'Antoine? He looks at everyone like that.'

I looped my arm through his as we strode back along the mossy pathway, our feet silent, the only other sound our breath in the still night air. It was as much for support as anything else. My legs still felt as wobbly as those of a new-born foal. Or of someone who's had their world kicked out from under them.

At the edge of the forest, I paused, tugging on Marcus's arm to signal him to stop. The barn huddled low in a hollow, a dark bulk that appeared abandoned. I could feel Marcus's mouth move against my ear.

'What's wrong?'

I shook my head, my senses shrieking. There was nothing to see, nothing to hear, and yet I knew something was off.

'I— Nothing.'

I was lying. Or was it my mind lying to me? I so wanted him to be here. To know for sure he was safe. I wanted it so much that I had conjured him out of the night, a wraith that resembled Jack. Only it wasn't him. It was, at best, a wisp of night mist, a sense of someone who was already many miles away. At least, I hoped so.

Run, I prayed silently to Jack. *Run*.

But what was the point of Jack running when the man at his heels was a traitor prepared to betray anyone, even his brother in arms? And for what?

Jack was the best of the best. He had stayed alive this far. There was no reason he couldn't stay alive a lot longer.

Fool. There was every reason. A reason that was by his side day and night, who might even now be leading him to his death or at least into German hands. And there was nothing I could do to stop him. All I could do was hope.

I closed my eyes for a second, trying to stop the world spinning out of control once more – shapes shifting, truth blowing apart and reforming like dust in the wind. Like the dust kicking up in the cornfield as the Germans raked it with their machine guns, sending more good men and women to their graves. Someone had betrayed us all tonight, bringing the Germans straight to us as we gathered to try to end this war at last. But who?

My heart cried into the darkness. There was no answering cry. No sound save the cicadas thrilling to the moon and the breath of my remaining brother beside me.

THREE

'He's been arrested.'

Maggie gasped out the words, the wheels still spinning on the bike she'd flung to the ground. Beyond her, the sky was flushed with the dawn that was dissipating into the golden sunlight of another glorious August day.

'Jack has been arrested along with two other agents. The Milice have them.'

'Where?'

'I don't know. That's all the information I have.'

I stared at Maggie, thoughts tumbling over thoughts as I tried to work out what to do. The Milice were, if possible, worse than the Gestapo at times – a bunch of vicious, Nazi-loving French police who delighted in arresting and torturing their own. They must be thrilled with their latest prize. A prize we had to snatch back to have any hope of winning this war.

I beckoned Maggie into the barn.

'The Milice have taken Jack along with two others,' I announced to the men ranged around the cavernous space, most of them still slumped in sleep. 'We need to make a plan.'

'A plan for what?' It was Antoine who spoke up, his eyes flat black pebbles in his thin face as he rose to his feet.

'To rescue them of course.'

Silence sang back at me, my words falling into the far corners of the barn.

'That's an order,' I added. 'These men are our brothers.'

Still silence. I curled my fingers into my palms. An unfamiliar, sullen silence. They might be my comrades in arms but I was still their leader. I had never known them disobey a direct order from me.

'We already have orders,' said Antoine. 'Those are to wait and do nothing until we receive the signal. Otherwise we could compromise the entire operation.'

'Oh for God's sake,' I cried, reaching for my jacket.

'Wait, Marianne.' Marcus, forever the voice of reason. 'Sit down a moment. We need to think this through.'

I took the chair he offered me with reluctance. Every moment we wasted was another one lost. The others took the remaining chairs at the battered table we used to dine, to plan and for everything else.

'Maggie, does Jeannot know?' I demanded.

'They rounded up the local Maquis too.'

'Hell.'

Without Jeannot, I had no one to call on for help. It was his farmhouse they'd burned down and the last I'd seen of him, he was creeping through the cornfield with his men, seeking an escape route. If anyone could escape the Germans, it was Jeannot. He was born and raised on this land and knew it like the back of his well-worn hands. The same hands that had silently and efficiently despatched more than one German soldier as well as members of the Milice.

As leader of the local Maquis, Jeannot was unparalleled. His capture was a mortal blow. The Maquis were all we had until the Allied forces landed in Provence. When that would be, we had no idea. The radio messages from London had been ambiguous. Deliberately so. From what I could decipher, the landings were imminent. Until then, we were on our own and now more so than ever. But there was one man here, in France, who knew exactly when the landings would take place and where. A man I loved with all my soul but also considered a priceless asset. And now he was in the hands of the enemy too.

I looked at my men ranged around the table, at Henri with his crumpled face belying his stoic bravery, at Marcus flashing me that wary glance I knew so well, at Antoine staring down at his hands and then back at Maggie, still fluttering like an anxious carrier pigeon by the barn door.

'Maggie, go and find out what you can about where they've taken them. All of them. The Maquis as well as Jack and the others. Report back here by 1400 hours.'

That gave her four hours. Enough time to cycle to the village and the town beyond.

She nodded and disappeared through the door without another word. I could hear the clatter of the bicycle wheels receding, Maggie already going full pelt. She always did, her chin lifted with a determination that was softened by a charming smile when necessary. That smile had saved many lives as Maggie deployed it on the Milice and Gestapo alike, her aura of sweetness backing up her cover story.

Maggie really was acting as the local midwife, but her medical skills were useful in other ways. She could kill with surgical precision and had done so more than once, the mouth that smiled so readily setting into a thin line of cool efficiency. If there was anyone who could find out what had happened to them, it was Maggie. I would trust her with my life. More importantly, I trusted her with Jack's.

'We have to find them,' I said, aware that my fingers were digging into my left palm. I unclenched my fist and flexed it. 'We have no other choice.'

No one needed to know just how vital Jack was to us, to the entire operation. It was better they didn't and enough to understand that loyalty came first.

Henri cleared his throat, but Antoine was already speaking. 'Marianne, we have many choices. We must not make the wrong one.'

I glared at him, biting back the retort that sprang to my lips. He was right of course. We did have other choices. But there was only one I was prepared to make.

'We were told to sit tight and wait,' he repeated. 'That is our job. To wait for further orders.'

'Since when have we sat and waited for anything?' I spat. 'If we thought like that, we'd all be dead. Besides, Jack has our orders. He was supposed to give them to us at the meeting.'

Another silence.

Then Henri spoke up. 'She's right, you idiots. When was it we turned into cowards?'

My heart lifted at his ringing tones.

'What do you want us to do?' Marcus broke his silence.

'We have to let London know what's happened,' I said. 'We also need to know if they destroyed everything at the farmhouse or if there's anything we can salvage. Maps, food, weapons. Anything at all. Henri, I believe Jeannot also keeps a cache of weapons hidden on the land? Do you know where?'

'I can find them,' he replied, getting to his feet.

'Good. I'll contact London. Antoine, you and Marcus take a look at the farmhouse. Abort immediately if you spot any Milice or Germans still on-site. We meet back here in one hour. We don't have much time.'

I glanced back over my shoulder as I lugged the radio set to the door. Antoine was still seated, alone, at the table. His obsidian eyes met mine.

'Antoine?'

Slowly, he got to his feet. Disobeying an order from a

commanding officer was still punishable even in these chaotic times.

I looked at my watch. 'I'll see you all back here at 11.20 on the dot.'

As I lugged the radio set into the woods, I tried to dismiss the doubts whirling round my head about Antoine. He would do what he was told. He had to.

Not for the first time, I wished I had appointed anyone but him as my deputy. Antoine was smart and he had a cool head, but there was always that simmering resentment. I was a woman. How dare I issue orders to him? Never mind that those orders came from on high. I was the wrong sex, at least in his eyes. Too bad that it was my sex that gave me the edge.

No one ever suspected a woman who cycled around with a basket full of farm produce for the old folk in the village and who regularly allowed the German soldiers to steal their share. Naturally, I had no choice but to let them have it, just as they had no choice but to succumb to a smile and a little chat. It was amazing what you could discover in a few words shared over a purloined goat's cheese and a couple of packets of ham 'for the boys'. I practically purred as they turned on what they thought was charm, their awkward attempts falling on deaf ears that were nevertheless shell-like and pretty. Or at least, that was what they said.

I would let out a little, ladylike laugh to acknowledge their awkward sallies and then speed off on my way once they were out of sight. Anything I garnered of value, I transmitted to London or shared with the Maquis. Sometimes both. We were in this together, and then again, we weren't. And now, with the local Maquis rounded up, the only allies I had were hundreds of miles away, safe in their offices in Whitehall and Baker Street. Or here, in the middle of the French countryside – the motley, brave assortment who were all that was left of my network.

FOUR

A good mile and a half from the barn, I opened the suitcase and set up the radio, aware that once I had sent my transmission, we had even less time to spare. We had to work with such speed these days. The Germans were on our signals almost before some operators had time to pack up their equipment, so increasingly desperate were they as our forces advanced through France. And that desperation only made them all the more deadly.

I perched the aerial as high as I could on a nearby larch, unfolded the silk handkerchief from my knickers where I'd tucked it and inspected the code. Once I was satisfied, I inserted the crystal into the set and tapped out my message.

'Mission aborted...'

Crouched in the undergrowth, with the ferns tickling my exposed calves, I switched to receive and waited for an acknowledgement.

A butterfly circled my head and then fluttered down to perch on the rim of the radio set, its wings translucent in the sunshine that filtered through the trees. All around me, the forest was alive with insect life, birdsong intermingling with the chirrup of crickets and the low hum of the bees. It was going to be a glorious August day in Haute Provence.

An image flashed through my mind of another summer day, this time on the Backs in Cambridge, butterflies flitting from one clover flower to another as Jack and I lay entwined in one another's arms.

He was murmuring the poem in my ear. My poem. The one he had written for me. The one I had first used as my code.

'And if I should wake and see you there...'

'You'd what?' I smiled lazily as I stared into his eyes.

'I'd do this.'

His hand travelled down my back, teasing my spine, wrapping itself around my waist, making me ache with longing.

'And this.' His kiss, butterfly soft on my neck. 'Then this.' A harder kiss, more demanding.

I rolled over and lost myself in another kiss, my breath coming in short pants now, my mind dizzy, spiralling somewhere I had never been. Somewhere I may never go again.

A click through my headphones jolted me back to the present. Message received.

I snapped shut the suitcase and started to march back to the barn. The others would be back at any moment. At least, I hoped they would. Last night was a stark reminder of how close we all sailed to the wind right now. Marcus was right. Someone had betrayed us. And that someone could not have acted alone if he was one of Jack's men. The exact location of the farmhouse was obscure even to a local. There was another traitor a lot closer to home.

Back at the barn, Marcus and Antoine were waiting for me. I could tell by Marcus's face that their sortie had not been a success.

'They have a couple of men guarding the place,' said Antoine. 'We got close enough to see what was left of it without being spotted, but basically there's nothing. It's all gone. Burned to the ground.'

'Well at least they didn't get their hands on any maps or information.'

'True.'

'Is it still burning?'

'Most of the fire is out. It's smouldering here and there. The guards are keeping well away from the actual structure. Some of the joists are still in place, but they look like they could come crashing down at any moment.'

There was no point trying to salvage anything in there, not with the Germans standing sentry. And nor could we save the men and one woman who had been part of that particular cell and who now hung lifeless outside, a stark warning to anyone who might try.

I glanced at my watch. Four minutes until my deadline.

At that exact moment, Maggie burst through the door. She untied the scarf from her hair and raked her fingers through it. Although she must have cycled back at great speed, she looked as unruffled as if she had just returned from a shopping jaunt.

'I have more information. Jack and two of his men were stopped at a roadblock and arrested when they found a great deal of money on them. They've taken them to the police station in Valréas.'

The money Jack had brought to the rendezvous to be distributed among the networks. Money dropped from London to finance guerrilla support of Operation Dragoon.

'How did you discover this?'

'I spoke to Madame in the *boulangerie* opposite the police station. Her lover is a gendarme and it makes her feel important to be in the know. As ever, she was very keen to tell me all the gossip while I bought her madeleines.'

Maggie tipped the contents of the packet she was carrying under her arm onto the table. Sure enough, a cascade of golden madeleines spread out across the paper in which they had been wrapped.

'She also said that they'll be handed over to the Gestapo tomorrow morning. Which doesn't give us much time.'

Less than twenty-four hours to stage a rescue, if we could even pull one off.

Of course we could pull one off. We had to. Once the Gestapo had their hands on them, they had almost no chance. It would be summary execution at worst – a bullet in the back of the skull, just like Edward. At best, transportation. But the Germans weren't so keen to risk that these days. They preferred to kill their prisoners there and then rather than send them on a train across France to Germany and Poland beyond. There was no time to spare and no stomach for it when the Allied forces were snapping at their heels.

'Who's holding them at the police station?' I asked. 'The Milice or the gendarmes?'

One marginally worse than the other, unless you got lucky. Both equally beholden to their occupying masters.

'The gendarmes, according to Madame.'

'Then we have a chance.'

'Marianne.' Antoine stepped forward, his face set, his voice even more so. 'There is no way we can rescue them from the police station. You know that as well as I do. It would be insanity to even try.'

I stared him down, his eyes opaque as they met mine. 'I am prepared to take that risk.'

'I am not.'

'Well let's put it to a vote when Henri gets back, shall we? Who here is prepared to try and save their comrades? Their fellow agents and Resistance fighters. Men who have risked their lives to liberate this country.'

'We can vote now.'

I followed Marcus's gaze to the door where Henri was carting in armfuls of weapons.

'*Et voilà.*' Henri dumped them on the table with a grin. 'Pistols. A Sten gun. Ammunition. I found them all. Vote on what?'

'On whether we rescue Jack and the two men arrested with him from Valréas police station.'

'But of course we do.' Henri looked around the assembled group. 'How can there be any question?'

'It is suicidal even to try,' snapped Antoine.

I rounded on him. 'You mean like all the suicidal missions they've carried out for all of us? For this country? What is wrong with you, man?'

The colour rose in his sallow cheeks, staining them with an angry flush. He lowered his gaze and walked out the door, closing it softly behind him. Even when infuriated, Antoine was frighteningly controlled.

'Go after him,' I said to Marcus. 'Make sure he doesn't go anywhere.'

I caught Henri's quizzical stare.

'Someone betrayed us,' I said. 'They had to have done. Why else would they hit the farmhouse after all these years and on the very night so many networks meet up?'

'And you think it was Antoine?' Henri's tone was incredulous.

I caught Marcus's warning glance.

'It could have been.'

I ignored their stares. Explanations and even recriminations could come later.

'So,' I said, 'what are our chances of taking the police station by force?'

'Absolutely none,' said Maggie. 'There are gendarmes at the door and more patrolling the exterior of the building. Then there are those inside on the front desk and guarding the cells themselves. The chief of police and his deputy in their offices. We're completely outnumbered.'

'What if we create a diversion? Say we blow up something elsewhere in the town so they have to send men to deal with that?'

'Then we would have to split up, which means we dilute our numbers even more.'

I looked at Henri. He was right. The only way to do this was through subterfuge and not force.

An idea began to sprout from a seed planted earlier. The memory of another poem written by Verlaine. One that had fooled the Germans into thinking the Normandy landings were imminent when verses from it were broadcast by the BBC.

'We must send a message that the Germans can immediately intercept and decipher. Maggie, I need you to do that but not from here. You have to take the radio set north of Valréas. Make it appear as if it's coming from another network. I'll tell you what to say.'

I picked up the radio suitcase and ushered Maggie out of the door, away from the barn. Antoine and Marcus were nowhere in sight.

'We need to make them think the Allies are about to land on the south coast any moment. Send a message that says: "Message received and understood. Fourth verse of Verlaine."'

'Verlaine? I don't understand.'

'It's what they broadcast before the Normandy landings. "Chanson d'automne". The Germans thought it meant the landings were due to start within forty-eight hours. In fact, it was the signal to start sabotaging the railway lines.'

Maggie's teeth flashed, white. 'Perfect.'

'Encrypt it using one of the old poem codes so they can decipher it easily. Set up the radio as far north from Valréas as you can get by 2100 hours, which will give the BBC time to include it in their late broadcast. Think you can do that?'

Maggie tied her scarf with great solemnity under her chin then winked at me. 'Of course.'

I strapped the radio set into the pannier on the back of her bicycle, covering it completely so that it appeared to be nothing more than bulky shopping or medical supplies.

'If they stop you, tell them it's an X-ray machine.'

She wheeled her bike around and gave me a wave. 'Don't worry about me. You go get our men.'

And she was off, disappearing down the track, her skirts flapping behind her as she cycled at speed, those bright curls bobbing under her scarf.

The dust she kicked up caught at my throat. Or maybe it was something else.

'Be safe,' I whispered.

I no longer believed in God. But I prayed now, to something, to anything. Maggie was the bravest of the brave. If she failed or was captured, the consequences could be dire for us all but especially her. I couldn't think like that. She would succeed. We all would. Or die in the attempt.

FIVE

It was a dog barking that alerted me. A single bark and then silence. I sat up from the hay bale where I had eventually sunk into a dreamless sleep and shook Marcus, who was still snoring softly beside me.

'Marianne, we must leave now.'

Henri was already awake, stuffing guns into his belt, grabbing what food he could as well.

I blinked through the grey darkness at the shapes emerging from the far corners of the barn and motioned with my hand towards the back wall where a smaller door gave on to the field beyond. There was no sound from outside, nothing to indicate anyone was approaching, but to go through the main door now would be foolhardy. Whoever was coming didn't want to be heard. They had probably killed the dog with a single shot. The farm the dog guarded was two fields away. That gave us minutes at most.

I led my men out the rear of the barn, brushing aside Marcus's hand. I was in charge – I would go first.

Outside, all was still. Too quiet. Luckily for us, the clouds hung low, obscuring the moon and sheltering us under a blanket of darkness. It wasn't until we reached the cover of the trees once more that I dared stand up straight.

We kept moving, plunging deep into the woods and away from any human habitation. The countryside here was rough, the terrain peppered with rocks and fallen branches over which we could stumble.

From the direction of the barn, I could hear faint shouts. I couldn't risk looking back or even pausing to count my men. Maggie. She would be back soon from her mission. She could walk straight into them. I swallowed, stifling the warning cry that threatened to burst from my lips. There was nothing I could do. She knew the score. We all did. And for the greater good, we had to keep going.

We crested a hill as dawn broke and only then did I stop and take stock, taking a slug of water from the bottle I'd snatched up and slung around my neck.

'Where's Antoine?' I snapped as my eyes flicked from face to face. They were all here save him. And Maggie.

'That bastard,' Henri muttered.

Our eyes met in grim acknowledgement.

'Let's keep moving,' I said. 'If he's with them, he knows all our escape routes.'

The ones we had carefully plotted out night after night, committing them to memory in case of a situation just like this. But not quite like this because I had never really thought that one of my own would betray us.

Fool, I whispered to myself. What an idiot. The first rule of war was never to trust anyone, not even your own. At least, it was if you were one of us. And I had considered Antoine one of us even as my suspicions grew. My mistake. I had given him the benefit of the doubt. Now that mistake could cost all of us our lives.

Could. But hadn't as yet. There was still a chance we could

outwit and outrun them, whoever they were. The Milice? The Gestapo? One and the same.

I was leading the others blind now, deliberately avoiding any of the routes we had so carefully laid out, heading across open country where we risked being spotted at any moment, run down with dogs, shot in the back as we ran. *No, Marianne. Don't panic. Keep cool. Remember your training.*

Apart from Marcus, the men I'd been working with in this cell were barely trained. What they knew, they'd picked up from me and my fellow agents, but they more than made up for that with bravery and native cunning.

Henri whistled between his teeth as we crested a ridge and stared down at the road below – two vehicles parked on a bridge so that they blocked it in both directions; soldiers standing at the ready, their uniforms horribly familiar.

Instinctively, we all dropped to the ground and began slowly to shuffle back. They were waiting for us, I was sure of it.

Safely back on the other side of the ridge, I gestured towards the river that wove like a ribbon, a beautiful blue barrier to our escape route, in the other direction. We slid down towards it as one, keeping low to the ground and moving as fast as we dared. One dislodged rock sent bouncing in the wrong direction would have them upon us.

All at once, I saw something move in the trees that lined the riverbank. Figures emerging, gesturing to us to hurry. Then hands reaching out, pulling us in.

'Down. There are Germans patrolling the other bank.'

I looked up into a familiar face.

'Jeannot. I thought they'd arrested you.'

His mouth stretched in a grim smile. 'They tried. We outran them. The Boches don't know this country like I do. We marched through the night and stopped here to get some sleep. Then we saw the pigs had arrived to set up their roadblock. Is that for you?'

'Probably. We holed up in the barn but evacuated when the farm dog started barking.'

'Good dog, that. Trained it myself.'

I didn't mention the shot.

'Jeannot, we need to get to Valréas. They've taken three of our men there. Two agents and one maquisard. They were stopped at a roadblock and searched which was when they found the money they were carrying. The money that was supposed to be distributed last night. They're holding them at the gendarmerie for now. We have to get there before they hand them over to the Gestapo.'

Jeannot whistled between his teeth. 'Even if you get to Valréas, how are you going to extract them from a police cell?'

'I'll figure that out when we get there.'

I peered across the river at the far bank. Nothing moved.

'They will be here,' said Jeannot, 'in a couple of minutes.'

Sure enough, with Germanic precision they appeared, a patrol moving through the trees, guns at the ready. No dogs at least.

I reached for my pistol. A hand descended on my wrist.

'No,' hissed Jeannot. 'Not here. There are more of them.'

He indicated with his head towards the bridge.

His grip on my wrist loosened and I let my hand drop to my side. He was right. To shoot now would be stupid in the extreme. Fatigue was fogging my brain and clouding my judgement.

'How far from here to Valréas?'

'Across country? Maybe ten kilometres. You will have to circle round to the east to avoid the Germans.'

I glanced at Henri, crouched beside my left elbow, listening to every word.

'All right,' I said. 'That will take us a couple of hours over this terrain. We have to get moving.'

'We'll come with you,' said Jeannot. 'You'll need all the help you can get.'

I looked at his solemn face, seamed by the sun, eyes alive with defiance, and smiled.

'*Allons-y, mes amis,*' I said. 'Let's go get our men.'

SIX

My fingers brushed the tips of the lavender bushes as we skirted the field, sending up bursts of the scent that already filled the air. Heat once more pulsed from the earth. The sun was rising in the sky. Ahead of us lay Valréas, its church towers and red rooftops ranging above the treeline that separated us from the town.

Jeannot indicated a large, white building to the right of twin spires, tracing a line with his finger. 'That's the gendarmerie. That tower you see is the town centre, more or less. There is a straight road that runs between the two.'

I stared at the jumble of stone and slate houses overshadowed by the mountain that rose in the distance. It was a typical Vaucluse hill town, its labyrinthine streets snaking around the churches that marked its heart, a place now made unholy by its German occupiers.

'How many German troops in residence?'

'I'm not sure. Since the Gestapo infiltrated the local Maquis, we have no recent intelligence.'

Not just infiltrated but massacred as many as they could

round up. It would be some small justice to whip our men out from under the noses of the Nazi-loving police.

'So we're going in there blind?' asked Marcus.

I rounded on him. 'What else can we do?'

He stared back at me, a muscle twitching under his eye.

'I don't want to lose a sister too,' he snapped.

'You won't. I know what I'm doing.'

'And what is that exactly?'

'I'm going to walk in there and demand they set our men free.'

'You will not.'

'I will.'

I glared up at him, the ten inches he had over me in height no match for my fury. 'I'm following orders, remember?'

He sighed. 'Yes, but not like this.'

'Do you have a better idea? The gendarmes and the Milice know that the landings are happening any day. They don't want to be on the losing side. The message I had Maggie send was quite deliberate. It's an echo of the one they sent before the D-Day landings. For all the police up here know, thousands of troops are even now landing on the Riviera beaches. At least, that's what I want them to think.'

'We're a long way from the coast,' said Jeannot.

'Doesn't matter. Once the Allies arrive, there will be reprisals. You think the police here want to be paraded through the streets after they've been arrested? Or face a military court and probable execution for war crimes?'

'Good point,' said Henri.

'So here's the plan. We create a diversion just as you suggested but one that reinforces their fear the landings have already happened.'

'How the hell do we do that?' asked Jeannot.

'Simple. You make a lot of noise about it. Run through the

town centre, stand outside the church shouting victory. Fire your guns into the air. Act as if we've already won.'

'Won't that bring the Germans running?'

'Exactly. That's why you have to keep one step ahead of them. Lead them away from the police station. Jeannot, you know the town well. They won't be expecting this so we have the advantage of surprise.'

Marcus looked at me with grudging respect. 'It could just work.'

'It will work.'

I sounded more confident than I felt. But we had no other option. The police station was too exposed on that main road to do anything but act with outrageous audacity. We were outnumbered and on the back foot. The only thing to do was face them down. In style.

The scent of lavender grew headier as we descended through the field towards the road below. Or maybe that was my breath quickening in tandem with my heart.

The lavender field gave way to vineyards that clung in orderly rows to the hillside. We stuck to the shelter of the trees, slipping through them in single file as the way through narrowed. I let Jeannot lead, the other men silently treading behind with the occasional crack of a twig snapping underfoot.

All of a sudden, I heard Jeannot swear under his breath. A fraction of a second later, I was staring into the barrel of a gun, a pistol aimed at my heart from point-blank range.

'What the hell...?'

'Arms above your head.'

A woman's voice. A pair of green eyes surveying us coolly from behind the pistol, her tones as rock steady as her grip.

'All of you,' she snarled as the rest of our party stepped into the clearing where men were emerging from the shadows of the trees, armed to their broken teeth. Then one of them let out a grunt of recognition.

'Jeannot. It's you.'

Beside me, Jeannot was engulfed in an embrace.

'Juliette, this is Jeannot,' said the maquisard who had his arm clamped across his shoulder. 'It was his farmhouse the Nazi pigs burned down last night.'

The woman barely blinked, still bristling with hostility. She was as fine boned as a sparrow, honey-blond hair drawn back in an elegant chignon. Even her fatigues appeared elegant, fitting her form with the kind of chic nonchalance only a Parisian could pull off. I unconsciously tugged at my baggy shorts, smoothing down the ever-present creases.

'What are you doing here?' she asked, gesturing with her pistol at me. 'And who are you?'

I thought about the options. There weren't too many.

'My name is Marianne. We're here to extract three men who were arrested at a roadblock last night. They're being held at the police station. We need to get them out before they hand them over to the Gestapo.'

'Then we're here for the same reason,' she said. Her voice, if anything, had dropped a few degrees in temperature. 'One of those men is my second in command.'

'I see.'

I held her gaze, determined to make her blink first. Sure enough, she did, but only because she took a step forward and pressed her pistol against my temple.

'I suggest you leave now before you screw this up for all of us.'

Her head snapped back as I struck with an open-handed jab to her chin, grabbing her wrist with my other hand and jerking it to send her pistol flying. To her credit, she stayed in control. But only just. Her eyes when she levelled them back on me shot beams of fury.

'I think not,' I said, my gun now aimed squarely at her forehead.

Around us, the men stood silent, their fingers twitching. They didn't know whether to reach for their weapons or stay still, hoping this moment would pass.

'You know, we could work together,' I said. 'Treat this as a joint op. After all, you have a man in there too. You need us as much as we need you.'

She didn't blink.

'We're too late.' A maquisard burst, panting, into the clearing. 'They've moved them already.'

'*Merde*. When? Are you sure it was them?' snapped Juliette.

'Not more than fifteen minutes ago. And yes, it was them. I saw them with my own eyes. Charles and two other men, all of them in chains. They loaded them into a prison van.'

I ran a hand through my hair, thinking fast. 'Do you know where they've taken them?'

'I have no idea.'

'Come,' said Juliette to her men. 'We need to find out what's happened to them.'

I picked up her gun and handed it to her.

'How do you propose to do that?' I asked.

She inspected her pistol and, for half a second, I thought she might turn it on me again. Then she tucked it in her waistband and glared at me.

'I have men on the ground,' she said. 'We will send word. Find out where they've taken them.'

'We don't have time for that,' I said. 'They might be taking them straight to the Gestapo as we speak.'

'They might. I will know for sure in an hour or so. Then we can decide what to do.'

'You need our help,' I said. 'There aren't enough of you to take on the Gestapo.'

Those green eyes glinted. 'There are nearly ten thousand of us spread among these hills. All of them my men. I think that's enough to take on the Gestapo. Now we really do need to get out of here.'

'In that case, can we come with you? Don't forget, two of those men are our agents. And we're all supposed to be working together to support the final invasion. That was why we were gathered at Jeannot's farmhouse. To act as one.'

I nodded towards Jeannot, who squared his shoulders.

'It's true,' he said. 'We have pledged to support the Allies in their effort to free France once and for all. We are brothers. And sisters.'

Juliette shrugged. She didn't look too sold on the idea of me as her sister but she had to concede the facts.

'As you wish,' she said.

Without waiting for any more dialogue, she strode through her men, pushing her way through the trees in the opposite direction to our approach then through the vineyards running roughly parallel with the road below. There was nothing to do but follow in her footsteps.

Twenty minutes later, we emerged in another clearing from which I could glimpse the road beyond. Under the cover of the trees, two trucks were parked, both the kind of farm vehicles that regularly chugged along these roads.

Juliette got behind the wheel of one, the maquisard who'd staked out the police station the other. I flung myself into the front seat beside her while my men piled in behind. She flicked me a glance but said nothing as she gunned the engine, its throaty roar indicating this truck had far more power than it had first appeared.

She put her foot down once we were well clear of Valréas, racing along the mountain roads and taking hairpin bends at breakneck speed. I gripped the edge of my seat and gritted my teeth. If she was hoping for a reaction, she got none.

Finally, we turned off the road and bumped along a rutted track that headed upwards, leading us to what looked to be a derelict chateau that sat almost hidden among the rocks and trees that rose from the ridge on which it was perched.

As we drew nearer, I could see that some of the windows gaped black, devoid of glass, and ragged holes peppered the roof. The outer wall greeted us like a maquisard's gap-toothed grin, but once through the vast wooden gates which were opened and shut for us with military precision, I saw the reinforcements that had been put in place. The chateau might look abandoned to fool the Germans, but it still offered sanctuary against all invaders as it had done for centuries.

I scrambled out of the truck and drank in the view. Far below, the river snaked through the fertile valley, the purple swathes of lavender contrasting with the gold of sunflowers, like a regal carpet laid at our feet.

The moment we stepped into the great entrance hall of the chateau, the smell of sweat and gun grease bit the back of my throat. Sacks and packages were being stacked and counted by a group of maquisards while others were stripping down and cleaning weapons. I counted Sten guns, pistols and revolvers among their armoury as well as a rocket launcher. These Resistance fighters were not only well organised, they were well armed.

'Quite an operation you have here,' I said.

Juliette nodded to the man who was ticking off a list. 'François here is organising food for the men. We have around four thousand here. The rest are in the countryside all around.'

I shot her a look. 'Four thousand? But where?'

'Three hundred here in the chateau. Others in farmhouses and hidden camps. We have a courier system to communicate. I can muster all those men in less than one hour. Or get information, as I told you.'

'So you're in charge of all of this?'

'Yes, of course.'

The hint of a smile in her eyes spoke volumes. For a brief

second, we understood one another. The loneliness, the constant need to prove ourselves stronger and braver than any man while never succumbing to temptation. Yes, we were surrounded by men, but to us they were soldiers to lead and command. It was how we had both survived this far.

'I have sent word,' said Juliette. 'We should know where they have taken them soon.'

'Thank God.'

She looked at me. 'These men, they are important to you?'

'They're vital to the operation. My orders are to keep them out of German hands at all costs.'

She looked at me a moment longer. 'Then we had better do so.'

I nodded and abruptly turned my head away. I would not, could not let another fighter see me cry, especially a woman. Once this war was over, I would have time to grieve the many things I had lost. The people who I would never see again, including my brother. And the man I could not bear to lose even though it seemed the fates would tear him from me anyway.

SEVEN

MARCH 1938, CAMBRIDGE, ENGLAND

'Wine?'

Without waiting for an answer, he filled my glass almost to the brim.

I slapped my hand over it. 'That's enough. Thank you.'

He raised his glass in response. 'As you wish. Cheers then. To your good health.'

He had blue eyes, the colour of pewter. Or maybe periwinkles, depending on the light. They were laughing at me now over the rim of his glass. Undeniably handsome in an offbeat kind of way, strong bones softened by an unruly tuft of nut-brown hair that fell across his forehead, as stubborn as I suspected he might be. At first glance, a charmer. But there was something about the set of his mouth, the dimples at each corner, that spoke of depths kept carefully hidden and a heart that was similarly guarded.

'I don't think we've been introduced,' I said.

'I'm Jack. Jack Hamilton.'

The faintest of accents. Scottish maybe.

'You want to watch that one,' said Edward. 'He has half of Newnham sighing over him.'

I looked at my brother, elegant in black tie and gown, protective as ever. I could feel my own gown, whisper soft against my skin. For once, Mother had rallied, insisting I have it made up in London. It was the most beautiful dress I had ever owned, jade-green slipper satin with a fitted bodice, falling in folds from my waist. My first formal gown for my first formal dinner anywhere, never mind at Cambridge. I loved Edward for his gallantry but I could look after myself.

'She's coming up to Newnham for Michaelmas Term,' added Edward, nodding at me.

I saw Jack's eyes sharpen a fraction.

'Reading what?' he asked.

'Natural Sciences.'

He raised his glass to me again. 'Impressive.'

'You think?'

'I do.'

I could tell that he meant it. And that he wasn't necessarily referring to my studies. Much later, he told me that he fell in love with me there and then. It took me a while longer. But then, I had more reason to be cautious.

Somehow, Jack contrived an invitation to stay with us in the country that summer. Mother was forced into her best behaviour, not least because he disarmed her with his ready smile. Which meant that Papa, too, visibly relaxed. This was a Papa I had never seen before, perhaps the man he'd been before he left for the Great War. I was born exactly nine months after his last home leave but didn't meet him until I was nearly two, far too young to remember his reaction to the family that had expanded in his absence.

Papa was one of the last to be demobbed, only returning after he had seen the last of his men safely depart from the Salonica front. My brother Marcus was born during the two and a half years he was absent, a fact that was scrupulously ignored by everyone in the family.

In the years that followed his return, Papa barely seemed to notice the son who could not possibly be his. I knew Marcus felt that. It was why he occasionally acted up, trying desperately to gain attention. Instead, Mother, too, would act as if he didn't exist, atoning for her sins by sweeping them under the carpet. It was never acknowledged or talked about, even as I grew old enough to understand what must have happened. Instead, we shrouded the truth in silence, as so many families did.

To be honest, Papa hardly seemed to notice most things except for now and then when his gaze would sharpen as it locked on to something I couldn't see or his hand would tremble at the distant sound of shotguns during the season. He forbade hunters on his land but he couldn't stop them stalking the woods beyond. Many times I had seen him fling himself to the floor and then, when he realised I was there, pretend to be looking for something he'd dropped. He would shuffle back to his armchair, patting his knee so that I would crawl onto it for a cuddle before Mother appeared and shooed me away.

With Jack there, that part of Papa returned. They seemed to warm to one another, and for once, home really felt like one, the lawns ringing with shouts and laughter as we all joined in games of cricket and croquet or leaped in the lake for a dip. Even Edward, my watchful big brother, seemed to approve.

'He's a good 'un,' he murmured in my ear as we watched Papa bowl Jack out, much to Papa's delight.

'He is, isn't he?'

I caught Jack's eye as he settled into a deckchair. He had let Papa win. It was a kindness that said so much about him. I could feel my heart softening, treacherously, by the day.

This was not a part of my plan. I was going to university to study, to be as well educated as any man, even if they wouldn't actually award me a degree. Falling for one of them was simply going to prove a distraction. But Jack was impossible to resist. By the time I went up to Cambridge, I had reluctantly started to love him back. I don't think there was a moment when that happened. It was only when he was leaving to go back home before the start of term that I felt an unfamiliar tug on my heart.

'So,' he said, 'I'll see you on the Backs.'

I looked into his eyes, bluer than ever against his tan, a few freckles dusting his nose. We were standing by the summer house where I liked to stack my books, plucking one from the pile to read each day in preparation for my studies. It was my favourite hideaway, separated from the lawns and flower garden by the orchard. My brothers knew better than to disturb me there, but Jack had no such compunction.

'Not if I see you first.'

He pulled my sun hat playfully over my eyes. 'There, now you can't.'

'You rotter. My hair.'

I had never cared about my hair a day in my life but I had to have something to throw at him.

'Your hair is beautiful,' he said, lifting a curl from my shoulder and caressing it between his fingers. 'So dark until the sun touches it, and then it bursts into flame at the tips. A little like you, in fact.'

I felt my breath stop in my throat. Heard my heart thudding in my ears.

He leaned forward, wrapping his fingers around the back of my neck as he drew me gently to him.

'No, it's not. My hair. It's a mess,' I stuttered.

'Do shut up.'

'Don't tell me to shut up.'

'All right. How about this?'

For a first kiss, it would do, but then I had nothing with which to compare it. There was a somewhat awkward meeting of noses. Eyes open or shut? I went with shut. He tasted salty and sweet at the same time. I would have to look up the composition of saliva.

When he drew his mouth away from mine, I saw he was trying not to laugh.

'Was I that bad?'

'On the contrary, you were perfect.'

'Really?'

'Yes, really.'

'Excellent.'

He threw back his head and let out the roar of laughter I had seen bubbling up. 'It's not some kind of exam, you know. I have never met anyone as competitive as you.'

'Then you'd better not take me on and hope to win,' I said.

I looked into his face, serious now, pupils so dilated his eyes appeared navy blue.

'Taking you on would be a win. Even better if you took me on too.'

He spoke lightly but I could hear a note in his voice. One I had never heard before.

'We'll see about that,' I said.

'I'll hold you to it.'

And he did.

EIGHT

'What are you smiling at?'

I looked up to see Marcus hovering in the doorway of the dusty salon off the main hall of the chateau where I had taken up the table, spreading out a map across it. Without thinking, I brushed my hand across my mouth. I could still feel it. That kiss.

'I— Nothing. Is there news?'

He shook his head. 'Not yet.'

'Damn it.' I stabbed at the map. 'They could be in any of a dozen places. There are so many prisons across the zone as well as internment camps.'

'We'll find them, Marianne. But you're not going to work it out by staring at a map.'

'What else do you suggest I do?'

I pushed my chair back and paced the room, thinking. 'Maybe we should forget about trying to rescue them and eliminate the danger instead. Go straight to the heart of it and kill Klaus Barbie. That would solve a lot of problems. Not to mention save a lot of lives.'

'I already told you: you won't get anywhere near Klaus Barbie. He's surrounded by his men at all times.'

'So? There must be a way. I wonder why Edward didn't try to kill him.'

'For that very reason. And for the fact the reprisals would be horrific. They killed seven thousand people after that attempt on Hitler.'

'The Allies will be in Lyon soon. The Germans will have other things to think about.'

I could see a muscle twitching in his cheek, like a pulse. Marcus was never usually this agitated. Then again, this whole situation was unusual. I wasn't used to my little brother taking the lead.

'Marianne, stop it. The very idea is crazy. Until the Allies get there, we need to stick to the plan and make sure they do. In the meantime, there's a drop tonight, according to Juliette. They're bringing in more supplies and a support team. We could help on the ground.'

'As if Juliette will let us help. That woman loathes us. Or at least me.'

'She doesn't loathe us. You have to see it from her point of view. The Resistance have fought long and hard alongside us. All of a sudden, they have to bow to some great, big foreign plan. It must be hard.'

'She knows that Operation Dragoon is the best chance of liberating the south and the whole of France.'

'Doesn't make it any easier. You of all people should understand.'

I sighed. 'When's this drop?'

'We're heading up to the plateau just before sundown. This is their op,' he added, seeing my face.

'Of course it is. You're right. The least we can do is help.'

My voice sounded artificially bright even to me. Better than breaking though. Every second Marcus stood there made it so much harder not to think of Edward, and once I started, I couldn't stop. Did he suffer? Was he frightened? Thoughts I couldn't bear to utter. Could hardly bear to think. I silently willed Marcus to leave, staring hard at the map once more, but he hovered by the door, refusing to take the hint.

'For what it's worth,' he said, 'I miss him too.'

Sibling intuition. Or maybe my expression just gave me away.

I lifted my head, staring not at Marcus but at the dust motes that danced in the air, whirling in a waltz of pain.

'We'll find him,' I said. 'This traitor. Claude. When we do, I'll kill him myself. He's taken everything from us. Edward. An entire network. So many good agents. And now Jack. Everything.'

Including my heart.

NINE

The drop was timed for close to midnight, while the full moon shone bright in the sky to light up the airstrip but the world, or at least the enemy, slept. Up on the scrubby rock table that formed a hidden plain, the air was almost still, a tiny breeze now and then wafting the scent of lavender up my nostrils from the long seam that had been planted to disguise the landing strip from curious eyes.

Right now though, the strip was lit by the torches we held to mark it out for the approaching plane. Bang on cue, I could hear the unmistakable sound of its engines coming in from the northwest. A Lysander flying blind, lights off as they always were, aiming for our torches and the signal they sent that all was well.

As it dipped and flew low overhead, packages bounced from its undercarriage – guns, more money and medical supplies to shore us up for what lay ahead. Then the plane banked and steadied above us, its engines briefly cutting out as three larger shapes dropped one by one, this time human. One landed on target at the far end of the strip, but the other two drifted off, disappearing into the scrub.

I could see torches bobbing as two of the reception

committee raced to rescue them. The one who'd landed at the end of the strip was striding towards us, his flying suit and parachute bundled under his arm, resplendent in full uniform. He held out his hand and took Juliette's, bowing low over it.

'Lieutenant Daniel Diaz at your service, ma'am,' he said, before bowing over my hand in turn. 'Delighted to meet you too, ma'am.'

'Likewise.'

'You're a Brit?'

'Well spotted.'

'Well then, we probably have some chums in common.'

Was he teasing me?

'We probably do.'

I stared up into his handsome, boyish face, his olive skin offsetting the even, white teeth that gleamed in the moonlight.

'Don't mind him. He says that to all the girls.'

A shorter, stockier man appeared at Diaz's side and thrust out his hand. 'Lieutenant Bob Meyer, OSS. It's a pleasure to make your acquaintance.'

In contrast to the Latin Diaz, Meyer was all floppy blond hair and puppyish energy. He reminded me of a Labrador I had once had back at home, although I suspected there was an added edge to this affable American.

'And this,' he added, indicating the man who stepped out of the shadows behind them, 'is our radio operator.'

He nodded at us, the suitcase he clutched a facsimile of the one I had strapped to Maggie's bicycle. Another radio was a godsend, as were the supplies that had been dropped along with the team.

'Want a hand?' offered Diaz, indicating the packages all around us on the plateau that the men were gathering up.

'Thank you,' said Juliette. 'That would be most kind.'

Diaz glanced at her, his eyes lingering. She stared up at him and then hurriedly looked away. I smothered a smile. The

Americans had been dropped in to help with the final push to rid France of the Germans, those glamorous uniforms they wore designed to boost morale. It looked as if they would be boosting rather more than that, at least in Diaz's case. I sneaked another peek at Juliette, who was ferociously ignoring him. It would be fun to see if this developed into something more than an *entente cordiale*.

We set to, lugging the lumpy parcels to the edge of the plateau where they were being piled together. A human chain snaked from there down to the chateau, passing the packages along in grim silence. Not a half-mile away, in the valley, the enemy slept, although they had sentries to keep watch and listen. The slightest sound might alert them to our presence up here. We could not afford a mistake now. Not when so much rested on our assistance with Operation Dragoon.

It was to be the final nail in the Nazis' coffin. The push from the south that dealt the death blow to a vast army already on the run from the D-Day landings. Squeezed between north and south and with the Resistance strengthened by Allied troops and training, not even the might of the German troops could withstand an invasion on this scale. Or at least, that was what we all hoped. And it was no more than hope. Even weakened and on the run, the Nazis were a formidable and ferocious enemy, as we had all learned to our cost.

I lugged one of the final sacks down the treacherous slope, fighting to keep a foothold as stones skittered out from under my feet, refusing all offers of help from the men. It was a point of principle. They had to see me as their leader now more than ever with the plans for the final preparations still locked in Jack's head. Until we had those orders to follow, we would have to improvise. As for the Yanks, I wasn't yet sure if they would be more hindrance than help. Only time would tell – the most precious commodity of all. And we were fast running out of it.

TEN

OCTOBER 1938, CAMBRIDGE

He was late. I stamped my feet, warding off the late October chill as people surged past me into the cinema – friends, couples and families chattering excitedly about *The Lady Vanishes*. I was excited too. And not just because the reviews were marvellous.

I glanced at the clock just inside the foyer and then at my watch. They agreed it was now seventeen minutes after the appointed time. Any moment now they would be starting the programme. I would give him five more minutes. Five minutes and then Jack Hamilton was history. My excitement was vanishing faster than any lady in a film.

'Marianne, I am so sorry,' he gasped, panting as he skidded to a halt beside me. 'I ran all the way. Was held up by my tutor. I'll make it up to you, I promise.'

I looked at him, taking in the contrite expression, the battered box of chocolates he was clutching.

'Are those for me?' I asked.

'What? Oh, yes. I thought we could share them.'

His breath was coming more evenly now, his composure

returning as he linked his arm through mine. Or that might have been cockiness. He seemed very animated.

'Shall we?'

He bought two tickets for the back row. I said nothing. It was only the second time I had ever been to the cinema and an outing with my brothers scarcely counted as an occasion. This, however, was something different. Our first real date, just the two of us without company or a chaperone. And I wasn't absolutely sure how to carry this off.

As soon as we sat down, I realised Jack had no such qualms. His arm snaked along the seat back behind us and dropped across my shoulders. A kiss in broad daylight was one thing, such close proximity in the dark quite another. There was no arm between us, nothing to stop his thigh pressing against mine. No wonder he'd chosen these seats. Well, I would give him a run for his money.

As he leaned in towards me, I caught a whiff of something on his breath, a hint of whisky veiled in a layer of mint.

'Does your tutor serve drink?' I murmured. 'Or does he conduct his tutorials in the pub?'

A momentary hesitation as he digested this and then he was attempting to nuzzle my ear once more. I wriggled away and stared at Margaret Lockwood's face filling the screen.

'I'm trying to watch,' I hissed.

'And I'm trying to kiss you.'

The woman sitting in front of us turned round and glared. I elbowed Jack in the ribs.

'Ouch.'

Unperturbed, he tried another angle, artlessly dropping his hand on my knee. I gave it a couple of minutes and then I dug my fingernails into it none too gently. To his credit, he said nothing but simply removed it. I smiled to myself and focused on the film.

Just as we got to the part where the music teacher reveals

herself as a spy, I realised Jack was snoring softly. I nudged him again in the ribs, harder this time. He jolted awake with a start, looked at me and then his head dropped onto my shoulder, where it stayed until the credits rolled.

As the lights went up, I gave him a good shake. He opened his eyes, smiled at me, yawned and stretched. Then he looked around, realisation dawning. 'Marianne, I...'

'Save it,' I said, thrusting the empty box of chocolates down the front of his coat. 'At least I enjoyed these.'

I was halfway down the street before I found the piece of paper he'd slipped into my pocket sometime during the film. I read it under a street lamp, my heart simultaneously sinking and bursting. It was a poem. The first he ever wrote for me.

I read it through three times before I refolded the paper and carefully tucked it back in my pocket. He might be an idiot, but he was an idiot who could write words so beautiful they made me want to weep. For that reason alone, I would forgive him. Eventually.

ELEVEN

AUGUST 1944, FRANCE

Maggie wrinkled her nose. Those bodies had been swaying from their gibbet for over eighteen hours now. Plenty of time for the summer sun to set them putrefying. She could see the two young soldiers sent to guard them were standing as far upwind as they could. They appeared to be not much older than her brother, boys barely out of school.

Carefully propping her bicycle against a tree, she smoothed down her hair as she sauntered towards them, her basket swinging from her arm. In it she had stuffed as many cherries as she could along with a cool flask of water from the stream. It was all she had and it would have to do. The rest was down to charm.

'You look hot,' she called out as she approached.

They instantly raised their weapons. Then one of them relaxed.

'I know you,' he said. 'You gave us ham at the checkpoint.'

'I did,' she trilled, trying to remember him. 'And I have some lovely cherries today. Along with some water. I thought you might want to cool down a little.'

She pulled aside the cloth covering her basket to show them.

The one who'd spoken licked his lips. The other still had his weapon half-dangling, unsure what to do.

'Relax. I know her,' said his companion, his eyes fixed on the cherries nestling plump and juicy in their wicker container.

Maggie placed the flask of water in the shade. 'I'll leave this here for you. Unfortunately, I need my basket but I'm sure we can find something for the cherries.'

She looked around, careful not to glance at the bloated corpses dangling only metres away. A plate, miraculously intact, poked from among the rubble. She picked it up and polished it with her cloth before setting the cherries on it.

'What happened here?' she asked innocently, concentrating on arranging the fruit.

'Place burned down,' said the more reticent soldier.

The other laughed. 'Oh come on. It was a bunch of filthy Resistance scum. These ones here, they were the ringleaders. We rounded up the others. Sent them off where they belong.'

He pointed his gun at the corpses and fired, sending one spinning, arms flapping as if he were still alive.

Maggie felt her guts lurch. 'I see.'

She placed the finished plate by the flask of water.

'But if they're all gone, why do you still need to guard the place?' She saw one of them frown. 'I mean, you poor things. Out in this hot sun all day.'

'In case the others come back,' said the boastful one. 'They're like rats. There are always more.'

Maggie smiled. 'Well, I'm sure you have it all under control. No one's going to get past you, eh?'

She ran a hand through her hair and pretended to fan her chest. 'My God, but it is hot.'

The soldier licked his lips again.

'Would you mind if I had a little of that water?'

'Go ahead,' he said, gesturing with his gun. A Beretta 38, Maggie noticed. Standard issue sub-machine gun for close quarters.

She poured a little of the water into her cupped hand and drank from it, peering up at him through her lashes as she did so. His friend was growing restless. She needed to move faster.

'I'd better be getting along,' she said. 'Babies to deliver. Do you know if it's safe to take the main road into the village? Or are some of these people still about?'

The soldier smirked. 'They're all safely in police cells. We got them all. Even the ones who tried to hide.'

'But of course you did.' Maggie smiled even as her heart sank. 'Well, see you later.'

The soldier's hand shot out and snapped around her wrist as she turned to walk away. 'Leaving so soon?'

She didn't like the new note in his voice or the look in his eyes. He had grown brave with her ego-stroking, convinced once more of his all-conquering position.

'I must.'

Her eyes flicked to the other soldier. She tried to pull her wrist from the first one's grasp but he held fast.

'Hans.'

A warning in the other soldier's tone. She felt his fingers loosen and drop.

'See you again,' he sneered.

Not if I see you first.

'*Au revoir.*'

She could feel his eyes on her back all the way down the lane. It was only when she reached the safety of the forest that her shoulders relaxed.

As she pulled her bicycle away from the tree where she'd left it, a figure stepped out.

'I thought you would never get away.'

'Oh my God.'

She would have dropped it with a clatter but for him grabbing the handles.

'What the hell are you doing here? They told me everyone was rounded up.'

'No,' said Antoine. 'Marianne and the others escaped.'

'Thank goodness.' Maggie's knees sagged with relief. 'Where have they gone?'

'That I am still trying to find out.'

'Why aren't you with them?'

Antoine's face stilled. When he spoke, it was with care. 'I was not here when they left.'

'Why not?'

Maggie's antennae were up. Her instincts, finely tuned by years of evading the enemy, told her something was off.

'I had to meet someone.'

'Who?'

Antoine sighed. 'It's better you do not know.'

Maggie felt the anger begin to uncoil from the pit of her stomach. 'Tell me.'

He stared at her, brought up short by the way she rapped out the words.

'*Allons*, we need to leave here.' He gestured back towards the burned-out farmhouse. 'Or our friends there might come looking.'

'I'm not going anywhere until you tell me.'

Another sigh. Antoine glanced at his hands and then back at Maggie. 'Very well, if that means you will come with me away from this place.'

A brief nod from Maggie.

'I went to see someone I know and asked him to speak to the chief of police.'

'Why?'

'So that I could find out where they would be taking the prisoners after they left Valréas.'

'You mean Jack and his men?'

'I do.'

'The chief of police and not the Milice?'

There was a big difference. Some of the local gendarmes, the chief of police included, were secretly sympathetic to the Resistance, fed up with their Nazi masters and deeply resentful of the Milice who did their bidding.

'Yes. All he could tell me is that they had already been moved on. As soon as he finds out to where, he will let me know.'

Maggie sucked in her cheeks. 'I see.'

'In the meantime, we need to gather together any stragglers here, although it appears it is only you and I who are left.'

Maggie studied his face. He had always had an atavistic air about him. Perhaps it was because he was gaunt and looked permanently hungry, although she suspected it was more likely due to the gleam in his eye. Antoine seemed forever to have one on the main chance.

'How do you propose we do that?'

'You promised you would come with me once I told you.'

She peered out, up and down the lane. It was empty. Not a solitary soul ever came this way. That was why it had been the perfect headquarters for the local cell. Still, it was her habit to be cautious. A lifesaving habit.

Maggie wheeled her bicycle through the trees and into the lane just after the bend that hid them from view. They walked in silence to the main road and turned towards the village. From a hundred paces away, they could see the roadblock on its outskirts. The road was straight here. It was too late to take a different route and arouse German suspicions. Instead, they carried on bold as brass, just as Maggie had done a thousand times before.

'Papers,' demanded the officer in charge.

'But of course.' Maggie deployed her best sweet smile and drew hers from her purse.

The officer glanced at them, then at her basket.

'You have nothing for us today?'

She let out a tinkling laugh. 'I did. I was bringing you some beautiful cherries, sir. From my own garden. But two of your soldiers demanded I hand them over. *Désolé*. I am so sorry.'

The officer's face darkened. 'Where was this?'

'At the old farmhouse on the road to Valréas, just outside the village. I'm afraid I turned up the wrong lane. Silly me. I should have taken the next one. Madame at the neighbouring farm is due to give birth any day. A breech, I fear.'

'Yes, yes.'

The officer waved his hand as if to indicate he'd heard enough, which was precisely what Maggie had been hoping. Men, in her experience, did not like to dwell on the messier sides of feminine life, and birth was one of the messiest.

He turned and began to issue orders. Maggie took the opportunity to wheel her bicycle past them, Antoine still walking silently by her side.

'Wait.'

They froze and stayed exactly where they were, backs stiffened.

'How many of them were there at this farmhouse?'

'Two, sir.'

The officer wheeled on his heels and snapped his fingers. A jeep drew up alongside him.

As it roared off towards the farmhouse, Maggie exhaled. 'Come on.'

TWELVE

They headed on up through the village towards the house Maggie used as a clinic as well as her home. Once inside, she set a pot of coffee to brew, moving with the quick, incisive efficiency her patients valued. Antoine watched from the door.

'Sit.' She gestured to one of the carved chairs set around the kitchen table. The cottage was old, its furniture in keeping. It made a change from the place where Maggie had grown up, a vast Norman manse that went with the ducal title her father held. It was also quite different to the Parisian apartment where she'd lived while studying medicine. Maggie was no more a midwife than the local butcher, but she was a sight more skilled. She knew how to deliver a baby and that was all that mattered. She also knew how to slit a throat.

'I know that Kommandant,' she said. 'He cannot bear anyone stealing. It's funny, isn't it, how even now a man like that can have his principles.'

'How well do you know him?' asked Antoine, still lurking in the doorway.

She glanced at him sharply. 'Not in that way, if that's what you mean.'

Maggie straightened her shoulders and glared at him. Antoine had the grace to look away.

'That is not what I meant. I simply wondered how you got your information.'

'By watching, Antoine. Observing what goes on around me. I go in and out of these people's lives. They trust me. Now that we no longer have a doctor in the village, they come to me when they're sick and need help. Yes, even the Germans. Many times I have been summoned to help one of their soldiers who has a bad stomach or some other complaint. Of course, I may just make sure they don't recover too quickly. You understand.'

Antoine returned her smile.

'You should do that more often,' said Maggie as she poured the coffee into wide breakfast cups.

'What?'

'Smile. It makes you seem more human.'

'I don't appear human to you?'

'You're very serious at times. Most of the time.'

'These are serious times.'

'I know. But a smile, a laugh – they can help things along.'

'I am not a pretty young woman. The Germans do not care if I smile at them. It does not work as it does for you.'

Maggie sighed. 'It's not just the Germans. It's your comrades. Your brothers and sisters in the Resistance. We're all so tired of this war. We need to pull together now more than ever.'

'Not so easy,' said Antoine, 'when your comrades have disappeared.'

He glanced at his watch.

'Something wrong?' asked Maggie.

At that moment, there was a tiny tap at the back door, so gentle that it could have been the breeze.

Antoine was on his feet in an instant. He nodded to the

man standing there and let him in, closing and bolting the door behind him.

Maggie also rose and stared at them both, arms folded.

The man was of medium height and such an average appearance she was immediately suspicious, his hair a forgettable shade of brown, his features unremarkable. Even his clothes were nondescript. He was precisely the sort who could disappear into a crowd, a trait both sides valued highly in their agents.

'Who is this? What are you doing in my home?' No time for niceties. And she certainly had no stomach for them.

'Special Agent Jim McMahon at your service, ma'am. I'm here to rendezvous with Antoine. And to meet you.'

Maggie kept her arms folded, ignoring the hand he held out. 'To meet me? Why? How did you know we would be here?'

She looked at Antoine.

'We had an appointment,' he said. 'Jim and me. In the village. But then there was the roadblock. It would have been too dangerous to meet in public.'

'So I followed you here,' said McMahon.

Maggie mentally kicked herself for not noticing a tail. 'You're American?'

'Yes, ma'am.'

'But you're not in uniform.'

'My unit operates in plain clothes, ma'am.'

'I see.'

She carried on staring at him, taking in the easy stance, the eyes that met hers without any trace of discomfiture.

'And who are "we"?'

'I work for CIC, ma'am. Counter Intelligence Corps.'

'So you're a spy.'

'I'm an intelligence officer.'

Maggie looked at Antoine. 'How do you know each other?'

A pause. An unspoken assent passed between the men.

'Antoine here is helping us out.'

'Is he now?' Scorn dripped from Maggie's words.

'May I sit down?' McMahon didn't wait for her reply but settled himself into a chair and eased back. 'That coffee sure smells good.'

She pursed her lips, but innate good manners compelled her to fetch him a cup and fill it to the brim before placing it in front of him with just enough force that it splashed his fingers as he reached for it.

'Pardon.'

Maggie took the chair furthest from McMahon and regarded him as he sipped.

'My that is good. Thank you.'

She tilted her head a fraction but refrained from smiling.

'So,' she said, 'you were telling me how Antoine is helping you out.'

Her emphasis on the last three words wasn't lost on either man.

McMahon leaned forward, the geniality falling away from his face as he spoke. 'Antoine isn't just helping us but the whole of France. This is a crucial time, ma'am, as I'm sure you know. Thanks to Operation Overlord we have the Germans on the run, but we need Operation Dragoon to finish them off. We must do everything we can to make sure it goes according to plan. That includes using any and all intelligence sources to keep tabs on what the Resistance is doing as well as the Germans.'

Maggie's face flushed a dark, angry red. 'You would spy on your own?' she snapped at Antoine.

'Antoine here isn't spying on his own. He's identifying spies.'

The geniality was back, along with a soothing tone.

'Oh really? How?'

'Maggie, you know very well that we have moles within this

network and others. Traitors who are responsible for many lives lost.' Antoine spoke so quietly she could barely hear him. He raised his head, his voice growing louder. 'How do you think the Germans knew to come to that farmhouse at that particular time? They have ignored it for four years and yet all of a sudden they are there just when all the networks are meeting. Coincidence? I think not.'

She fiddled with the handle on her cup, allowing his words to sink in. It was exactly what Marianne had said. There was no such thing as coincidence and certainly not in situations such as this.

'Who do you think it is?' she asked.

'I do not know.' Antoine spread his hands. 'Genuinely. The British seem to think it's one of Jack's men, but I am not so sure. I think there are others.'

'We have intelligence reports that indicate information has been passed from a particular source,' said McMahon. 'But nothing is certain.'

'So is this why you're still here instead of with the others?' asked Maggie, turning to Antoine. 'To work for the Americans?'

'I work for France,' said Antoine. 'For a France free of these invaders and whole again, not divided by the communists and the fascists who want to turn us one against the other.'

His face was white, his eyes burning from what looked to be deep pits of exhaustion. *We're all exhausted*, thought Maggie. *We have endured so much*. Maybe Antoine's mind had snapped under the strain or perhaps he genuinely believed he was doing the right thing.

'What is it you want with me?' She could feel McMahon observing her, watching to see what she would say or do. 'Let me guess – you would like me to work for you too.'

His smile immediately wiped five years from his face, making him seem almost boyish. 'You're as intelligent as Antoine here told me.'

'And you're as patronising as I would have expected from an American. May I remind you that this is still my country and you are in my home.'

McMahon threw back his head and laughed. 'As feisty too. Ma'am, I salute you.'

'In France we say madame. Or mademoiselle. But you may call me Maggie.'

'Very well, Maggie. My apologies. I very much realise this is your country and that is why we're all working to give it back to you. We're on the same side here. We hate the Nazis every bit as much as you do.'

'You hate the communists too.'

He laughed again but this time there was an edge to it. 'We do. So what do you say, Maggie? How about we all help one another?'

'You first.'

It was like playing chess with her brother, thought Maggie. Only her brother was a mathematician and an excellent strategist. McMahon's eyes certainly gleamed with intelligence, but she rather thought he was better at reading people than the odds.

'OK. I could start by telling you where your friends have gone.'

Her heart lifted. 'You know where they are?'

'Sure.'

He pulled out a packet of cigarettes, tapping one into the palm of his hand. She waited as he lit up, determined not to show her impatience. If he knew how much she wanted that nugget of information, he would put an exceedingly high price on it. Far better to let him think that it was of little consequence to her where they'd gone.

'Thing is,' said McMahon, narrowing his eyes as he exhaled away from her, 'this is a quid pro quo. I tell you where they are and I'm going to want you to do something for me in return.'

'Well, there's a surprise.'

Another guffaw from McMahon. 'I like you.'

'I'm not so sure about you, but do carry on.'

'OK, here's the deal. I tell you where they are and I even help you get there. In return, I want you to introduce me to your friends.'

'So they'll trust you?'

'Exactly.'

'What if I don't trust you?'

'Then you would be wise. You don't know me from Adam. But I hope to prove to you that you *can* trust me, for your sake and that of your friends. It's important that you do.'

'Why is that?'

'Because right now, we all need to work together. This is a crucial moment. Our chance to turn things around and win this damn war, at least here in France.'

She looked at Antoine, his eyes lowered, apparently examining the woodgrain of the table.

'Do you have anything to say, Antoine?'

'I do not think there is anything I need to add,' he said. 'Maggie, these people genuinely want to help. We need to do this. You need to do this. If not for you, then for France.'

'For France.' She scoffed. 'Since when have you done anything for anyone but yourself?'

He flinched as if she'd hit him.

'I lost my whole life to the Germans,' he whispered. 'My wife. My children. All of them gone. Taken to the camps. I have no idea where. I do not know if they are alive or dead, but what I do know is that the Germans are determined to kill as many of us as they can before they are done. Especially people like me.'

She gazed at him, at his clever, intense face. At his hand on the table, stretched towards her, trembling with emotion.

Realisation washed over her. 'You're Jewish?'

'I am.'

'Antoine, I never knew.'

The story of this war. Of the Resistance. They knew so little of one another, quite deliberately. It meant information couldn't be tortured out of them, but it also meant that personal tragedies, such as Antoine's, went unshared. He had borne his burden quite alone. She wanted to reach across the table and enfold him in an embrace. Instead, she gently touched his hand and then rose to lift the coffee pot from the range.

'I'll make us fresh coffee,' she said. 'And then, Agent McMahon, you will fill me in on what we do next.'

'Jim, please,' he said. 'Now that we'll be working together.'

She swung round from the range and surveyed him, sweeping her gaze down to the coffee cup he tapped with one impatient finger and back to the genial grin that told a different story.

'As Antoine said, Jim, I work for France. A free France. Whatever that takes. We may be working for the same results, but that is all.'

'Whatever you say, Maggie.'

She met him smile for smile, her eyes wide and guileless. Let the American think he had won. Before this war was over, she swore she would wipe the floor with his all-conquering grin.

THIRTEEN

FEBRUARY 1941, CAMBRIDGE

'What will you have, Marianne?' asked Edward.

'I'll have a glass of port please.'

'Marcus, come and give me a hand at the bar.'

I watched my two brothers stroll away together, so different and yet in some ways so alike.

'He's settling in well,' said Jack. 'You'd think he'd been here forever.'

It was true. Cambridge suited Marcus, the ancient stone walls absorbing and embracing him, its spires allowing him to dream as he had since he was a little boy.

'I think he loves it,' I said.

The pub door banged open and a tall, rangy figure burst through. He bounded up to Edward, clapping him around the shoulders. I saw him shake hands with Marcus as Edward introduced them before he turned and strode over to us.

'Guy. Good to see you,' said Jack. 'This is Marianne.'

He took my hand and held it a fraction too long. 'Marianne. I've heard so much about you.'

'Really?' I raised an eyebrow at Jack and glanced up at

Edward, who was depositing our drinks on the table. 'All good things, I hope.'

'The very best.'

He beamed at me and I felt the full force of his charm. Unlike Jack's, it was manufactured – or so I felt.

Guy took the chair to my left while Marcus squeezed in beside me on the bench under the window.

Edward raised his glass. 'Cheers, everyone. To happier times. And victory.'

We clinked our glasses, the sound ringing like a knell through my heart.

'When are you off?' asked Jack.

'Any day now,' replied Edward.

I looked at the two of them, my boys. My men. Except one of them was leaving, his papers in his pocket, off to be trained at some location he couldn't name.

'Then we will all have to look after Marcus until you get back,' I said.

'Absolutely,' said Guy.

'I don't need looking after,' said Marcus. 'I'm perfectly capable of looking after myself.'

As if to prove it, he lifted his pint to his lips and sank it in one, leaving a foam moustache along his upper lip.

'Evidently,' I said, reaching forward with my handkerchief to dab at it. He swatted my hand away and growled, just as he'd done since he was old enough to object.

'Marcus, what's your subject?' asked Guy.

'I'm reading English.'

'Splendid. So am I. If you need to borrow any books, just ask. I have some which are hard to find.'

'Thank you. I will.'

Marcus looked abashed but pleased. He wasn't used to the attention.

'I also belong to a writer's group, if you're interested,' added

Guy. 'Actually, there's a reading this evening, if you'd like to come along.'

He smiled at the rest of us around the table. 'You're all welcome of course.'

'Thanks, mate,' said Jack. 'But I'm taking Marianne to the cinema.'

'I'm busy saying goodbye to someone,' said Edward.

I threw him a sharp look. 'Oh yes? Who?'

'Never you mind.'

He gazed into the middle distance with that enigmatic half-smile of his. That was big brother all over, unable to hide his sweetness even when he was playing the man of mystery.

'She's a lucky woman, whoever she is,' I said, squeezing his forearm.

'So's Jack,' said Guy. 'A lucky man, I mean.'

I could have sworn he was blushing, his cheeks ruddy with clumsy gallantry.

'Thank you,' I murmured.

He was an odd one, but good-hearted. A dreamer, like Marcus, under that exuberant exterior.

'Steady on, old boy,' said Jack. 'You'll be sweeping her off her feet next.'

'No chance of that.' I smiled up into his eyes.

Jack was the one. I knew that in my bones. In that part of me I couldn't name, that sense that was absolutely certain. We were meant for one another. Nothing and no one could ever change that.

FOURTEEN

I woke to the cool insistence of steel pressed against my throat.

'Where's the money?' hissed Juliette.

I played for time. 'What money?'

'The money the Americans brought with them tonight. I know they gave some of it to you.'

'They didn't. Look, do I really have to disarm you a second time?'

I sat up, not even bothering to swipe the knife out of her hand. She hesitated. At this point I would have gone for the kill.

The linen sheets rustled as she moved, sitting back a fraction so she was at arm's length. I could still get that knife out of her hand if I needed to, but I wanted to hear what she had to say. Then she dropped the knife on the bed, a mischievous grin transforming her entire face.

'We need to talk,' she said.

'Is this how you always start conversations?'

'I was testing you.'

'And did I pass?'

'Of course. At least you didn't try to kill me again.'

'We both know I could have done.'

'Yes, but then you would have been without me and my men. And you need our help.'

'That's true.'

We looked at one another in the dark, my eyes fully adjusted now so I could make out the solemn expression in hers.

She held out her hand. 'Friends?'

I took it and shook it. 'Friends and fellow soldiers.'

She laughed and pulled a flask from her robe, taking a swig from it before offering it to me.

'I'll drink to that,' she said.

I took a swig too, feeling the burn of cognac on the back of my throat.

'My guess is that you didn't just sneak in here in the dead of night to shake my hand and bring me a drink though,' I said.

'You're right. I wanted to talk to you about that money.'

I held out my hands, palms up. 'I swear to you, Juliette, I don't have any of it.'

'I believe you, but we do need to get hold of it. I have to feed my people. Many of them have families who are starving. They can't fight for France if they're hungry and worried about their loved ones.'

I looked at her, at this woman who not only led an army but looked after the fighters and families in her charge. She was running on empty too, but she didn't care. All she wanted was to free her country and protect her people. It was all she had ever wanted.

'What can I do to help?' I said.

'You can make sure we get enough money to supply food to all those who need it.'

'Consider it done.'

'You mean that?'

'You have my word. The only way we can win this war is together. We're on the same side.'

'Are we? Really?'

'Yes, really. I admire what you're doing here. You're doing far more than many men could do, and you're doing it on your own, without backup. That takes guts.'

'It takes everything, as you know.'

'I do.'

Our eyes met and, in hers, I saw understanding. More than that, kinship.

She picked up the knife and ran it gently down my forearm, tracing the veins.

'We're all sisters under the skin,' she said. 'Although if you betray me, I will not hesitate to use this.'

'I know. And likewise.'

She threw back her head and laughed. 'I don't doubt it.'

FIFTEEN

He braced himself before the first punch, tightening his stomach muscles and breathing out so that his organs were protected. Then he detached, pulling his mind away so that it felt as if this was happening to someone else, somewhere else. He heard their shouts and threats from that place far away. A place where he was walking, hand in hand with Marianne, her heart-shaped face turned up to him as they talked, her hair dancing around it, dark as a raven's wing.

'Names – give me their names.'

The guard's shouts penetrated his thoughts.

Another blow, this time to his kidneys. A bolt of pain shot through him. He pulled back even further, letting his mind soar once more. Another time, another place. This time the prison camp rather than a cell, sharing a smoke with one of the other chaps. 'I hear you have a girl. Tell me about her.'

'She's brave. Fierce even. But once she lets you in, she's like a warm bath you want to sink into forever. Gentle and yet strong. So strong. You can see it in her eyes. The way she looks at me sometimes, it makes me feel as if she can see it all. The real me. The parts I keep hidden even from myself. She has beautiful eyes. The same colour as whisky. A mouth that smiles even when she doesn't feel like smiling. She's great with her men. Good at keeping up morale.'

'Her men?'

'I've said too much.'

'On the contrary, you've said just enough. I would love to meet her, your girl.'

'Perhaps you will.'

His head jerking back with a sharp crack, the sound ringing through his skull. Hadn't seen that one coming. He was too busy remembering.

A couple of days after their shared smoke, the other fellow was dead, mown down as they broke out of the prison camp. He would never meet Marianne, more's the pity. Never see that lovely smile of hers or hear her say his name. But he would see her soon. He could feel that in his bones, even as they rattled under the onslaught of blows.

'A name. Give me a name,' the guard yelled in his face, his spittle landing on Jack's cheek.

Jack shook his head and laughed. The guard stared at him as if he had lost his mind. Perhaps he had. He had certainly lost his heart. He murmured something.

'What was that?' barked the guard.

Jack mumbled it again, the guard grabbing him by the hair and jerking his head back so he could hear.

'Say it again,' he snarled.

'I said go to hell.'

One more punch, this time to his jaw, and he was spiralling away, spinning, lights dancing, dazzling, before his eyes until the curtain of darkness dropped over them and he was gone, falling into merciful oblivion.

SIXTEEN

Light sliced across the cell as the door swung open and Jack stumbled through. He righted himself just as Guy reached out a hand.

'Steady, old chap.'

'I'm all right.'

'You don't look it.'

Jack sank onto the edge of the iron bed that was screwed into the wall, raised a hand to his jaw and gingerly pressed along it. 'I don't think it's broken.'

'Here.'

Guy was holding out the vest he'd soaked in the cold water that ran from the tap in the corner of the cell. Aside from that, their beds and the bucket that served as a toilet alongside it, there was nothing else to occupy the eight-by-twelve-foot space that served as their temporary home.

Jack applied the vest to the swelling that was already bruising on his cheekbone. 'Thanks, mate.'

'Any word of Charles?'

'None.'

As a Frenchman and suspected member of the Resistance,

Charles would probably get even more special treatment. Jack sent him a silent prayer of solidarity. It was all he could do. Such bad luck to stumble into that roadblock. Even worse to have all that money on them. The money that was vital to the operation. He wanted to kick himself hard yet again.

Of course, if they didn't get out of here then the money was immaterial. The information he carried in his head was priceless by comparison.

Jack dropped that same head in his hands and peered through his fingers at Guy, who was staring out of the tiny cell window. Moonlight illuminated the rooftops of the prison blocks and the barracks beyond, the vast silver disc sitting low in the sky.

'It's a full moon,' said Guy. 'I wonder if there were many drops tonight.'

'I should imagine so,' said Jack. 'They're running Jedburgh as well as the normal ops.'

'Not long now,' said Guy, 'until we give them another kicking.'

'No.'

He wished he felt as sure as he sounded.

Jack moved the vest to his eye socket, which was turning as purple as the bruise on his cheek. The Germans were always thorough but tonight's going over had been especially brutal. At least he'd had Marianne for company, if only in his thoughts.

And it seemed Guy could read those thoughts. 'Back in that cornfield... did you see her?'

Guy appeared relaxed, his question casual. And yet something in Jack sounded an alarm. It always did where Marianne was concerned. The torch Guy carried was barely concealed at times. He was pretty sure Marianne had noticed too but chose to pretend not to. She was always kind to Guy. She was kind to everyone so long as they deserved it.

He suppressed a sigh. 'No.'

The image of her standing, a slight figure backlit by flames, was seared into his brain. A few rows of corn, that was all that had rippled between them. That and a thousand unspoken words. He could remember other fields, other times. Memories he couldn't bear to uncork, not here and not now. Like genies, they were safe only as long as they were trapped in the glass of the past, glimpsed only to get him through the beatings. Just a few yards and he could have touched her, held her. It was too much.

'Think they'll move us out in the morning?'

Guy was still staring out of the window, apparently transfixed by the moon. Jack's response was swallowed by the sound of the cell door opening once more.

'You. Come with me.'

The guard beckoned to Guy, who straightened his shoulders and, without a backward glance, strode into the prison corridor. As the clang of metal upon metal reverberated around the space where he'd stood, Jack murmured, 'Good luck, my friend.'

If he'd been religious, he would have crossed himself. But all belief in God had died long ago, not so much on the battlefields, where at least the fight seemed fairer, but behind the lines, waging the secret war that would bring them so much closer to victory. Just as Marianne was doing, wherever she was now.

'Stay safe, darling girl,' he whispered. It was the closest he came now to prayer, an invocation he repeated every night wherever he was. One he had murmured even as he'd led his men out of that cornfield, leaving behind him the one person he longed to save above all others. Although Marianne was more than capable of saving herself.

Stories had reached his ears hundreds of miles away, borne by lips that spoke admiringly of the Englishwoman who not only led her own network but did so with such guts and panache. Of course she did. She didn't know any other way of being. Marianne was a woman like no other. His woman. And if nothing else, he would live to reclaim her. As she would him.

SEVENTEEN

Maggie gazed out through the car window at the perimeter walls of Digne prison. Even at this distance, they looked impenetrable.

'You're sure they're in there?' asked Antoine.

'According to our intelligence, yes,' replied McMahon. 'We have someone on the inside.'

'I'm sure you do,' she muttered. 'So what do we do now?'

'We watch and wait.'

'For what? For them to throw their bodies over the wall?'

McMahon glanced over his shoulder at her, crouched in the back of the car. The headlights were off. They had coasted into position on a side street tucked beneath the cathedral almost next to the prison. Gazing up at both, the contrast between the roseate window of the cathedral offering hope and the forbidding prison walls seemed to Maggie to be particularly cruel.

'Do we know when they're moving them?'

'Our informant could only tell us they are waiting for orders from Montluc.'

An involuntary shudder ran through Maggie. The very name spoke of such brutality and suffering, whispers of which ran through all the networks in Vichy France. Montluc was Barbie's prison, the place from where he summoned agents and *résistants* alike to be tortured until they couldn't talk even if they wanted to, which they almost never did.

Maggie studied the prison walls in front of them again, taking in the three buildings that loomed beyond them, rising starkly in the moonlight, their windows black, barred squares that resembled eyes staring back at her. Which one was Jack's? she wondered. Was he even now looking out, staring up at that same full moon? She hoped for his sake that he was. And for Marianne's. More than once, she'd caught Marianne gazing at that shining silver orb, her face unreadable.

'There – I see him,' murmured McMahon.

Instantly, they were on the alert, watching the figure emerge from the guardhouse and make his way down from the prison, strolling towards the cathedral as if he didn't have a care in the world. McMahon was already slipping out of the car, noiselessly padding up the street towards the side doorway where the man stood, invisible unless you knew he was there.

'He's good,' murmured Maggie.

'I hope so,' said Antoine.

She glanced at him, taking in the worry creasing his face. 'You don't like this, do you?'

He shook his head and raised a finger to his lips. They had kept their voices barely audible but Maggie understood. Even walls had ears.

'Let's go,' said McMahon, sliding back behind the wheel and disengaging the brake so that the car began to roll backward down the street. It was only when they reached the bottom of the hill that he dared turn on the engine and purr as gently as he could out of town, driving by the light of the moon until they were far beyond the boundaries and racing along the open road.

'Where are we going?' asked Maggie, breaking the silence that had engulfed them since Digne.

'To see some friends of yours,' said McMahon.

The road flashed past as they picked up speed, eating up the miles. The roads were empty, the Germans huddled in their camps, unused to the terrain and unsure of what was coming. Good. They had them on the run, at least mentally. Soon they would have them on the run physically too, as they had in the north. And she would play her part in that as they all would. They were so close now to a free France. A truly free France. Above them, the moon shone with promise, lighting their way to freedom, to friendship. To the people who were more Maggie's family than her own.

EIGHTEEN

'Marianne. Get up.' I heard Juliette's voice from a long way off. 'We have visitors. Friends of yours.'

I blinked. It felt as if seconds had passed since I'd sunk into a deep and dreamless sleep once Juliette had left my room, taking her knife with her. I pushed aside the bedcovers, trying at the same time to push through the fog that clouded my mind.

'What? Who?' I rasped as I flung on my clothes.

'Come – they are downstairs.'

Like me, Juliette must have had two hours' sleep at most, yet her eyes were bright, energy crackling from her as we descended to the hall where I saw three people standing in the grey light that filtered through the windows high above. I recognised the spring of Maggie's curls before I made out her face, falling on her with cries of delight.

'What are you doing here?' I murmured as I enveloped her in my arms. I could feel her exhaustion in the heaviness of her limbs and in the way she rested her head briefly on my shoulder. I glanced at the two men who were with her.

'Antoine,' I said.

He nodded.

'It's good to see you.'

My words sounded hollow, even to me. Truth be told, I was more surprised to see him than anyone. I'd thought I might never see him again, except perhaps overseeing my arrest or otherwise unveiling himself as a traitor. Yet here he was, with Maggie and another man who now took a step forward.

'Special Agent Jim McMahon,' he announced, holding out his hand.

I shook it, noting the insignia on his collar. 'Special Agent?'

'Yes, ma'am.'

'We have news,' said Maggie. 'We came here straight from Digne. They're holding Jack and the other men in the prison there. Jim here has a contact on the inside.'

McMahon cleared his throat. 'I just met with this contact. He informed me that they're transferring Jack and the other two officers to Montluc prison in Lyon. Klaus Barbie is very keen to question them.'

I drew a deep breath. 'When are they moving them? Are you sure this man is telling the truth?'

'He doesn't know exactly when but he thinks it could happen any day now. He's a longstanding contact of ours and completely trustworthy,' said McMahon. 'His son died in the Battle of France. He hates the Nazis as much as anyone.'

'Then we have to intercept them before they get anywhere near Lyon.'

McMahon shook his head. 'Impossible. We're not going to get anywhere near a prison convoy on these roads, much less intercept one.'

Juliette looked at me. 'I disagree.'

'He's right,' said Diaz, descending the stairs dressed in full uniform in spite of the early hour. He walked straight up to McMahon. 'And you are?'

'Special Agent Jim McMahon.'

Diaz glanced at me. I caught a warning in his gaze.

'How did you find us?' he asked McMahon, a slight edge sharpening the friendliness of his tone.

'Intelligence,' said McMahon.

I looked at Juliette and gave her the tiniest shake of my head.

'From?' Diaz wasn't giving up so easily.

'I'm sure you know that's classified.'

Diaz smiled. 'Of course.'

The smile dropped and there was a glint in his eye I hadn't seen before.

'Thing is, Jim,' went on Diaz, 'this is wartime and, as you know, we share intelligence in this theatre. So I'll ask you again – who told you we were here?'

'And I already told you that's classified. Now, if there's nothing else, I must be getting along. Good day to you all.'

McMahon turned on his heel and was halfway to the door before Diaz caught up with him.

'You tell your friends,' said Diaz, 'that if they try any other funny business, I'll be waiting for them. We all will.'

I felt my back stiffen. Something was going on here that sent thrills of alarm running up and down my spine. The two men stared one another down as if they hated each other, rival lions, each wanting to lead.

'I have no idea what you're talking about,' said McMahon.

His eyes shifted from Diaz and settled on me. 'I almost forgot,' he said, pulling an envelope from his pocket and thrusting it into my hand. He smiled. Or at least, his mouth did.

'I think you'll find that interesting,' he murmured.

And then he was gone, the door shutting silently behind him, frighteningly in control until the last.

I let out the gush of air I'd been holding in my chest.

'What the hell was all that about?' I asked Diaz.

'Those CIC bastards think they can do anything they like.'

The envelope in my hand was searing the flesh of my palm.

'Aren't you going to open it?' asked Diaz.

I could feel everyone's eyes upon me, burning with curiosity.

I thrust my thumb under the flap and tore it open, extracting a single sheet of folded paper from within. I read it once. Then again, my heart cracking with every word. There were barely half a dozen of them but that was enough. They confirmed the true identity of the double agent known as Claude, caught by the disinformation he'd been fed to pass on to his German masters. There was no mistaking the poem code he'd used to send messages from Lyon. The same one he'd whispered in my ear.

'My God, Jack, why?'

I wasn't even sure if I'd spoken aloud, but I felt the ripple in the room, the sharpening of focus. It couldn't be true. Not Jack. I wanted to retch, to fall to my knees and vomit out every last thing in my stomach. This couldn't be happening.

A kaleidoscope of thoughts and memories. Jack holding me, kissing me, fighting by my side. Blue eyes shining, true. Words spilling from his lips, truer. I had never known him to lie. But then, how would I know? This was a night for worlds turned upside down and beliefs blown to smithereens. I felt my heart shatter, like a star exploding in the galaxy, the white heat of pain blasting through me until it solidified into shards of ice.

'Marianne, are you all right?'

Maggie's voice, full of concern.

'Yes, yes I'm fine.'

I could feel the fury now, surging through the pain. That smile back there in the cornfield was not one of love but betrayal. The smiling assassin. And now I wanted to kill him.

'I am absolutely fine,' I repeated, crumpling the piece of paper in my fist, digging my nails into my palm until I felt the pain bite.

'Well, come on. What are we waiting for? We have work to do.'

I headed for the door, biting back the howl I was stifling in my throat. *Stay angry. Focus on the mission. Follow orders.* I would do all of that and more. But once this was done, once we had liberated France, I would hunt Jack down, wherever he was and whatever it took. I wanted to see the look in his eyes when he knew it was me who had come for him. Me, the woman he had sworn to love forever. The same woman who now hated him with every beat of her broken heart.

NINETEEN

'We must get you to Lyon,' said Diaz. 'Set you up with the local network.'

'There's no network left in Lyon,' said Marcus.

'Exactly. Marianne needs to take over there. Make contact with the agents still in place.'

'What agents?' I asked. 'I thought everyone was rounded up.'

Including my big brother. Thanks to Jack.

Diaz turned to Marcus. 'Any chance you could find our radio operator for me? I need him to send an urgent message about this. Haven't seen him all morning.'

Marcus looked a little taken aback, but good manners won out. 'Of course.'

'Thanks, buddy.'

Diaz waited until he'd pulled the salon door to behind him before resuming. 'We have a couple undercover they didn't catch,' he said. 'One is working a joint op along with us. A top-secret one.'

'And the objective of this op?' I asked.

Diaz looked at our small group, weighing up what to say next. 'To kill Klaus Barbie.'

The breath caught in my throat. Exactly what I had suggested to Marcus. And someone was already in place, working on it, apparently with the help of the Americans.

'How do you know all this?'

'That's classified, ma'am,' said Diaz. 'What I can tell you is that I was stationed in London for quite a while before I was sent here – in Baker Street as it happens.'

Baker Street, shorthand for SOE headquarters.

'I want in,' I said.

'Me too,' said Juliette.

I looked at her. 'This is an SOE op.'

'You heard him. It's a joint op. Besides, you need me. I know the local Resistance. It was you who said we need to work together.'

Touché.

'We're all going to work this,' said Diaz. 'It's why they sent us, don't forget. To support you and everyone else in the run-up to Dragoon.'

The arrogance was back and it grated. Or maybe it was simply the fact he was treading on my toes.

'Very well,' I said. 'But we need to make a plan and move swiftly. Who are these agents already in the field?'

Diaz hesitated again.

I looked at Antoine, standing next to Maggie. They had arrived with McMahon. Or rather, Antoine had arrived.

'How did you two find one another?' I asked.

'What?'

'You and Maggie – how did you meet up? Last thing I knew, Maggie was on her way to send a message and you were nowhere to be seen.'

'Antoine was waiting for me near the farmhouse,' said Maggie. 'I went there to find you. Instead, there were a couple of German soldiers still guarding the place. We went back to my house, and McMahon followed us there. He had an assignation already arranged with Antoine.'

Now we were all looking at Antoine.

'Would you care to explain how and why?' I asked.

Antoine remained silent, his thoughts flitting across his face.

'Maybe I can explain,' said Maggie.

She glanced at Antoine but he stared steadfastly ahead. My fingers itched for my gun. Anything to break through that stubborn silence.

'Antoine told me that he is, in fact, Jewish. His entire family has been taken. McMahon promised to help find them in return for some favours.'

'What kind of favours?' I asked.

'Information.' At last Antoine spoke up. 'But I gave him nothing about us or the network or the Maquis.'

'So what did you tell him?'

His eyes dulled, becoming flat and impenetrable once more.

'Who did you betray, Antoine?'

My gun was in my hand now, level with his heart.

'Marianne.'

Diaz spoke my name softly. I ignored him.

'Come on, Antoine. You must have something to say for yourself.'

'I betrayed no one. I would never do that. I passed on information we already had about the Boches. Nothing important. I needed something to trade, to get information back from him. You don't know what it's like losing everything and everyone that you love.'

Actually, I did. Well, almost everyone. Marcus was still here with me. I lowered my gun.

'And did he help you?'

'Not really,' whispered Antoine. 'All he could tell me was that they had been transported.'

I could see the muscles working in his cheek as he fought to stop himself from breaking down.

'That bastard,' said Diaz. 'He strung you along, buddy. Don't you worry. We'll find your people.'

'They are in the camps,' said Antoine, his eyes bleak, the hollows beneath them deeper than ever. 'No one comes back from those camps. I have heard the stories. We all have. People are dying there. The Nazis are killing them even as they arrive.'

'Not all of them,' I said. 'Those are just rumours, Antoine. No one knows for sure. We'll find them. I promise.'

'I hope so,' he said. 'They are my whole life.'

'Don't lose that hope.'

My words sounded hollow, even to my ears. There were some losses that eradicated all hope. Things that were too hard to bear. People who could never be replaced, no matter how hard we tried.

TWENTY

'So,' I said, 'these agents.'

'You'll love them,' said Diaz. 'They're both women.'

'I think I know of one,' said Juliette. 'She runs an establishment popular with the Gestapo, if it's who I think it is.'

'Correct,' said Diaz. 'She owns the best brothel in Lyon. It's a favourite with all the German officers as well as half the Vichy government.'

'And the other?'

'Is embedded in the Grand Hotel where her objective is to seduce Klaus Barbie.'

'Dear Lord. She must be one brave woman.'

'She is.'

I heard a note in Diaz's voice. He knew her, above and beyond the demands of duty.

'And after she has seduced him?'

'Her orders are to assassinate him.'

I stared at him. 'That is a suicidal mission.'

'It almost certainly is since the network was blown. She's now operating entirely on her own, without backup.'

'Then we must give her some. When do we leave?' I asked.

'Not so fast,' said Antoine. 'We have to put a proper plan in place first.'

'We wait to do that and Barbie will have tortured our men to death before we ever reach Lyon,' said Juliette. 'There's no way this agent will succeed in assassinating him alone. If she even tries, they will kill her too. I'm with Marianne. We should leave without further delay.'

I glanced at her, grateful for the support. 'Agreed.'

'Even so,' said Diaz, 'we need to proceed with caution.'

'Caution be damned,' I said. 'You're not in charge here. I am.'

Diaz flashed one of his incandescent smiles. 'So you are,' he said. 'Ma'am.'

'Call me Captain,' I said. 'Or Marianne. Anything but ma'am. It makes me sound positively ancient.'

Truth be told, I felt positively ancient at times but there was no way I would ever let him know that.

Diaz saluted. 'As you wish, ma'am. Captain. Marianne.'

I wanted to laugh at his earnestness. Except that I wasn't entirely convinced of his sincerity. Diaz shrouded dangerous undercurrents in layers of charm. Some women might have found it irresistible. I thought he was too cocky by half.

'So these two agents are not working together?'

'They're working separate missions. The madam has been running her brothel for a while now while the other only recently arrived at the Grand Hotel with the aim of targeting Barbie.'

'This Grand Hotel,' I said. 'Do we have contacts there?'

'I understand the manager is sympathetic to the Resistance.'

'Juliette and I could embed there too. Pretend to be hotel workers. Help our agent carry out her mission. With Barbie dead, the SS in Lyon will be all over the place. And it stops him getting his murdering hands on Jack and the other two men.'

Despite my rage, my burning desire for vengeance, it was still somehow a thought I couldn't bear.

'Absolutely not. It's insane to even suggest it,' snapped Antoine.

'Which is why it might just work,' said Diaz.

'Which is why it *will* work,' I countered.

'Barbie will never fall for it. He's a cunning bastard,' said Antoine. 'They'll shoot you before you get within a hundred yards of him.'

'It's my choice,' I said. 'My network. I decide what happens.'

'It's not just your decision,' said Antoine. 'This affects all of us. We could all be killed.'

'True,' I said. 'But we could also succeed. Which means Operation Dragoon will not be compromised and we can get the Nazis out of France once and for all.'

'You're right, ma'am,' said Diaz.

'I thought I told you to cut that ma'am nonsense,' I snapped.

'Sorry.'

He didn't sound it. Diaz was gloriously unrepentant. It was what got him through every day intact.

'We could succeed,' I repeated, raising my voice a fraction. 'And frankly, we have little choice but to try anything and everything.'

They all looked at me. Even Antoine fell silent.

'What this relies upon,' I went on, 'is meticulous planning. Juliette, do you have contacts within the Lyon Resistance? What's left of it?'

'I do,' she said. 'I will send a message to the *résistants* in Lyon to let them know we are coming. We will need accommodation. Up-to-date intelligence on Barbie and his movements.'

'Excellent,' I said. 'We can't descend on Lyon en masse. It makes us too conspicuous. We'll need to split up and work separately with watertight cover stories. Juliette and I can simply slip into being invisible women working at the hotel. The local network can assist with that. Maggie will act as courier to liaise between us all.'

'What about the rest of us?' asked Diaz.

'You are our backup,' I said. 'It's harder for you to become invisible, especially in that uniform.'

I could see Diaz itching to bite back. Luckily for him, he didn't.

'We can make use of you with the Maquis,' said Antoine. 'That is the whole point of the Jedburgh teams after all. To inspire the Resistance with our Allied friends in uniform.'

Operation Jedburgh was the first time we'd really worked with American agents. The fact that the Jeds, as we called them, wore uniform helped reassure the *résistants* in the run-up to Dragoon.

'It is indeed,' I said. 'And we need to deploy the Maquis between here and Lyon to sabotage the Germans in any way possible. Especially anything that will delay them transporting our men to Montluc. Now is the time to strike.'

'And the time to strike Barbie,' said Juliette.

Above her smile, her eyes glittered.

'That is an order,' I added, looking straight at Diaz. I still outranked him.

He regarded me through narrowed eyes but said nothing.

'I'm sure that Juliette's men will give you all assistance.'

'They will do whatever you need,' said Juliette. 'My men have been waiting for this day. They gathered here precisely for this purpose. To get rid of the Boches at last. To regain our country.'

The venom in her voice was as controlled as ever and all the more deadly for it. I saw Diaz glance at her with open admiration. He had good taste.

'We need to move out as soon as possible,' I said. 'We really don't have much time. We reconvene in the great hall in one hour. Remember, not a word goes beyond this room. We operate and issue orders on a need-to-know basis.'

'Let's do it.'

The energy Diaz exuded was electric, galvanising the rest of our small group.

'Do what?'

I looked round to see Marcus with the radio operator in tow.

Diaz shook his head as if to sound a warning, his eyes flicking to the radio operator lugging his equipment.

'I'll fill you in later,' he said. 'I need to talk to my radio operator now.'

'As it turns out,' said Marcus, 'he had an urgent message for me. I'm to return at once to Paris and report to the network there. They're a man down and there's no one else to take over.'

I stared at him, my heart sinking. 'When are you leaving?'

'Today.'

'We'll miss you.'

'And I you, but duty calls.'

'Of course. How are you getting to Paris?'

'On the afternoon train. I have all the right papers if anyone stops me. It's the same cover story I used before.'

A clutch of dread.

'Be careful, Marcus.'

'Aren't I always?'

I gave him a level look. 'No.'

'I'll get one of the men to drop you near the station and you can walk the rest,' said Juliette. 'You are less likely to be noticed that way.'

'Thank you,' said Marcus. 'That would be a great help.'

I threw my arms around him, holding him tight, not caring what the others thought. 'Come back to me soon,' I whispered.

I had held him so many times like this, especially when he was a small boy back in the orchard at home. Now he was a grown man but I still felt that need to protect him. He was my baby brother, now and always.

As I watched him go off to pack his things, I couldn't ignore the niggle in my gut.

A niggle I had long ago learned to heed. I only wished it had served me with Jack.

I beckoned to Henri, drawing him aside. 'I need you to do something for me,' I murmured. 'But this is strictly between us.'

Even here he still smelled faintly of pork fat. It was an oddly reassuring smell.

'But of course,' he said. 'Anything.'

'I want you to be the one to take Marcus to the station. Make sure he's safe. Then I need you to keep a close eye on the Maquis operations. Trust no one. Alert me if necessary.'

'No problem.'

That was what I loved about Henri. About so many of the men. Their unquestioning loyalty. It was how we operated, as a family. But even in the best of families, there are bad apples. The rotten fruit in the barrel. The same rot I could smell in the air around me. The rot we had to cut out before it proved fatal.

TWENTY-ONE

SEPTEMBER 1942, ENGLAND

The apples in the orchard shone like jewels, rubies scattered among the green of the leaves. Or at least, that was how they appeared through my eyes, glistening with the patina of pain I was already burying in my heart.

'I understand,' I said. And I did. I knew he had to go just as I also knew I was going too.

'I report tomorrow morning – 0800 hours,' he said.

'At the barracks?'

'No.'

Something about his tone warned me off asking anything more. He must have seen the flicker of surprise and hurt on my face because he sighed.

'I'm sorry,' he said. 'I wish I could tell you more, but I can't. You know how it is.'

I knew only too well. It had been the same with Edward before he was deployed somewhere in France. Now Marcus was itching to join him.

'I do,' I said.

It was impossible to say more than that. I was already choking back the tears. Of course Jack wanted to do his bit. We all did. But I still couldn't bear to see him go, wondering if I would ever see him again.

I reached out and stroked his collar between finger and thumb, focusing hard on the crisp, white cloth, hoping to keep those tears at bay. I could see the pulse beating at his throat. Almost hear the blood pumping through his veins. Jack's blood. My lifeblood. The two intermingled.

'Don't go,' I whispered, the words falling out of my mouth before I could stop them.

He reached up, his fingers intertwining with mine and pulling my hand to his heart.

'I will think of you every day,' he said. 'And every night.'

He glanced up, over the tops of the trees to where the moon was still visible in the sky, a silvered ghost against the blue.

'When I look at that moon, I will think of you and you must do the same.'

I looked at it then, almost full, a fat harvest moon. That was when I knew for certain.

'You're going on the full moon, aren't you?'

His flinch was imperceptible to anyone but me. 'I have no idea what you're talking about.'

'Yes you do. You're going on the full moon... and so am I.'

That blood I had seen pumping so vitally through his veins drained from his face. 'What do you mean?'

'You know what I mean. We're obvious choices, you and me. Your mother is French. My papa did two diplomatic tours in France. My brothers and I even attended school there for a while. It's why they chose Edward and why they will want Marcus too. *Nous parlons français couramment, mon cher*.'

He stared at me, disbelief written across his face. 'No. No, you can't go. You won't go. I absolutely forbid it.'

'You forbid it?' It was my turn to be shocked. 'Who are you to tell me what to do? I am going to serve my country and help the people of France, and neither you nor my parents nor anyone else is going to stop me.'

'Do your parents know?'

'Not yet.'

'Then I'll tell them. Get them to stop this insanity.'

'They won't care. Or at least, Mother won't. She probably won't even notice I've gone. That's why I have to go, don't you see? I can't end up like her, having wasted my life. I want to do something good to help this world. Something important.'

'Isn't what we have important?'

'It is, but it's not enough. Not for me. I have to be my own woman. Not just some wife and mother.'

I stopped, gulping in a breath. He was no longer radiating fury. Instead, I could see the hurt in his expression, hear it in his voice.

'Then you must go,' he said. 'If that's not enough for you. If I am not enough.'

'You are more than enough. It's me. I need more from life. A life I would like to spend with you.'

There. I had said it.

He squeezed my hand tighter then raised it to his lips; I unfurled my fingers, caressing his cheek. He bent his head, our lips meeting, saying everything that needed to be said. I would never know if he kissed me to stop me from uttering another word or because he wanted to. I think it was the latter. What I do know is that by the time I came up for air, everything and nothing had changed. I was Jack's. I had always been Jack's. Just as he had always been mine.

I pulled him towards the summerhouse, urgency over-coming fear. He stopped dead inside the door, gripping me tightly by the shoulders, eyes boring into mine.

'Are you all right? We don't have to do this.'

'Yes we do. We really do.'

I kicked the door shut and turned the key in the lock. Then

I reached up and began to undo the buttons on my dress, my fingers fumbling, my eyes never leaving his.

'Let me.'

His fingers were surer. More practised maybe. As they brushed against my flesh, I felt electric shocks thrilling through me. A deep, pulsating heat was rising in my belly, fuelled by the fire in my groin. I was at once wet and burning for him at the same time, melting and opening to something I had never known. He was easing my dress from my shoulders, kissing me as he peeled it from my body and let it fall to the floor. I could hear the birds singing above the rushing in my ears, the soft groan that escaped from my throat as he pulled one of my breasts free and caressed it with the tip of his thumb, circling it, then bending to draw my nipple into his mouth.

We sank to the floor together, the boards rough under my back, but I didn't care. I reached for him, undoing his belt, pulling him free, loving the surge of triumph as he moaned at my touch. He was hard under my fingers, harder still as I wrapped them around him. I had no idea what I was doing; I knew exactly what I was doing. Some primeval instinct guided me even as I stumbled.

He pushed himself up on his elbows, naked as I was by now, cushioned by the clothes onto which we had rolled, his flesh searing mine where it met.

'You sure?'

In answer, I lifted my head, drawing him in for another kiss, our tongues intertwined, then drawing him into me, stifling a grunt of pain, feeling him hesitate, pulling him in deeper still, beginning to move with him in a dance that was as old as time, forcing my eyes open to look into his face, then closing again as I surrendered to the moment. To him. Desire, terror and love washing over me, sending me tumbling in a rolling wave that ended in a glorious, liquid-limbed exhaustion, my cheek pressed against his chest while his fingers twined through my hair. He stroked it back from my face as he lifted it for another kiss and I met him there, eager for more. He laughed softly even as his hands began to roam once more across my flesh.

'Temptress,' he teased.

'Hardly,' I countered.

Later, much later, I rose from the floor to stand naked before the tiny mirror that hung by my bookshelves. I gazed at my flushed face, searching my eyes to see if they had changed, if there was a new knowingness behind them.

'You are so beautiful,' said Jack from behind me.

My eyes met his in the mirror. 'Promise me that you will always remember this.'

He reached around me, pulling me back into the safety of his chest as he dropped a kiss on my head. 'How could I ever forget it?'

I looked at us both there for a moment, his head bent into my neck before he raised it. His eyes so blue. So very blue.

'I love you,' he said. 'I have always loved you.'

'And I you.'

The words bounced back at us from the mirror, an echo that, had I only known it then, would have to sustain us for many years.

Later still, I stroked his cheek, feeling his stubble graze my fingertips, tracing the outline of his mouth, thrusting my finger inside it, luxuriating in the heat from his tongue as he sucked on it greedily before transferring his attention to my nipples once more. More confident now, I straddled his hips, arching against him, my head thrown back. He thrust up into me, my heat closing around him in turn. It was perfect. We were perfect. We fitted, one into the other, melding together so that neither of us knew where the other began or ended, only that we moved to the same rhythm, feeling it quicken and then reach a crescendo that consumed us both, drowning out everything except our cries of ecstasy.

'Don't do it.'

I was dozing against his chest, his words reverberating through the muscle and bone that guarded his heart. It took me a moment to realise what he was saying.

'I have to.'

'No you don't.' His arm tightened around me.

'You know I do. And you know why.'

I opened one eye. It was darker now, the shadows lengthening so that the summerhouse was in complete shade.

I looked at my watch and yelped. 'Christ. They'll be ringing the dinner bell any moment.'

I scrambled to my feet, scooping up my scattered clothes and tugging them on as fast as I could. Once we were both dressed, I smoothed Jack's hair where it stood up in tufts at the back. In turn, he gently raked his fingers through my curls. We faced one another, on the surface much as we had been just a few hours before while knowing to our very bones that everything was different. He was leaving first thing in the morning. This might be our last time alone together.

'So I'll see you down the road,' I said.

'I hope not.' His eyes were still dark with concern.

'Just try and stop me. I will find you. You will find me. Unless I cock it all up and they send me back to work in some munitions factory.' I tried a gay smile and failed, my mouth wobbling treacherously.

'My darling girl, I know you better than that. You'll be brilliant. You always are.'

He knew me better than anyone, did Jack. He was my lodestone. My north star. The one I would look out for every night as I gazed at the moon. And I would be his.

TWENTY-TWO

AUGUST 1944, FRANCE

Lyon was still beautiful, even under Nazi rule, its domes and spires rising above tree-lined boulevards bisected by the sparkling waters of the Saône and the Rhône. We parked up in woodland a safe distance from the city. There, a taciturn maquisard handed Juliette and me a bicycle each while Maggie climbed into the cart that stood ready, her radio equipment carefully buried under piles of peaches and melons.

'*Bonne chance,*' I murmured as I hugged her tight before she clambered up.

She smiled down at us from her perch beside the driver. 'See you at the hotel.'

And then they were off, Maggie giving us a final wave as they clopped at a brisk trot towards the city centre and the Grand Hotel where *monsieur le fermier* was ostensibly delivering his fruit along with the 'niece' he could then introduce to the hotel manager.

Juliette and I mounted our bicycles and followed a respectable distance behind. The cart had already disappeared ahead of us, and we cycled together along the winding road that took us into the heart of the city, the streets all but empty at this hour of the morning.

The buildings around us rose, dark shapes against a cloudless sky, blotting it out completely in places as they crowded together, dense now, some facades majestic, others crumbling, bombed out and run-down. This was a city that had suffered much but hid it well under a veil of respectability. A bourgeois, Vichy veil. I glanced at the houses and apartment buildings as we passed, wondering which hid the *résistants* and which harboured those loyal to the occupying army.

We stopped in front of a house a couple of streets from the banks of the Rhône, near one of the bridges that crossed into the city centre. Juliette dismounted and rapped once on the door. I could hear a bolt being shot, and then the door opened a couple of inches.

'I have just delivered some peaches and melons,' she murmured.

'Were they ripe?'

'They were perfect.'

The door swung wider. The compact man who stood there beckoned us in, looking over our shoulders before he shut and bolted the door once more. He took our bicycles from us, leaning them against the wall, and then ushered us into a salon where a smiling woman awaited.

'I will put your bicycles in the courtyard,' he said, 'and your bags in your rooms. My wife will look after you in the meantime.'

'Welcome,' she cried. 'You must be hungry. I have prepared *petit déjeuner*.'

She bade us sit and pressed coffee upon us before disappearing into her kitchen, re-emerging with brioches piled high on plates along with dishes of home-made preserves.

'Apricot jam,' she said proudly, 'made from my own trees. And this one here is cherry. Eat up. There is plenty more.'

I bit into my brioche, warm and oozing with butter. '*Merveilleuse*,' I mumbled.

It truly was. So light it almost melted against my tongue while its honey-rich sweetness wrapped around my taste buds like a hug.

'These are superb, madame,' said Juliette, dabbing at the crumbs on her plate with her fingertip so she could lick them off.

Madame beamed in delight. 'I will fetch some more,' she said, bustling off with the coffee pot to refill.

I caught Juliette's eye. 'Thank goodness we're going to be doing plenty of cycling,' I said. 'And a lot of it uphill.'

Madame reappeared with a plate stacked with croissants.

'Almond,' she announced. 'My own recipe.'

'My wife is famous for her baking,' said Monsieur, drying his hands on a cloth as he rejoined us. 'Your room is ready whenever you are. I'm afraid we only have the one spare so you will have to share.'

'You are more than kind,' said Juliette. 'We are truly grateful.'

'It is we who are grateful,' said Madame, her eyes filling as she surveyed us, one hand plucking at her apron. 'You young women are so brave. I wish I were young again. I would do what you do in a heartbeat. Instead, I am an old woman and all but useless in the fight against those bastards.'

She spat out the last word, her face crumpling.

Her husband laid his hand on her shoulder. 'There, there, Mathilde. Do not upset yourself. We have our guests.'

'On the contrary, madame,' said Juliette. 'You are the reason we keep fighting. You and all our compatriots. As for what you do, you have just fed your army. The most vital job of all. You are a particularly important part of this fight, and don't you ever forget that.'

A single tear trickled down Madame's cheek even as a smile lit it from within.

'Please,' she said, 'call me Mathilde. Mère Mathilde. Consider me your mother while you are here. And this is Bernard.'

'I would be honoured, Mère Mathilde,' said Juliette.

'I too,' I said.

'Excellent.' Bernard clapped his hands together, evidently a little embarrassed by this display of emotion. 'Shall I show you to your room and then we can discuss our plans?'

'That would be very kind.' Juliette brushed imaginary crumbs from her skirt as she rose and followed Bernard from the salon.

I turned to smile at Mathilde, still hovering. 'For the first time in an awfully long time,' I said, 'I feel as if I have a home.'

She looked at me and then her face broke once more into that beautiful smile. 'I am glad,' she whispered.

Our room was small but immaculately clean, the twin beds arranged either side of a window that overlooked the street below, with a clear view of anyone who came knocking at the front door.

'Our grandchildren sleep here when they come,' said Bernard. 'But we have not seen them for a long time. Since the start of the Occupation in fact.'

His face sagged for a moment. Then he collected himself and bent beneath one of the beds, pulling aside the counterpane that hung to the floor.

'See here,' he said, levering up a floorboard that looked exactly the same as the rest, 'this is where you can put your things. You simply press down on this end here.'

I peered into the space beneath the floorboards. 'Perfect.'

'I'll leave you to it,' said Bernard. 'Anything you need, please ask.'

'Thank you. For everything.'

Juliette had already bagged one of the beds so I dumped my things on the other, the one over the hidden storage space. A quick splash at the basin and we were done, stowing our things as instructed and tugging the counterpanes tight to leave no trace of our presence. Downstairs, Bernard had been joined by another man whom he introduced as André.

'How did you get in?' I asked as I shook his hand. I hadn't seen or heard anyone approach the front door from the spy post that was our new bedroom.

He looked taken aback and then smiled. 'You are observant, madame. There is a rear entrance through the courtyard. It leads to the traboules. The secret passageways of Lyon.'

'I've never heard of them.'

'Centuries ago, people in the city used them to access water more easily. Later, the silk workers and craftspeople would carry their goods through them to protect them from the elements. You see, we are close to the river here. Many of the streets in this part of the old town run parallel to the river. The traboules connect them through passages, stairways and court-yards like the one out back.'

'How very handy,' I said.

'Especially for the Resistance. The traboules allow us to move around the city unobserved as well as hide from the Boches. They have no idea that they exist.'

'I believe you know some of my colleagues in the Resis-tance,' said Juliette.

'I do, madame. They have spoken of you.'

André was looking at Juliette with naked admiration.

'So,' she said briskly, 'what do you have for us?'

He pulled a packet from his inside pocket. 'New identity papers. You, madame, are now Juliette Martin. And you, madame, Marianne Durand. Sadly, Monsieur Martin was killed at the front and Monsieur Durand is missing, presumed dead too. You are relatives who have come to work in Lyon.'

'Wonderful,' I said, looking at the papers he'd handed me. They were immaculate in every detail, down to the worn paper on which they were printed and which had evidently been folded at the same place for some time. Along with each was a short biography, neatly typed, to be destroyed as soon as we had memorised the details.

'You have both secured positions at the Grand Hotel,' he went on, 'where you begin work this afternoon.'

'Excellent,' said Juliette. 'How far is the Grand Hotel from the École de Sante Militaire?'

'The Gestapo is no longer headquartered there,' said André. 'They moved into 32 Place Bellecour, a building on the corner of Place Bellecour and Rue Alphonse Fochier after the École de Sante Militaire was bombed.'

'I see.'

'But Monsieur Barbie still likes to dine in the same places. Including the Grand Hotel.'

'Good,' I said. 'Easy for him to rendezvous with particularly special guests of the hotel.'

'Exactly. I believe one of those guests is a Countess Christina von Strassburg, former mistress of the commander of the German Home Army. Unfortunately, he took a bullet to the heart, so she is now looking for a new patron.'

'Poor woman,' I said. 'I expect she is lonely.'

'Absolutely,' said André. 'But at least now she has made Barbie's acquaintance, she does not have to dine alone.'

'How fortunate,' said Juliette. She glanced at me and I thought I saw the ghost of a smile.

'Of course,' went on André, 'as employees of the hotel, you are expected to help out as and when necessary. That includes assisting the waiting staff when they are short.'

'Handy,' I said. 'Although I suspect I may be the worst waitress they have ever employed.'

André laughed. 'I doubt Barbie will notice. He will be otherwise occupied.'

'Let's hope so.'

'And now I must leave you.' André picked up his hat and pulled it low over his forehead. 'Good luck.'

His sharp gaze encompassed us both. Then he was gone, slipping out the back door and into the courtyard where the traboules afforded him the perfect route to head back into the city, hidden from the eyes of the Nazis.

I turned to Bernard. 'Is there a map of the traboules?'

In response, he pulled aside an unremarkable painting of sunflowers that hung on the wall above a bookcase. Beneath was a map stuck to the wall, parts of it delineated in blue, outlining streets, stairways, passages and courtyards.

'We have mapped as many as we can,' he said. 'Some have not been used for thousands of years, but we opened up those that we could. Others are more commonly known and used. Especially in the old town. You see here. And here in the Croix Rousse.' His finger traced the area which bordered the river, including the street on which his house stood. 'We believe there are around 400 traboules in total,' he added. 'They are a godsend to those of us in the Resistance.'

'I can imagine.'

'André will take you through them later,' said Bernard. 'For your appointment at the hotel. You are due there at 2 p.m. to meet the manager and collect your uniforms.'

'Then we have no time to waste,' said Juliette. 'We must learn our new stories and make ourselves presentable.'

Mathilde appeared, shyly handing each of us a pile of clothes. 'I took the liberty,' she said, 'as I saw how little you had brought with you.'

Her eyes now twinkled where they had been damp before. I

got the impression she was relishing this. A chance to kick back at the Nazi occupiers who had ground Lyon under its brutal heel for so long. We would not let her down. We would not let our men down, not even Jack, despite his treachery. Most of all, we would not let one another down. We lived or died together, come what may.

TWENTY-THREE

The manager of the Grand Hotel was just as I imagined him to be – elegant in his tails, imposing without being intimidating. Above all, discreet. I glanced around his office, an orderly command centre to one side of the reception area. From here, he could see everything that happened in the heart of the hotel, the lobby, including who came and went.

'You will work as chambermaids,' he said. 'That way you have direct access to the rooms and to particular occupants. I'm assigning you the VIP floor, including the presidential suite.'

Out of the corner of my eye, I saw Juliette nod in approval.

'The presidential suite is reserved for visiting high-ranking German officers and officials as well as members of the Vichy government. It is most important that you give those guests whatever they need.'

'I know what I'd like to give them,' I said.

The manager raised one reproachful eyebrow. 'We may hate them,' he said, 'but we never let them see that. For them, the Grand Hotel is a welcoming place, a sanctuary that allows them to do what they like, away from their colleagues and spouses. Which means we are able to gather a great deal of valuable information on them. Information we pass on to our colleagues. Understood?'

'Understood,' I said.

'Here are your uniforms. The receptionist will show you to the staff changing room. Meet me back here as soon as you're ready. The rooms have already been cleaned for today so I'll put you on duty in the public areas. You'll get a good feel for who comes and goes from there.'

Juliette remained silent. We'd exchanged no more than a few words since we departed the safe house for the hotel. I reached out and brushed her hand with mine. She flashed me a smile in return. Lyon felt threatening, a hotbed not just of Nazis but the Vichy government and its unpaid spies. The Grand Hotel was our sanctuary too. As well as the trap we were setting for Barbie. Of course, the trap was already baited, although we had yet to meet this particular piece of cheese. I wondered what she was like, the agent embedded here. Diaz had been sparing with the details apart from the name she went under, Countess Christina von Strassburg. Quite some cover.

In the event, I didn't have long to wait.

She swept into the hotel lobby as if it were her personal fiefdom. The bellboy panted behind her, lugging the shopping bags she'd deposited with him at the door. She stood, dazzling in a closely fitted Fath dress that showed off her enviable figure, her summer jacket skimming its lines, acting as the perfect frame.

She was tall, perhaps a couple of inches taller than me, and held herself with immense dignity, but it was her face that stopped me in my tracks. She was, quite simply, the most beautiful woman I had ever seen, the light from the central chandelier casting a glow around her platinum hair and playing over cheekbones carved from marble.

'Countess von Strassburg,' she drawled to the concierge. 'Are there any messages for me?'

He bowed low, his eyes never leaving her face. 'But of

course, *Comtesse*. There is one, along with a bouquet I believe.'
The concierge was all smiles, his hand a flourish in the direction
of the receptionist. 'Marianne here will give those to you and
help you to your room.'

I moved forward from the pillar where I'd been discreetly
standing, as instructed, and took the room key from the receptionist along with an envelope and a vast bouquet tied with a
satin bow.

'Follow me, madame,' I said. 'The boy will bring up your
bags.'

He duly took the service lift while we waited for the gilded
doors of the guest lift to open. The moment we were inside and
they closed once more, I spoke to her in English.

'Countess von Strassburg, the weather is truly lovely today.
Almost as lovely as a day by the Serpentine.'

She went very still, those beautiful eyes narrowing as they
assessed me. 'Do they still have swans there?' she asked.

Her voice was smoky, tinged with something more exotic
than the standard cut-glass British accent.

'Swans and ducks as well as plenty of vegetables. Everyone
is digging for victory like mad.'

Her shoulders relaxed a fraction. 'Call me Christine. Did
Baker Street send you?'

'In a roundabout way.'

The lift doors opened once more. The bellboy was just
emerging from the service lift, but other than that, the corridor
was empty. I could hear my skirt swish as I followed Christine
to room 233. The bridal suite. How ironic.

As I opened the door for her, I saw that the suite was, in
fact, beautiful in its faded luxury. A carved marriage bed took
pride of place, lace curtains falling from the canopy above it.
The walls were lined with blue toile, and the French windows
gave on to a tiny balcony that overlooked a courtyard at the rear.
I wondered if the traboules connected here too.

I turned from the window to see Christine press a coin into the bellboy's hand. He practically genuflected, backing out of the room without ever taking his eyes from her face.

The minute he'd left, I dumped the bouquet in the basin, took out my duster and began methodically to sweep the room, checking for listening devices as I pretended to clean. Anyone listening would have heard nothing more than the sounds of a chambermaid going about her work. When I was satisfied the room wasn't bugged, I pocketed the duster and perched on the dressing table.

'We don't have much time,' I said. 'There are eyes everywhere, as I'm sure you know. Fill me in on how far you've got.'

She pulled a cigarette from its packet, inserted it between her lips and flicked open a slender silver lighter. Cartier, if I wasn't mistaken.

'With what?' she asked. Her eyes were amused but wary.

'Klaus Barbie.'

'Klaus has become a dear friend.'

'How dear a friend?'

She smiled and took another drag from her cigarette. Her nails were polished, I noticed, the deep red matching that of her lipstick.

'Tell me,' she said, 'where did you train?'

I hesitated for just a second too long.

'You think they've turned me, don't you?' she said. 'Perhaps they have. You're right to be cautious. But I need to know you're the real thing too if you understand my meaning.'

I stared at her. Checkmate.

'Wanborough Manor. Arisaig. Beaulieu.' The standard SOE training circuit.

'Do you remember Dangerous Dan?'

I was instantly back at Arisaig, the rain driving through me as I aimed punches and kicks at my instructor.

'Who could ever forget him? He and Sykes taught me

everything I know about close combat and silent killing. I can hear Sykes now: "Just kick him in the balls and chop him in the side of the neck."'

'When were you at Beaulieu?'

'The summer of 1942. I was sent out here not long after.'

'You've lasted two years in the field?'

'Off and on. This is my second tour. I was sent to replace a courier who had been captured. Then the leader of my network was arrested too so I took over.'

'You lead a network? How old are you?'

I bristled. Her stare wasn't unfriendly, but I was all too aware she was assessing me and finding me wanting.

'I'm twenty-four. I'll be twenty-five next month.'

'Good God. You must have been scarcely more than a child when they recruited you.'

She took a final drag of her cigarette and stubbed it out in the marble ashtray that sat on the occasional table beside the armchair into which she sank, crossing one perfect leg over the other before giving me a slightly warmer smile.

'I trained people like you,' she said. 'Or rather, I trained men like you.'

'What do you mean?'

'Let's just say I was a test they had to pass.'

I stared at her, the faint echo of a memory beginning to resound in my brain.

'I heard about you,' I said. 'But I didn't believe you existed.'

'Oh I existed all right. And I wasn't the only one. Without me, we could have sent agents into the field who would have blabbed at the first hint of a pretty face or a glass too many.'

'So you taught them not to?'

'No. I tested their capabilities. I was, if you like, their final hurdle. A professional tripwire. An *agente provocatrice*. If I could seduce them, that was one thing. If I could seduce them and get them to talk, quite another. Then they were out.'

'Where did you do this?'

'Anywhere and everywhere,' said Christine. 'Mostly I would pretend to bump into someone by chance. They would usually send them to dine with another officer or contact in a restaurant where I would happen to be, acting as an old acquaintance. Or they would introduce me as a French journalist who could help them with their mission over here. The good ones never bought it completely. The bad ones were too busy looking into my eyes to care.'

'So you would draw them in and then what?'

'Oh, you know. We would retire somewhere more comfortable. Or private. Almost always these restaurants were in hotels. Sometimes I would take them back to my flat.'

'And you slept with all of them?'

'Not at all. Officially, I didn't sleep with any of them.'

'I see. And unofficially?'

Christine's face grew serious. 'I stick to the official line. You have no idea how important this was, to know if they would succumb in the face of temptation. These were men we were sending out into the networks. Men with the names and whereabouts of other agents as well as the details of operations. We couldn't risk all those lives through careless pillow talk or because someone couldn't hold their drink.'

'Did most of them pass?'

'The ones who failed were the ones who were too eager. A bit like puppies, you know. All slobber and no finesse. I hate puppies.'

I was beginning to understand why they'd sent Christine to carry out this mission. If anyone could seduce Klaus Barbie, she could and with deadly efficiency.

'Were you ever attracted to any of them?'

'Never,' said Christine. 'Although plenty of them liked me enough to tell me far too much.'

'What about Klaus Barbie? Does he tell you anything?'

She opened her mouth and then shut it again, putting a finger to her lips. Her head was cocked, listening. I heard it too, a barely audible tap at the door. She moved to the dressing table and flipped open her vanity case, extracting the pistol that was hidden beneath a false-bottomed layer of powders and potions. A Welrod, specially designed to be extremely quiet in use. It could be slipped inside a sleeve, even that of a negligee. The perfect weapon for close range.

She crossed to the door, standing by the lintel, her gun aimed above the doorknob, which was slowly turning. I heard the key rattling in the lock.

'Room service,' someone called out. A voice I knew.

Then the door swung open and Juliette appeared, bearing a tray on which there sat several covered dishes.

Christine kicked the door shut behind her.

'I didn't order room service,' she said, the gun held low at her side to conceal it.

'It's all right,' I said. 'She's with me.'

Juliette placed the tray on the occasional table and whipped off the covers. On each dish there lay another pistol – short-nosed Brownings rather than Welrods.

'Here,' she said to me, stuffing her pistol into the holster she wore under her skirt. 'The Germans are conducting a search of the hotel. They're right behind me. The manager just had time to warn me and give me these.'

'Who are they looking for?'

'Apparently they received a tip-off that members of the Resistance are working here. Possibly even enemy agents.'

'Someone has betrayed us already?'

Immediately my thoughts spun to Edward's network, busted wide open by another betrayal. Jack's betrayal. Only it couldn't be him this time. Who then?

'Wonderful. Now you've led them straight to me,' said

Christine. 'Well, the only thing to do is brazen it out. And, if necessary, to shoot our way out.'

At that moment, there was another knock at the door, this time a loud, demanding rap. Christine nodded to us both, slipping the Welrod up her sleeve.

'Open up.' His accent was guttural, his tone pure SS.

Christine flung the door wide. 'Can I help you?' she purred.

A beat and then I heard the officer stammer. 'M-Madame. It's you.'

'It is indeed. Don't I recognise you from somewhere? Ah yes, you work for Hauptsturmführer Barbie. I've seen you with him. I'll be sure to tell him you dropped by like this.'

I heard a second voice but didn't dare look up from the bouquet I was assiduously arranging while Juliette fluffed the bath towels as if her life depended on it. Which it well might if these SS officers suspected for one second that we were their targets.

'Come on,' said the second man. 'We are sorry to disturb you, madame.'

A pause. I held my breath. Then an audible clicking of heels.

'Yes. My apologies. Good day to you, madame.'

The soft sigh of the door shutting.

'Well,' said Christine, 'that was close. Welcome to the Grand Hotel.'

With that, she threw herself down on the bed and lit up another cigarette. 'Now,' she said, 'tell me exactly why you're here. Or I might have to shoot you myself.'

TWENTY-FOUR

'We're here to help you,' I said.

Christine blew a smoke ring then sat up, ground out her cigarette and swung her legs over the side of the bed. They were spectacular legs, I noted. No doubt one of her favourite weapons.

'I don't need your help,' she purred.

'Oh but you do. Right now you have absolutely no backup. The entire Lyon network has been blown. There's no one left. That's why we're here. To replace them.'

She blinked, lifted the cigarette again to her lips and relit it on the second attempt, throwing the lighter aside in irritation at her shaking hand. It was the only sign that she was rattled by what I'd said.

'When?'

'Five days ago. You hadn't heard?'

'Nothing. Bloody Germans kept that quiet.'

She was blinking rapidly, her thoughts assembling and reassembling.

'So Barbie didn't say anything about it?'

'Not a word. Bastard.'

She exhaled a long, furious plume of smoke. 'Any idea how the network was blown?'

'Someone betrayed them to the Gestapo.'

That stillness again, coupled with the intense alertness I'd seen in the lift.

'Any idea who?'

I didn't blink. 'Not yet. My network was also blown, at a rendezvous of networks and Resistance I organised. We were raided by the Germans, and one of our men was detained at a roadblock along with two others. They found the money they were carrying, which was intended to finance a large operation. He and the others are being held at Digne prison, but they're bringing them here, to Montluc, now that Klaus Barbie is ready for them. Apparently he has been otherwise occupied.'

She took another furious puff. 'Not with me, I can tell you. He's been busy carrying out raids. Barbie is no fool. He knows defeat is inevitable. He wants to clean up as much as he can before the Allies get here.'

From the way she ground the cigarette into the ashtray, I could tell she would love to do the same to Barbie.

'His way of cleaning up is to transport as many undesirables as he can, as well as wipe out any opposition. He has his men out all the time, hunting people down. You heard what he did to those poor children in April?'

I shook my head.

'At Izieu. It's a small town not too far from here. Forty-four children, all Jewish refugees. They were hidden there in a farmhouse. He sent his troops in to drag them out and put them on a train to the camps. Not a single one left.'

'How did he know they were there?'

'An informant. Someone betrayed them.'

Just as someone had betrayed the Lyon network and now us. Except we had got away with it. For now.

I felt her gaze focus in on me.

'They sent you to replace the Lyon network?'

She'd recovered some of her composure, her tone flatter and more assured. For a moment there I thought we'd seen a spark of real emotion. If we had, she'd snuffed it out before it could burst into life.

'They did.'

'You?'

My fingers itched to give her an open-handed slap. The kind that would shut her up for good.

'You don't think Marianne is qualified to do so?' Juliette's voice was soft, but the undertone was all too apparent.

'She's hardly more than a child. They could at least have sent someone with experience.'

'Marianne has led her own network for the past two years. A very successful one. Until they were betrayed. It seems a lot of people are when they are involved with you.'

Juliette was actually sticking up for me. For a moment, I wanted to throw my arms around her.

Christine's eyebrows shot up, but her cool smile stayed in place. 'What exactly does that mean?'

'It means that you are not above suspicion,' said Juliette. 'No one is. We don't know for sure who gave the Lyon network away, but we intend to find out.'

I bit my tongue. I could feel the pressure mounting at my temples. So much to think about. So much I didn't want to think about, including the brother I had not yet had time to mourn.

'He was my brother,' I said. 'The leader of the Lyon network. Edward was just a couple of years older than me. I assume you didn't think he was a child. Apparently Klaus Barbie shot him in the back of the head a few days ago because he refused to talk.'

She blinked again, a slower blink this time. 'I'm sorry,' she said. 'He was a good man and a brave one.'

'Perhaps you understand now why they sent me?'

'I'm beginning to.'

'As for Juliette, she has ten thousand maquisards under her command. All prepared to do whatever it takes, as are we. That's why we're here, to help you carry out the assassination of Klaus Barbie. That will stop him murdering any more innocents before the Allies get here, including the men they're bringing to Montluc.'

She looked at us both, her eyes as clear as cobalt glass and just as hard.

'Good of you to offer,' she said. 'But I'm doing just fine on my own.'

'It's not an offer,' I said. 'It's an order. Or I may just have to report you for insubordination.'

TWENTY-FIVE

I had to hand it to Christine. She worked fast. It took her a few seconds to digest my words. A couple more to come to a decision.

'What do you want to know?' she asked.

'Tell me about Barbie. What's the state of play?'

'Barbie comes here almost every evening for dinner since the Resistance bombed his favourite restaurant, the Café du Moulin à Vent.'

'Oh dear, poor lamb,' I said. 'And are you his new favourite dish?'

She almost smiled. Almost. 'I'm working on it.'

'How far have you got?'

'Barbie is a tough nut to crack. He doesn't trust anyone, especially not a woman, but I think I'm slowly winning him round.'

'Excellent. When are you next seeing him?'

'Tonight, as it happens. For dinner here.'

'Then I'll make sure we're on dining-room duty. You need to find out anything you can about the men they're holding at Digne. Specifically, if he knows that they're agents or *résistants*.'

'I'm sure he has strong suspicions. He suspects everyone. I'll find out as much as I can, but I'm warning you now, it won't be easy.'

I looked at her more closely, at the shadows under her eyes and the pinched edges of her mouth. She'd been operating alone for weeks now, forging a relationship with the most brutal of men and with only the occasional contact from Edward and the Lyon network. Now even that was gone. I could understand why she was so reluctant to throw in her lot with us.

'Barbie wouldn't think twice about killing me if he even suspected what I'm up to, and he would enjoy doing so. I don't believe that man has an ounce of humanity, never mind a heart.'

The flatness was back and along with it an infinite weariness. Christine had been staring into the abyss of Barbie's soul for so long now. I wondered if we were asking too much.

'If anyone can do it, you can,' I said.

Like the sun coming out, Christine's smile lit up her face, obliterating the shadows that had darkened it. 'Of course I can, darling,' she said.

'What is your plan?' I asked. 'For killing him?'

'I don't have one as yet. My orders are to do whatever is necessary.'

'Who gave you those orders?'

'I can't tell you that.'

I held her gaze, the faint sense of unease that had been there since the chateau resurging. There was more going on here than I knew and it made me nervous. Too many secrets inevitably gave way to lies.

'I see.'

'No, you don't. Believe me, I wish I could tell you, but I can't.'

We'd see about that.

'Let's go,' I said to Juliette. 'Find out if the coast is clear.'

I listened at the door for a few seconds before easing it open.

The corridor was empty. I beckoned to Juliette and we walked as casually as we could to the service lift, half-expecting to see SS officers appear every time the doors opened on the way down.

In the lobby, all was quiet. I approached the concierge's desk.

'Are there any messages for Madame von Strassburg?' I asked.

The concierge peered at me over his spectacles, his moustache lifting a fraction as he favoured me with a professional smile. 'Indeed there are. This just came for Madame.'

He handed me a folded sheet of paper. I gave him a half-smile and slipped behind the pillar to open it. On it was written one word: 'Run.'

TWENTY-SIX

We paused for breath in the traboules, pressing our backs against the cool stone walls as we gulped in the air. Dusk was falling, but the heat of the day lingered. It was a sultry evening. Too hot for my blood.

'We must be nearly there,' I said.

I unfurled my fingers. I was still clutching the note, now a crumpled ball in my fist. Run. But where? Our only choice was our safe house, but we could be running into danger rather than from it.

'We could have done with a little more information,' I said. 'God knows if the Gestapo are on our tail or if they're still waiting for us back at the hotel. Or even if it's them at all.'

As we emerged into the courtyard behind Bernard and Mathilde's house, I held up a warning hand.

'Look – there,' I hissed.

A figure was standing at the upstairs window, the one that overlooked the courtyard.

I shrank back into the shadows, pulling Juliette with me, and we watched as the figure turned and moved out of sight. I thought I heard distant shouts and then the sound of a door slamming.

The minutes passed, ticking as fast as the beat of my heart.

The sound of footsteps came towards us, not from the house but through the traboules. I had my pistol aimed between his eyeballs, finger on the trigger, before I realised who it was.

'You're here,' whispered André. 'Thank God. I was hoping you would understand from the note.'

I felt the rush of relief. 'What's happening?' I murmured.

'The Gestapo raided the house earlier this evening. They arrested Bernard and Mathilde but it seems the bastards came back for a second look, probably to try and catch you.'

'How did they know we were here? We only arrived today.'

André's mouth was set in a grim line. 'An informant, no doubt.'

'They came to the hotel too.'

'I heard.'

I glanced around. 'One of the neighbours, you think?'

'Maybe. Maybe not. In any case, we need to get out of here.'

'Wait,' I said. 'What about our things?'

'Leave them.'

'We can't. We hid them away before we left for the hotel. There's a chance the Gestapo didn't find them.'

'I said leave them. It's too dangerous to go in there.'

'They left a few minutes ago. If we go in now, we can find them before they return. If they do.'

With that, I was striding across the courtyard to the back door. I heard André's grunt of alarm but I didn't care. Without our things, the Gestapo had no proof of our existence, nothing to link us to Bernard and Mathilde. Besides, I now had no clean underwear, let alone a toothbrush. And I was buggered if the Germans were going to get their hands on my most personal garments as well as my lockpicks and knife.

The back door had been left unlocked. André reluctantly

stood watch as we made our way through the kitchen. The house was silent apart from the odd creak or groan as it settled back after the indignities of the raid. Furniture and ornaments lay smashed on the floor, and papers were strewn all around. I bent and picked up a little porcelain statue of the Madonna that had proudly sat on Mathilde's mantlepiece, putting it back where I remembered seeing it, running my thumb over a tiny chip as if I could somehow make it whole again.

I glanced at the sunflower painting above the bookcase. Mercifully, it appeared undisturbed, the secrets of the traboules still safely concealed beneath. The bookcase was empty, the books spread over the floor beneath it like a carpet of knowledge, papers ripped out of some as if they might contain secrets their violators could scarcely comprehend. At the foot of the stairs, a rag doll lay along with a wooden whistle and toy drum while the wicker basket that had once contained them had been smashed to bits by what looked like a series of vicious kicks.

Upstairs was a similar sight, the bedding torn from the beds and clothing heaped on bare mattresses, wardrobe doors swinging open to reveal empty interiors. Whatever they were looking for, they had done a thorough job. Whoever they were looking for. In our bedroom, I eased up the floorboard beneath my bed. Our bags were still there, untouched.

I pulled them out, handing one to Juliette, before replacing the floorboard with care.

'Let's get out of here,' I said.

Downstairs, André was standing stock-still, alert as a bloodhound locked on to a scent. 'Hurry,' he hissed.

At that moment, I heard it – the sound of jackboots thudding on the pavement. A crash as they kicked the front door open. They were back, just as I'd suspected they would be. Only there was nothing more for them to find. No evidence to link Bernard and Mathilde to suspected enemy agents. It might just save their lives. Might. Already we were across the courtyard and into the traboules, André carefully closing the back door behind us even though it cost an agonising second or two.

'Follow me,' he whispered, taking a different route this time, leading us through the labyrinth of the traboules and then along a maze of small streets until I lost all sense of direction. Finally, we came once more to the river and paused in the relative safety of the plane trees that lined it. André's eyes swept the bridge and I followed his gaze. There was no sign of the enemy. Still, we waited. He glanced at his watch.

'I'm taking you to Madame Suzanne. She will look after you. But we need to wait here a while until the patrols pass. They do so on the hour.'

'Who is Madame Suzanne?' I asked.

'She runs the finest brothel in Lyon, popular with German officers and members of the Vichy government. Madame and her young ladies are an excellent source of information for us. They are also remarkably good at sabotage.'

Diaz's words came back to me. So this was the other remaining agent.

'We've heard of her,' I said. 'I believe she has helped many *résistants*?'

'Not just *résistants* but Jews escaping the Occupation and others who needed to get out of France. Her girls often spike the drinks of their clients. They never suspect. Instead, they give Madame Suzanne extra supplies, including gasoline. She uses that in cars to help people escape. She is a formidable woman.'

'An asset to the Resistance,' said Juliette.

'Luckily for her,' said André, 'her work with the Resistance has remained a closely guarded secret.'

All at once, Juliette's face was blasted with white light, her features bleached out by its intensity.

'*Merde*. They are early. Down.'

André was already crouched at the base of the tree, beneath the beam of the searchlight. It passed over us a couple more times, each time receding more until it faded into the distance. I heard a church clock chime and then another. Seven o'clock. Dinner time. But there was no dinner for us. My stomach growled in response to my thoughts.

'Come on.'

We followed André across the bridge, keeping our heads low and our pace even. It felt as if the bridge stretched forever in front of us, the water below inky black in the deepening dusk. As much as we wanted to, we couldn't run and arouse suspicion. Instead, we tried as best we could to look like ordinary Lyonnais heading home.

On the other side of the river, André turned an immediate left and left again, wiggling through the backstreets and alleys. There were no traboules here and so we had to keep up that same even pace, walking as close to the buildings that loomed above us as we could, the empty streets echoing with our footsteps.

Everyone was already home, sitting safely at their respective dinner tables. Some would have enough to eat. Others wouldn't be so lucky. Now and then I caught a glimpse of light escaping from a drawn curtain or blind, but otherwise the streets of Lyon were dead, its citizens keeping their lives as hidden as the secrets some concealed behind closed lips.

'Up here.'

André was standing at the foot of a spiral staircase that led up the outside of a tall townhouse. It looked like a fire escape. I didn't stop to question him but followed him up, trying to keep my tread light on the metal steps. Behind me, Juliette swore under her breath. I glanced over my shoulder to see her skirt had caught on one of the wrought-iron curlicues. The sooner we were out of these blasted maids' uniforms the better.

At the top of the staircase, André tapped twice and then twice again on a door. We waited for what felt like an eternity before I heard a key turning in a lock.

'A delivery for Madame,' said André. 'Fresh from the countryside.'

The door swung wider, revealing a rectangle of light and, beyond it, a narrow corridor. Silhouetted against the light, the figure of a woman.

'Leave it with me,' she said.

'Go on in,' said André. 'You are in good hands.'

I had no choice but to believe him.

The woman looked us up and down as she shut and locked the door behind us, slamming three bolts into place before summoning us to follow her along the corridor with a wave of her hand. Outside another door, she stopped, rapping on it just the once.

'Yes?' I heard a voice call out.

'Delivery for you, Madame.'

A moment later this door, too, swung open. A slim brunette stood there, her head held in a way that always reminded me of a ballerina, as did her stance. She scarcely came to my shoulder and yet her elegance and poise made her seem much taller. Christine was sex appeal personified but Suzanne exuded something more. Fires burned in her that pulled you in, just as flames do. She wasn't overtly sexual, but she possessed an indefinable magnetism, a life force that would not be denied.

Her dark hair was swept up into a chignon from which loose tendrils escaped. They framed a sweet face which was belied by the scorching intelligence that shone from her eyes. Her clothes were elegant and clearly expensive, the red lipstick she wore the only indication she might be rather more than the average rich Lyon housewife.

She smiled and held out her arms. 'It's wonderful to see you again,' she said, enfolding me in a hug. 'I had no idea it was you they were sending to Lyon.'

'A-And you,' I stuttered in joyful amazement.

It was so good to see a familiar face, even in these strangest of circumstances. The last time I'd seen Suzanne, she'd been waving us off from Beaulieu as fully fledged agents. Now here she was, running a brothel in Lyon as a cover. The machinations of SOE never ceased to amaze me.

'You know one another?' asked Juliette.

'We do. Marianne here was my favourite student. Not just talented but brave.'

I could feel myself blushing. 'I had a great teacher.'

'So you trained Marianne for SOE?'

'I did but I missed being out in the field so here I am. Now, I understand you need a new safe house. You are more than welcome to stay as my guests.'

'Who told you?' I was still trying to absorb the fact that my former instructor in the dark arts of spy craft was standing right here before me.

She stood aside, ushering us into what looked to be her office, a telephone sitting on a walnut desk on which paperwork was spread.

'I am fortunate to have a telephone,' she said. 'We know the Germans listen in, but we have a system. The manager at the Grand Hotel is as good a friend as André and generously shares his supplies when necessary. You are my latest delivery of fine wine. My customers get through a great deal.'

'I'm sure they do,' I said.

'Don't worry. You won't be staying here. I have an apartment not too far away.'

'We're very grateful, madame,' said Juliette.

'Not at all. Anything we can do to defeat those Nazi pigs. Here.' She scribbled an address on a piece of paper and held it up for us to read. 'Memorise that. I will meet you there in one hour. It is three streets from here. Pauline will show you the way.'

She pressed her finger down on a bell that sat beside the telephone on her desk. I turned to see the same woman who had let us in now hovering by the door, a couple of parcels in her arms.

'Your clothes,' she said. 'From the Grand Hotel.'

I looked from her to Suzanne. 'Impressive.'

'We try.'

'Did these come with some fine wine?'

She smiled. 'They did. And now I must attend to that wine. I will see you in one hour.'

I remembered André's words. Was she about to doctor the wine? Probably. Beaulieu was known as the finishing school for SOE, and Suzanne had certainly made sure we were finished in style. Still, I wasn't prepared to put all my trust in her straight away. A lot could have happened in the two years since I'd last seen her. An agent could be turned in ten minutes. My gut told me to trust her, but I had long ago learned to listen to my head as well. It was what had kept me alive this far. And I intended to stay alive for a long while yet.

TWENTY-SEVEN

Suzanne's apartment was beautifully appointed, located on the mezzanine floor of a nondescript building on the Rue Boileau.

'It is perfect for our purposes,' she explained. 'There are two exits from the building, and you can get directly from the kitchen into the courtyard if necessary. I do not anticipate that anyone would come knocking, but you never know.'

I glanced at her. 'Indeed.'

'You will find fresh clothes in the wardrobes. We keep spares here just in case. There should be something to fit you both.'

'You're well prepared. But then, I would expect nothing less.'

She smiled. 'You remind me of someone,' she said. 'Someone I met since I last saw you.'

'I do?'

I waited but she said nothing more, although I could sense her scrutinising my face.

'I look like my brother,' I said. 'Edward. The leader of the Lyon network. Until it was blown. You probably met him.'

No harm in telling her now that Edward was gone.

'Of course,' she murmured. 'Do you know what happened to him? After he was arrested? We tried to find out but heard nothing.'

'He was executed. Shot in the back of the head by Klaus Barbie.'

My words were as brutal as the act. Deliberately so. It helped somehow.

She stared at me in shock. Her eyes dropped for the briefest of moments, her chest rising and falling as she composed herself. Then she looked up, all business once more.

'I will leave you ladies to settle in, but there is just one more thing. I understand Monsieur Bernard and his wife have been taken to Montluc prison. From what I hear, the Gestapo don't know for certain about you or the link with the Grand Hotel, but they may, of course, find out.'

'Do you know who the informant is?'

She shook her head. 'Not yet.'

'And the raid on the Grand Hotel today?'

'Coincidence, as far as I know. They arrested one of the kitchen staff. It seems he was spotted distributing leaflets on behalf of the Resistance.'

'So we can go back in there,' I said.

'You could, but is there any pressing reason why you should?'

'There is. We have another agent embedded there. Without any backup.'

I could tell by the sharpening of her gaze that she already knew all of this. Nothing escaped Suzanne, not at Beaulieu and not now. So much for the two agents knowing nothing about one another.

'Then perhaps you should but not as a pair. The Gestapo were looking for two women, remember. Go back one at a time. Do not be seen together. Make sure you wear different street clothes. You might want to change your hair. Put it up. Dye it maybe.'

Almost unconsciously, I touched the strands that framed my face. 'Good idea.'

'You'll find hair dye in the bathroom here. Make-up too, if you need it.'

'You really have thought of everything,' I said.

She didn't smile in return.

'Remember that there are several Resistance sympathisers working at the hotel. They will help you all they can, but equally you cannot compromise them.'

There was a clear warning in her voice.

'Do you think the Germans are still watching the hotel?' I asked.

'They are always watching, as are their collaborators.'

I looked at my watch. 'If I hurry, I can make it back there in time for the end of dinner service. I need to check on our other agent.'

Suzanne waved a gloved hand. 'I too must go. Good luck.'

Her perfume lingered in the room long after she departed, a heady mixture of roses, frangipani and something else. Perhaps it was just the indefinable essence of the woman.

'She's quite something,' said Juliette.

'Isn't she? I love the idea of her girls spiking their customers' drinks.'

'That's not all they do. From what I heard, they also get them hooked on heroin and spread venereal disease among them. She has a tame gynaecologist, another member of the Resistance. He provides fake white cards to prove that they are clean when they are anything but.'

I stared at Juliette. 'You're joking.'

'I am not. They have managed to turn a considerable number of the Gestapo and certain government officials into drug addicts as well as riddle them with gonorrhoea and syphilis. Can you imagine what their wives have to say about that, never mind their mistresses?'

'That's brilliant. Simply brilliant.'

'What was she like as a teacher? Suzanne?'

'Brilliant at that too. She taught me so much. Turned me into a real agent where before I just knew the mechanics. It's one thing to know how to kill people, quite another to learn what really makes them tick so you can use that to your advantage.'

'Did you ever think she'd be using a brothel as a front?'

'Nothing would surprise me about her,' I said. 'And now I'd better get going.'

The thought of Suzanne sabotaging the Gestapo with gonorrhoea kept me buoyed up all the way back to the Grand Hotel, swathed in a headscarf and light coat I'd found in the apartment. Under the headscarf, my hair was now a dull black, its waves flattened into a bun that sat at the nape of my neck, the overall effect making me seem both older and more French. It was the quickest way to change my appearance, and my hair was still damp from the dye, the harsh vermilion lipstick I'd slashed across my mouth only adding to the effect. I deposited my new outfit in the changing room, making sure my pistol was tucked tight in my waistband before emerging in my uniform once more.

'Are there any messages for Countess von Strassburg?'

The concierge raised an eyebrow at me but said nothing.

'I have one here as it happens,' he said, handing me another folded piece of paper. 'Apparently it is urgent.'

'Thank you. I'll make sure it's delivered immediately.'

I could hear the distant sound of glasses and silverware clinking in the dining room. Good. Dinner was still well underway. I slid behind my favourite pillar next to the grand piano and turned my back to the foyer. The note was written in Maggie's unmistakable hand.

Your packages are about to be despatched. Expect them Friday, I read.

Today was Tuesday. That didn't give us much time.

'Mademoiselle?'

I looked up to see the manager hovering.

'We need some help in the dining room.'

His meaning was unmistakable.

'Yes, of course. At once.'

I hurried after him through the double doors, my senses screaming.

I was about to see him for the first time.

Klaus Barbie. The Butcher of Lyon.

The man who had murdered my brother.

Our target.

TWENTY-EIGHT

According to the manager, Barbie always insisted on the same table in both the hotel bar and restaurant, one which had a clear view of the entire room as well as the entrance to it, where two of his men stood guard. Two more sat at an adjoining table while he drank or dined with his lieutenants, unless a better option presented itself. Or herself.

Christine kept him waiting a good twenty minutes before she made her entrance, gliding past his men guarding the double doors to the bar as if they simply didn't exist. She paused just inside the doorway, giving the entire room enough time to take in her cocktail dress, another Fath with a plunging neckline and a bodice that clung to every curve before gently flaring into a skirt that hinted at what lay beneath. She lingered there, giving Barbie time to appreciate the goddess that graced his presence, before finally moving to the lectern on which the evening menu was placed.

The maître d' greeted her with a deep bow. 'Madame. How are you this evening?'

'Very well, thank you. I am joining Monsieur Barbie for dinner.'

'Ah yes. Please follow me.'

As he led her to her table, every eye in the room followed her as one. Christine's hair was artfully swept up in a diamanté comb. The tiny jewels glittered in the light from the chandelier as she inclined her head a fraction. It took Barbie a moment to register. Then he got to his feet. She bestowed a gracious smile upon him and a wider one on the waiter who pushed in her chair before spreading a napkin on her lap.

She studied the cocktail list. 'I think just my usual.'

'Of course, madame.'

This entire pantomime wasn't lost on Barbie. As the stares slowly subsided, she sat, idly stirring the cocktail the waiter ceremoniously placed in front of her, ignoring his admiring gaze. A Gibson. It was going down far too fast. *Take a breath, Christine. Pretend you're about to fire a gun.*

The cocktail helped. She could feel her heartbeat returning to normal, her breathing growing less shallow as she steadied herself. He was just a man after all. Just another man. A man growing impatient. And now she, too, had a deadline to meet.

'You are looking very lovely tonight.'

Only Barbie could make it sound like a threat.

'Thank you,' she murmured.

He reached across the table and placed his hand on hers, resting it there in a way that felt more like a warning than a caress. Her hand started to tremble. Quickly, she removed it, placing it on her lap and staring as haughtily as she could at Barbie.

He laughed. 'Not feeling too friendly though.'

His eyes pulled her in, lupine pits of darkness. The eyes of a feral beast. But tonight they glittered as if with a fever, the whites mottled and pink. He was drunk, she realised. Or at least well on his way to it.

'We don't know one another that well,' she said, softening her words with a coquettish look.

'Yet.'

He snapped his fingers for the waiter. 'Champagne. Your finest. Madame deserves nothing but the best.'

'Thank you,' said Christine. 'But don't you think you've had enough?'

Her words fell into what felt like an endless silence. The entire room seemed to hold its breath. Even the piano player in the corner lifted his hands, his last chord dying on a sigh. Had she overplayed her hand?

Barbie's thin lips parted for a moment and then they widened in a wolfish grin. 'Never enough of you, my dear.'

His clumsy gallantry sounded fake, as he no doubt intended. He was toying with her, she realised, every bit as much as she was trying to reel him in. It was time to slacken the rope and let things play out.

Christine emitted a tinkling laugh. 'You may regret saying that.'

'I doubt it.'

All of a sudden, he appeared stone-cold sober, and as she stared into the void of his gaze, Christine could feel herself teeter. She snapped back just in time. There was no way on earth she would let him see her falter. He was rubbing her foot with his, enjoying her discomfort. She moved, forcing herself not to kick back hard. Barbie sober was bad enough. Drunk he was positively dangerous.

'Bread, madame.'

Christine recognised her voice immediately. She kept her eyes on Barbie, pretending not to notice the waitress.

'Water, madame?'

'Thank you.'

Christine felt a few drops splash on her lap.

'Madame, I am so sorry. Let me get you a fresh napkin.'

The napkin was whisked away to be replaced with another. And something else. A small square of what felt like paper tucked underneath. Christine casually moved her hand to her lap. A note. Equally casually, she tugged her napkin into place, secreting the note in her stocking top as she did so. Now all she had to do was keep Barbie at bay.

'Everything all right, my dear?'

The man missed nothing.

'Yes of course.' She smiled seraphically. 'Now tell me about your day. You seem a little stressed. Can I help at all?'

The invitation in her voice wasn't lost on Barbie. *Not too fast, Christine.* Not too slow either. She had to keep him dangling until just the right moment, although Barbie was no easy fish to land. But then, what shark ever was? Come to that, his gaze as he turned it on her reminded her of a shark – flat, cold and dead.

'I'm sure you can,' he said, reaching for the champagne bottle.

Christine instinctively pressed her thighs together.

They're all the same underneath, she thought. *Strutting like peacocks seeking a mate. Dropping their display the moment they think they have you hooked.* She needed to tug that line a little more.

'There is something I wanted to tell you,' she said, swilling the wine in her glass before taking an appreciative sip. The Grand Hotel kept an excellent cellar.

Barbie took another slug of his champagne. 'Go on.'

'I... well, I haven't told you this before, but there was a specific reason I came to Lyon.'

'Which was?'

'To meet you.'

A pause as he studied her, his eyes still expressionless, the pupils pinpricks against the granite.

'Why did you want to meet me?'

'Let me explain... you see, in Paris it was impossible once dear Hans – General Gottmann – died. The Allies, as you know, are advancing. Women like me, we are now considered objects of hate. All I want to do is return to my family in Alsace and perhaps to find sanctuary beyond, in Germany. But for that I need protection. The only place I could think to come was here, where the Vichy government still rules. Or rather, where you do.'

It was a calculated attempt at flattery, her words deliberately hesitant and stumbling. He liked vulnerability. It excited him.

'A good decision.' Barbie took another slug of his wine.

'So you see, that is why I wanted to meet you. It's just that I didn't expect to so soon. And now we are friends.'

Barbie broke off a piece of bread from the basket and crumbled it between his fingers, letting the crumbs fall onto the tablecloth. His fingers were long and tapered. The fingers of a philosopher or of the theology student he had once aspired to be. He snapped those fingers now, summoning the waiter, and ordered for them both.

Christine bit her tongue. No man had ordered for her before. Ever. One or two had tried and had soon been shown the error of their ways. But, in this case, she would just have to smile and take it.

Barbie raised his glass in a toast. 'The Fatherland,' he said.

'The Fatherland,' she dutifully repeated.

'And to you of course.'

'And you.'

She met his gaze and held it as they toasted one another, stifling an insane urge to laugh. Or to cry. Here she was, in a stuffy French hotel dining room, playing games with a vicious Nazi despot. Except these games were deadly serious. And she had to win them at all costs.

'I think we are going to be very good friends, you and I,' said Barbie.

'I hope so.' She smiled back, not too eagerly.

A memory flashed, unbidden, in her mind then – fishing in the Thames with her big brother, his hands holding hers as he taught her how to hold the rod steady.

'Like this, Christine. Rest your fingers on it gently so you can feel what the fish is doing.'

She could feel this fish biting. But fish could take the bait and then wriggle free, swimming off with the spoils. She had to make sure he was firmly on that hook, but with guile rather than anything too overt.

She crossed her legs under the table, briefly brushing his knee with hers as if by accident. The table lamp illuminated the pearls against her chest as she reached across to offer him some more bread.

'You must eat up,' she said. 'A man like you needs his energy.'

Barbie glanced at her and then grunted, a small sound that spoke of anticipation. She sat back once more, primly addressing herself to her food. Softly, softly catchee monkey. Or even fishy. In the meantime, she would watch him writhe on the end of that hook.

Something deep within Christine stirred, a sadness that she'd thought long buried. If only things had been different. If only she didn't feel marked out in the way that she did. But the past was the past. There was no changing it.

She took a sip of her wine, gazing over Barbie's shoulder at another time and place. At another Christine. At the innocent girl who was still there, buried somewhere she could never reach.

TWENTY-NINE

She was handling him well. Or as well as anyone could handle a man like Klaus Barbie. He wasn't as he looked in his photographs – shorter and slighter in the flesh, with a curiously studied air of calm, his grey suit well cut but nothing special. He looked more like a bank manager than a brutal murderer, and yet there was something about him that chilled my blood. Maybe it was his eyes, small and strangely pale, forever darting like a caged beast. Now and then they fixed on Christine, marking her out as his prey. Or so he thought.

I watched her excuse herself and leave the table. Eyes followed her as she glided from the room, glancing sideways from plates and over raised glasses. All except Barbie, who turned and beckoned to one of his men sitting at the table nearby, his arm resting casually on that of a brunette siren.

They conferred for a few moments, the tall, hawkish man bending to Barbie's level. I studied him surreptitiously. A proud nose that, along with his blond hair, gave him the perfect Aryan profile. Harry Stengritt, Barbie's right-hand man. He and Christine would have looked good together, although, if I wasn't mistaken, the brunette bombshell was Stengritt's mistress, Lydie Bastien.

Christine was back from the ladies' room, slinking to her table with what looked to be a shade more purpose. As she slid into her seat, she flicked me a glance. I knew then that she had read my note.

I was instantly at her side. 'Madame?'

'I wonder if you have any aspirin? I have a slight headache.'

'But of course, madame. If you care to come with me, I can find you some.'

She smiled apologetically at Barbie and Stengritt. 'Would you excuse me for another moment? It's been such a hot day. I'm probably just dehydrated.'

Without waiting for an answer, she rose and followed me back through the double doors towards the reception area where I retrieved the first aid kit, all too aware that Barbie's men were placed throughout the lobby area as well as the restaurant.

Christine swallowed the tablet I gave her and then clutched at the reception desk.

'I feel a little faint,' she said, clamping her hand to her forehead.

'Here, madame.' I took her by the arm, leading her to an armchair set on its own well away from any lurking Gestapo. I fetched her some water, bending low so I could hear her murmur.

'They're bringing them to Lyon on Friday?'

'Yes.'

'That doesn't give us much time.'

'I know. And now they're looking for two women whom they suspect to be agents so Juliette and I must work separately. Which means we must all be more careful.'

She lifted her head, mopping imaginary perspiration away with her handkerchief, pressing it to her lips as if to wipe those too. 'Understood.'

Then she got to her feet with a radiant smile. 'I feel so much better now. Thank you.'

I very much doubted it.

I followed a discreet distance behind as she returned to the dining room, watching her brush Barbie's arm as she took her seat, leaning across as if to hang on his every word. Stengritt was back at his table, observing almost as closely as I was. Did he suspect her? I had no idea. The Nazis suspected everyone. But we had one advantage, and she was deploying it for everything she was worth.

Klaus Barbie might be a murdering bastard, but he was also a man. And I did not believe there was a man alive who could resist Christine when she turned the full force of her magnetism on him. If he saw a trap, he was walking straight into it. I could only hope the trap didn't close on us instead.

I watched as Barbie placed a possessive hand on Christine's shoulder, stroking it as you would a cat. Slender hands. Fine fingers. Fingers that fit easily around a trigger.

I closed my eyes for a second, trying to obliterate the image of a bullet blasting into my brother's skull from point-blank range. Jack would die more slowly. He would die knowing why. He would understand with his last breath how much I hated him.

THIRTY

The moonlight sliced through the barred windows, casting elongated shadows across the cell floor. He was trapped by those shadows, pinned down by their weight. And they weighed heavy. Especially in his heart.

Another day spent waiting and wondering. They should have been in Lyon by now, although he wasn't complaining. This place was a paradise compared to what he'd heard about Montluc. Jack made a quick calculation in his head. Today was 8 August. Which meant that a week today, on the fifteenth, the landings would take place if everything went to plan. Operation Dragoon was going ahead and he hadn't breathed a word. Or rather, gasped one out under the torturer's fists.

He pressed his fingers once more along his jawline, feeling the swelling where the blows landed with admirable precision. They went for the same spots each time, reopening wounds, adding to the bruising that Guy informed him was now an impressive deep purple. Guy had got off more lightly. The bruises on him were mostly confined to his torso. Divide and conquer – a well-used Nazi tactic. At least, that was what it looked like. But they couldn't open Jack's real wounds, even as they barked at him to reveal his secrets. The Nazis were running scared. Good. They knew something was about to hit them, just as they rained down their blows. But they had no real idea what or when. Jack smiled to himself in the dark.

It was in the dark he'd last seen her, her hair edged auburn by the flames that had all too briefly illuminated her face. His heart had stopped when that shell landed. Jolted back into life when he saw her get up and dust herself off. Then she was gone, sprinting for the woods, leading her men to safety. She'd made it. Of course she had. He would feel it if she hadn't because the world would be that much emptier. Not as empty, though, as his heart. Or his soul.

Marianne was different to the others. He'd known that from the moment he'd set eyes on her. She had instantly and irrevocably filled a gap he hadn't even been aware existed, the part of him he thought he'd kept hidden. But she had found it and, without even knowing, poured herself into the hollow that had been there since he was a very small child. God knows how since their first real date had been a disaster, falling asleep like that in the cinema. He blamed the whisky. Or maybe it was the beer. Whichever it was, he'd drunk far too much of it beforehand. Nerves of course. She'd done that to him. She'd also forgiven him. Eventually. But he'd never done it again.

A gentle snore came from the other side of the cell. Guy was bearing up well, but then he had always been remarkably resilient. Funny how things turned out. They had roomed together at Cambridge and now they were here, rooming together once more. Jack let out a snort that was half-despair, half-laughter. Guy stirred at the sound, throwing the rough blanket back as he turned towards Jack.

'It's OK, old chap,' murmured Jack. 'Go back to sleep.'

An unintelligible mumble as Guy's eyes drifted shut again.

In repose, he looked more intense than ever, his fine bones etched deeper by the moon shadows, the lashes that lay on his cheeks ridiculously long for a man. The ladies absolutely loved him of course. He managed to pull off that trick of appearing vulnerable while at the same time cutting a swathe through them. Jack had to hand it to him. Guy would have made a great actor, although his heart was set on the Foreign Office.

It was that same talent for acting that made Guy such a superb agent. They had carried out dozens of successful operations together before their luck had run out and their safe house had been raided. Although it had returned when they'd been transferred to the internment camp from the prison where they'd first been incarcerated and from which it would have been impossible to escape. As impossible as this one, in fact.

So close to promised victory and here they were, cooped up in a cell when they could have been out there, setting the stage for Dragoon, making sure everything was ready just as they'd planned. Such bad luck to have run into that roadblock.

He watched Guy's breathing slow as he slipped deeper into sleep. Still, he and Guy had had an almost miraculous run. The average agent lasted no more than a few months in the field. Couriers and radio operators even less. He had managed nearly four years with just a couple of brief postings home, wherever home was now. Some days it felt more as if he belonged here, especially early on when he and Marianne had been running their network together. They made a good team. Naturally. But it was more than that. She was the only woman he had ever met who could put aside her femininity so easily and assume a place among her men.

They respected her for it – he could see that on their faces. He fancied he had seen that too, back in the cornfield as they followed her unquestioningly into the woods. Marianne was a cool-headed leader, brave but not foolhardy. She would have got them out of there, he had no doubt of that. And he loved her all the more for it, that courage under fire. She was more than his equal and, in so many ways, far superior. When all this was over, they would make a great team again. He had to believe that. Otherwise, he doubted he could go on.

THIRTY-ONE

'Your tea, madame.'

I pulled back the curtains, letting the morning light flood the room. Christine groaned and sat up from her pillows, pushing the hair back from her face.

'Thank you.'

'How did last night go?'

I'd clocked off at the end of my shift like any normal hotel worker. They'd been the last to leave the dining room, Barbie ordering yet more champagne while his men sat by, stifling their yawns.

She smiled wanly and took a good gulp of her tea. 'After dinner they insisted on singing around the piano. I managed to fend him off. Last I saw, Stengritt was half-carrying him out of the door.'

'Did you manage to get anything else out of him?'

'Nothing of any use. He was too far gone. Even when Barbie's drunk, he's well aware of what he's saying, and he's a mean drunk. He could have turned at any moment.'

'Do you think he would try and hurt you?'

'If he got the chance. Which he won't.'

She reached for her cigarettes and lit one up, alternating puffs with mouthfuls of tea.

'I'll try to find out what Barbie intends to do when they arrive,' she said. 'I'm dining with him again tonight. It would be useful to know if they're planning to take them straight to Montluc or to their headquarters first.'

'You think he would interrogate them right away?'

'He might. He's well aware that his days here are numbered. You can see it in his face. He looks like a man who knows his time is almost up. And I think he's determined to destroy everything and everyone he can before that happens.'

She spoke quietly but her words struck like shrapnel embedding in my soul. It was one thing my hating Jack – quite another imagining the brutality he would suffer at Barbie's hands. The same brutality Barbie had meted out to Edward. And it was Jack who had betrayed him. A shadow dropped briefly across my mind. No time to think about that now.

'Do you think you can get him to tell you?'

'I'll do my best.'

I looked at her pale, determined face. 'I know you will.'

She flashed me that smile of hers. It was so brilliant that it almost hid the layers beneath. Almost but not quite.

'But I won't be able to do that until this evening, unless...'

She took another drag, thinking.

'Unless?'

'I could be wandering near their headquarters on some pretext this morning. Contrive to bump into him.'

'He might possibly be free for lunch?'

'Exactly. And he's a man of habit so if I appear around noon, he'll be on his way to do just that.'

'Perfect.'

She slid out of bed and began to apply cream to her skin.

Last night's make-up was still in place, smudged beneath her eyes. She wiped it away and began methodically reapplying it.

'Are you sure you can handle this?' I asked. 'I mean, really sure?'

The colour on her cheeks was all rouge. Underneath, the pallor remained. Christine's skin was naturally pale but this was something else. Tiredness, certainly. Maybe more. I'd seen the bravest of agents crumble when they pushed themselves beyond endurance. We couldn't afford for Christine to crumble. Not now.

'Don't worry,' she said. 'I'm not going to chicken out. We'll save our boys and make sure Dragoon goes ahead.'

'I never thought you would,' I said. 'Chicken out.'

'Yes, you did. I would have thought the same.'

She suddenly seemed so much smaller, fragile but still alluring in her silk nightgown with its lace panels. She was an absolute mistress of the art of seduction. And yet she was so very human too. I wondered what it cost her to assume this role, because role it most certainly was. Christine may have been blessed with more sex appeal than almost anyone I'd ever met but I suspected it was a curse as far as she was concerned.

She drew herself up under my gaze, transforming as I watched into the goddess she deployed so effectively in the field. She might not be invincible, but Christine sure as hell was giving it all she'd got.

I stepped forward and wrapped my arms around her, feeling her resistance to my touch.

'Thank you,' I said awkwardly as I stepped back, dropping my arms to my sides.

She dipped her head, a swan observing a goose. 'For what? It's my duty.'

Not for the first time I wondered what drove Christine. This went far beyond duty. It was almost a sacred calling. Or an obsession. The kind of thing that was fuelled by love or hatred.

Perhaps both. Maybe she, too, had lost someone, although that didn't wholly explain the dark seam I glimpsed running through her, a seam that glinted like mica out of a darkness I could only imagine. This wasn't grief or even the fire in a warrior's belly but a burning, blazing desire for revenge. Retribution. I could understand that. It made us sisters under the skin.

THIRTY-TWO

She touched my hair, crimping it between her fingers. 'You need more curl. Here at the front. And leave it loose, like the local women do, or you'll stand out.'

Suzanne's own hair was swept into her customary chignon. I guessed the rules were different for a woman like her. Or rather, for the woman she was supposed to be.

'Less lipstick,' she added. 'Otherwise people will think you are one of my girls.'

She turned her attention to Juliette, elegant as ever in spite of her simple cotton dress and lack of any adornment apart from the earrings she always wore.

'Lose those,' said Suzanne, looking at the earrings. 'They are too good for someone who works as a chambermaid. They make you seem so Parisian.'

'I am Parisian,' said Juliette, reluctantly removing her earrings.

'Yes, but Parisians do not fit in Lyon. It's a parochial place. Especially now.'

She was right of course. I had spent too long out in the relative safety of the countryside, as had Juliette. In Lyon of all cities, we had to blend in.

Suzanne gave us a final once-over before nodding in approval. 'I am calling everyone together for a meeting this evening,' she said. 'It's important you get there safely.'

'Who's everyone? I thought the Resistance here was more or less blown along with the network.'

'Scattered maybe, but we are regrouping. And now we have you here to lead us.'

Instead of my brother. I wondered if the sharp pain in my chest whenever I thought of him would eventually dull into something more bearable.

As if she'd read my mind, Suzanne added, 'I considered him a good friend – Edward.'

I stared at her, my eyes pricking.

'He was a fine man,' she went on. 'So courageous.'

'When did you last see him?'

'The night before he was arrested.'

'And how was he?'

'He was... Edward.'

I heard the tiny catch in her voice. Then she shook her head as if shaking off a memory she couldn't bear to contain.

'I mean, he was in good spirits, as ever. He was such a cheerful person but no fool. Your brother was always cautious. It's why I still find it hard to believe they caught him, of all people.'

'He was betrayed,' I said, unable to keep the bitterness out of my voice.

'That was what I heard.'

'You don't believe it?'

'Oh I believe it. It happens. But to Edward? That is the part I find hard to believe. Everyone loved him.'

Including you. The thought flashed across my mind, unbidden. But once it was there, it made perfect sense. The way she spoke about him. The look in her eyes. Had he felt that way too? I didn't dare ask.

'Anyway,' she said, squaring her narrow shoulders, 'all the more reason to stop those Gestapo bastards getting what they want. We will make sure both those men and Operation Dragoon are safe, one way or another. What is happening with the agent at the Grand Hotel?'

'She has Barbie firmly in her sights.'

'Good.'

I wasn't giving any more than that away, not even to Suzanne. Cardinal rule of the Resistance and SOE – operating on a need-to-know basis. Except I was pretty sure Suzanne knew far more than she was letting on.

'She's a good agent. She knows what she's doing.'

'I hope so,' said Suzanne. 'But there is no guarantee that she will succeed.'

'There isn't, which is why we must try to stop Barbie getting his hands on our men in the first place. That means intercepting the convoy or, at worst, rescuing them from wherever they take them.'

'That won't be easy.'

'I know. But I think we can do it.'

'You would need to find the right place to intercept it. That convoy will be heavily guarded.'

'Yes but we have the element of surprise on our side. They won't be expecting us to attack. Especially if we do it right here, in Lyon.'

Her eyebrows moved a fraction higher. 'Why here? Why not out on the open roads?'

'It's too risky out there. They drive in a specific formation that's designed to ward off an ambush. Here in Lyon the roads are narrow and they can't keep up that formation. You also have the traboules, which we can use as an escape route. In the countryside, there are mainly open fields. Trying to escape across those makes you an easy target.'

'True. And, as you say, we have the traboules. Our men here know every inch of them.'

'Exactly. So we could stage an ambush near one of the entrances and get our boys away before the bastards know what's hit them.'

'André can help you find the right place. I will send him to take you on a reconnaissance tour. We will need plenty of men to add firepower if we are to have a street fight with the Germans.'

'We have our American friends as well as our other men on standby,' said Juliette. 'Ten thousand of them.'

'But do they even know where you are right now?'

'I left a message for Maggie with the concierge,' I said. 'To let them know that Juliette and I are safe with you.'

'Was that wise?'

'What do you mean?'

'Are you absolutely sure you can trust all your people?'

'I trust Maggie with my life,' I said. 'The rest have loyally served with me or Juliette for years. We have Maquis camped all the way from Lyon back to Digne. Our team at the chateau includes my other brother. Maggie will make sure to tell only those who need to know.'

'Very well then. If you're sure.'

She didn't sound convinced.

Suzanne rose and reached for her hat. 'I will let you know when and where the meeting is taking place. In the meantime, I will ask André to be here as soon as possible. We only have three days to get this organised. We need to move fast.'

She waved a hand at the basket she'd brought; it was laden with cheeses, meats, bread and fruit along with a good bottle of wine.

'Now eat,' she said. 'You will need your strength.'

'So will you,' I replied.

The look on her face told me everything I needed to know. If there had been any doubt in my mind that she and Edward had been lovers, it was dispelled by the depth of the loss I saw etched there. I knew that pain. It echoed my own.

THIRTY-THREE

The traboule opened into a backstreet near the Place Bellecour.

'I want to show you something,' said André.

He had already led us through the maze of hidden passageways – some arched Renaissance tunnels, others paths that traversed covered stairways and courtyards – until we arrived here at the Place Bellecour, in the heart of Lyon. At the corner of a street that led into the vast, dusty red square he paused and indicated a burned-out building, its windows boarded up.

'This was the Café du Moulin à Vent,' he said. 'Twelve days ago, the Resistance bombed it. It was a favourite meeting place of the Gestapo, including Barbie. We deliberately made sure to set the explosion late at night when it was closed and empty so there would be no innocent casualties. In retaliation, the Nazis brought five of our men from Montluc who had nothing to do with the bombing and executed them here in front of the café. They left their bodies to lie on the pavement in the sun, as a warning.'

André was already walking away, careful not to draw attention. Both Juliette and I wore headscarves and carried shopping baskets, looking as much like good housewives out replenishing supplies as we could manage.

Pausing on a side street just off the square, André pretended to examine the shopping list we had prepared.

'The large building over there is 32 Place Bellecour,' he murmured. 'Current headquarters of the Gestapo and home of Barbie's Department IV.'

I averted my face as we walked past, my eyes sliding sideways to take in every detail I could. It was an ordinary enough office building.

'They installed cells in the basement,' André went on, 'to make repeated interrogations more convenient. They also have what we call the Gestapo kitchens. Those are the torture chambers Barbie likes to use.'

I suppressed an involuntary shudder. Jack had undergone the same training as me, as all of us. But still nothing could prepare you for the reality of torture. Although surely if he was one of theirs, they wouldn't bother to torture him? It didn't make sense. Why play out this elaborate charade? To convince us he was still working for us as well? I had been so focused on my anger, on getting revenge for his betrayal, I hadn't let myself think about anything beyond that, but here it was – a niggle of doubt, my instincts whispering that something was very wrong. Was there some way he could be innocent, despite that damning evidence?

Up another side street, André darted into a doorway that was marked out only by a tiny, chalked symbol of a lion on the wall beside it, so small you would never see it unless you knew it was there. The mark of the traboule. Once safely in its confines, he stopped.

'That restaurant we just passed is the new Gestapo favourite, Restaurant Daniel. It is where Barbie likes to lunch most days, unless he is out on an operation or otherwise occupied.'

André ground out his words through clenched teeth. A muscle was working in his jaw, the same muscle that had tightened at the sight of the Café du Moulin à Vent.

'These men who were murdered outside the café, they were your friends?' I asked.

'They were my brothers,' said André. 'In this fight we are all brothers. I knew two of them especially well. One was the regional chef de l'Armée de la Resistance. The Gestapo executed them in cold blood, for the world to see. It was unforgivable. Like everything else they do.'

'We will avenge your brothers,' said Juliette.

'I hope so.'

André sounded infinitely weary.

'I promise we will,' I said.

'That is a fine promise,' he said. 'But Barbie is an extremely dangerous man. Many have tried to outwit him. None have succeeded.'

'That's because they were men,' I said. 'Attempting a direct approach. When all is said and done, Klaus Barbie is also just a man. And all men have their weaknesses.'

'Then I hope, madame, you have found his.' André didn't look or sound convinced.

'I think we can do it,' I said. 'Have faith.'

'Faith.' He spat out the word as if it were a particularly bitter pill. 'I once had faith but no more. Another of the men they executed outside the café was responsible for the spiritual well-being of the Christians in the Resistance. A good man but that did not help him. This is a godless war fought by godless people. Don't waste your time praying. No one is listening. The only thing I believe in is liberty. Now come, we must continue.'

We followed him in silence through more passageways, the dim light filtering across the vaulted ceiling that stretched above our heads. It came from the archway where we emerged once more, passing through a small walled courtyard into yet another narrow street, all part of the labyrinth that was Lyon. A church stood directly in front of us, its white spires stark against the bright blue sky.

'The marketplace is just up there,' said André. 'When it is open, this street effectively becomes a dead end. That means the convoy will have to pass along here to get to Place Bellecour. Which makes it the ideal place to stage an ambush.'

I looked along the street. It was hemmed in on both sides by buildings, the entrance to the traboules conveniently situated at one end with the marketplace at the other. Perfect.

'Here I must leave you,' said André.

I turned to thank him, but he had disappeared. Even in broad daylight, André was a man of shadows, no doubt already slipping through his beloved traboules.

Something caught my eye – a detail in the stained-glass window of the church. It was a lamb curled up at the feet of Jesus, its tiny head lifted to look at him. The shaft of light in which the lamb lay reminded me of Christine's hair, silver bright as it danced around her face.

The Lamb of God. Or a lamb to the slaughter. I wondered if Christine believed in God. Somehow, I already knew the answer.

THIRTY-FOUR

Christine was in position at 12.50 p.m. precisely. She strolled under the trees along the western side of the Place Bellecour, admiring the imposing statue of a man on a horse that stood proudly in the centre of the square. She kept her eyes on the statue as she approached the small party advancing towards her, apparently so transfixed she didn't see Barbie and his men until she almost walked straight into them.

'Oh, pardon,' she exclaimed before executing a convincing double take.

'Madame, a surprise and an honour,' said Barbie.

Christine, in turn, feigned delight. 'What luck,' she exclaimed. 'I was just thinking about you.'

'You were?'

A cat slunk up to Barbie, wrapping itself around his legs and mewling. He picked it up and cradled it in his arms, stroking the grey fur that almost matched his suit. Christine watched as the cat arched against his caress. It was an oddly disturbing sight.

'Yes. You mentioned a restaurant near here last night and I

was trying to find it. You said they served a particularly good *salade* Lyonnaise.'

'Ah yes. Restaurant Daniel. I am on my way there now, as it happens.'

He put the cat down and it sauntered off to a sunny spot where it stretched out, luxuriating in the warmth.

Christine clapped her hands together. 'But that is simply marvellous. You can show me the way, if you would be so kind.'

Barbie's knife-blade lips stretched in a knowing smile. 'I can do more than that, madame. I must insist you join me for lunch.'

'Are you sure? Do you not have important matters to discuss?'

She glanced at the two Gestapo officers with him, recognising the fair-haired one from the previous evening. Harry Stengritt. Right now, he was regarding her as a hawk would a mouse.

Barbie waved a dismissive hand. 'Nothing that is more important than you, my dear.'

His flattery was as insincere as his charm, but she nevertheless smiled demurely.

'Well, that really is very kind of you,' she said, forcing herself not to flinch as he took her arm. She could feel the eyes of people on her as she passed, the unspoken hatred behind them. *I am one of you*, she wanted to cry. *I am doing this to save us all.* Instead, she kept her gaze fixed on the square and then the street ahead as she chatted gaily.

'I do so love Lyon,' she said. 'It hasn't changed all that much since I was here last.'

'When was that?'

His tone was genial but she detected a sharpened note.

'Oh, before the war,' she said. 'I came with my husband. A short visit but we so enjoyed the opera and the ballet. And the food of course. We always stayed at the Grand Hotel.'

'Your husband?'

'Yes. Sadly, he was killed in the Battle of France. Fighting for the Fatherland.'

'I see. My condolences. You have been most unlucky.'

'I know,' she sighed. 'First my husband and then dear Hans. But, you know, I believe my luck may have changed.'

His smirk showed her that he had gobbled up her bait.

'Well, Daniel's food is excellent and, I believe, famous throughout Lyon. Fortunately, we can enjoy it much as it has always been.'

I bet you can, thought Christine. The Gestapo ate while people starved. But at least restaurants like Daniel's could supply information in return. Apparently, Monsieur Daniel was one of those who kept his ears open and his mouth shut.

He greeted them effusively now, his beaming smile taking in Christine as he insisted they try the new sausage he'd received that very morning from his own family farm in the countryside.

She nibbled politely at its meaty mass while the men carried on the conversation they had obviously been having when she appeared, staring into the middle distance as she pretended to be absorbed in her own inconsequential thoughts. They were saying nothing of real interest but still she could hear the restraint in Stengritt's voice.

All of a sudden, he tailed off completely.

'I'm sorry?' She turned in his direction, dimly aware that he had addressed her with a question.

'I asked if you could speak German,' he said in French. 'I understand you are from Alsace.'

'Not very well, I'm afraid,' she said. 'My mother insisted I attend a convent school. She was a very devout Catholic. Unfortunately, the good sisters were entirely French.'

'You did not speak it at home?' Stengritt's brows drew together, making him appear more hawklike than ever.

'Sadly, my dear papa was often away on business... Maman only spoke French. Her people were originally from the south-west, near Toulouse. Poor Papa is now dead or he would have gloried in the return of Alsace to the Fatherland.'

Barbie was nodding in approval, fanatical as ever about the Führer and the Fatherland. Stengritt, however, was not to be distracted.

'I see. But surely you spoke German with your previous, ah, companion? I understand he was a general in the Luftwaffe.'

He really wasn't letting this go.

Christine forced herself to answer sweetly. 'I tried. Of course I wanted to speak of the Führer in our mother tongue. I was having lessons when darling Hans was killed. My problem is that I simply do not have a head for languages. I find it so hard to remember anything.'

She ran a hand through her platinum waves. Her message couldn't be clearer.

'No matter,' said Barbie. 'I am sure your German will soon improve. I, personally, shall teach you.'

I'm sure you will, she thought, once more feigning delight.

'Would you? Well that would be marvellous. But an important man like you is far too busy to teach me. I can look around for someone who has more time on their hands.'

'I insist.'

There was something in his voice and eyes that brooked no argument. The same ruthlessness that had him torturing men, women and children beyond the point they could speak, never mind offer up information.

'You are very kind.'

Christine swallowed the rest of her saucisson, feeling it scrape against the sides of her throat.

'May I present our dishes of the day?'

Thank goodness for Monsieur Daniel magically appearing by her elbow. The waves of suspicion wafting her way from

Stengritt were suffocating. She had to do something – and fast, before he bent Barbie's ear.

'We have a fine, plump chicken cooked with slivers of truffle. *Volaille demi-deuil*, based on Mère Fillioux's original recipe with our own twist.'

'Perfect for you, my dear,' said Barbie. 'Chicken in half-mourning.'

'Indeed,' Christine murmured, smoothing the skirt of her lavender dress, a permitted shade for someone still apparently grieving. Even these days, the traditions of mourning were observed. Especially if you were aiming to convince the enemy of your fidelity for one of their dead heroes.

A fine Beaujolais accompanied the chicken. The Gestapo certainly knew how to enjoy themselves. No clutching a ration card outside an empty shop for them. They were happy to pillage the finest Lyon had to offer, including its women. Some were delighted to collaborate. Others not so willing. Christine had heard the tales of how the Nazis treated their women. Not all officers were gentlemen and, by the most horrific accounts, certainly not Barbie. The breath caught in her throat, and she looked about the restaurant, as much to distract herself as anything.

There were a couple of other women in the restaurant, both evidently dining with their husbands. Members, no doubt, of the Vichy government. She wasn't sure what was worse – a poor woman so desperate she offered herself up to the enemy or a woman like the matron pecking at her food two tables away, her shoulders quivering with disapproval at the sight of Christine.

Hypocrite.

The Vichy regime had sold out their countrymen far more than those girls hanging off the arms of German officers.

She stole a glance at Stengritt, deep in conversation once more. He was every bit as ruthless as Barbie, using his mistress to seduce and turn a member of the Resistance. If Christine had trained the Resistance, it would never have happened. But the Resistance and SOE were poles apart on that score.

While SOE had the luxury of their training, the Resistance had to learn as they went along, often starting up in cafés and restaurants like this. The walls in certain Lyonnais establishments held many secrets. Just as the Germans liked to annex a place such as this, so the Resistance met in the bouchons and corner cafés of the old town, in back rooms and darkened corners as well as in the traboules. Monsieur Daniel was, according to the intelligence, a prominent member. He certainly ran a tight ship.

An excellent, crisp salad succeeded the chicken and was then followed by a dish of Monsieur Daniel's home-made sorbet before the cheese course was produced. Christine took the tiniest sliver of a pungent white cheese, conscious that the afternoon was ticking away and she still hadn't winkled any information out of them. The men were deep in discussion regarding logistics and the movement of troops. Barbie was insistent that they hold their ground, even in the face of the approaching Allies.

'The Führer will send support,' he declared. 'We have three armies stationed just over the border, in Switzerland. He will not leave us to fight the Allies alone.'

Good luck with that, she thought. Word had it that the Germans were in full-scale retreat on several fronts, squeezed into tight corners. When that happened, rats tended to turn and run. At least in her experience.

All at once a name pricked her ears. Digne. They were talking about Jack and his fellow prisoners. She kept her movements casual and her shoulders relaxed as she savoured the cheese, sticking to her role of table ornament, listening as hard as she could. Friday. They'd said it twice now. They were definitely bringing them on Friday from Digne.

The next sliver of cheese was poised on the end of her knife when she heard Barbie insist that they were brought straight to the Gestapo headquarters.

'If they are, as we suspect, enemy agents then I will get it out of them, along with everything they know. We do not have any time to waste.'

She kept the knife moving towards her plate, making sure her hand held steady. She could feel Stengritt watching her out of the corner of his eye. She lifted the cheese to her mouth and savoured it. It tasted like sawdust.

The coffee cups had been cleared. It was evidently time to go. As Barbie rose, she remained in her seat, staring at the table-cloth. A risky move but she had to play the game out. Finally, he remembered his manners and moved to stand behind her chair.

'Thank you.'

She slithered gracefully to her feet, shrugging on the coat that Monsieur Daniel held out for her. It was important to keep Barbie's respect, even to insist upon it. To do otherwise might well prove fatal in more ways than one. For now, she was the aristocratic former mistress of a high-ranking German hero, killed in action. And Barbie had better remember that.

Thankfully, Barbie had no connection with the deceased General Gottmann and could only go on his reputation as something of a lady's man. It no doubt made him even more of a hero in Barbie's eyes. The man had probably had several mistresses as well as a long-suffering wife at home in Germany.

Outside the restaurant, Barbie remembered his manners once more.

'I must leave you,' he said. 'We have urgent business to take care of.'

'But of course.' She smiled. 'Thank you for lunch.'

'It was my pleasure. I hope to see you at dinner.'

'Eight o'clock. I won't forget.'

Another smile and a little wave as the men strode back towards the Place Bellecour. Then she turned and headed for the Grand Hotel as fast as propriety and good field craft would allow. She might not want to work with the others but, for better or worse, they were in this together now. And Barbie wasn't the only one with urgent business. It was time to put plans into action.

THIRTY-FIVE

The moonlight filtering through the barred window stirred a memory. Another night. Another place. The hush of blackout in Chelsea, the sirens for once silent in the darkened streets. The house too, was silent, shrouded in dust sheets. No one had been there since the start of the war. A stolen night huddled under a childhood eiderdown, her parents safe at their country house. A last night with Marianne. A last and a first. They had never spent a whole night together before. It felt wrong and right at the same time, creeping up the stairs like two naughty children although there was nothing childlike about the way they reached for one another.

All at once Jack felt her stiffen and pull back.

'What's wrong?'

She let out a long, shuddering breath. 'Absolutely nothing. Everything's perfect.'

She pressed herself against him once more, the heat of her body setting light to the fuse. Then fire consumed both of them, the flames reaching higher even as they cried out, ebbing to the warm glow in which they lay, sated for now.

Jack stroked her hair back from her face with his free hand, lifting her chin for another kiss. She met him there, eager for more, sighing in pleasure as his hands began to roam across her flesh, her skin soft as a butterfly's wing beneath his fingers, trembling at their touch.

'Temptress,' he teased.

'Hardly,' she countered. Then she threw herself over him, pinning him down, her hair falling over her face, tickling his as their lips met.

'I'll show you temptress,' she murmured.

'Please do.'

Grey dawn was creeping round the blackout curtains by the time she had finished showing him. She never ceased to astonish him, this wild, wanton, wonderful woman. He tightened his arm around her, feeling her burrow deeper into his embrace.

'Marry me,' he murmured.

She went very still. 'Ask me again when you come back from wherever it is you're going.'

She left the 'if' unspoken.

'I'll never stop asking you. And I am coming back.'

She pushed herself up on one elbow and gazed down at him, her eyes searching.

'I know you are.'

'Then say that you'll marry me. Now.'

'I might.'

'Tease.'

'First temptress, now tease. Which is it to be?'

'Can I have both at the same time?'

'Anyone ever tell you that you're greedy?'

'Greedy for you maybe. I can never have enough of you.'

'Prove it,' she said.

So he did.

THIRTY-SIX

There was a brass plaque by the front door that proclaimed it to be the surgery of a Dr Gaspard, Chirurgeon de Gynécologie. I rang the bell. A young man answered. He looked like any one of the university students and intellectuals who gathered in darkened corner cafés to plot against the regime.

'We have appointments,' I said. 'For the evening surgery.'

'You were referred?'

'Yes. By Madame Suzanne.'

He stood aside and ushered us through a waiting room, up the stairs and into a salon where a group was gathered. They ranged in age from late teens to the goateed man who turned out to be Dr Gaspard. He was handing round tiny cups of coffee from a tray placed on a low table. Books lined one wall, arranged with precision on carved wooden shelves. The paintings on display looked to be original, the rich oil colours glowing from within gilded frames.

Juliette and I perched on a chaise longue. André was deep in conversation with Suzanne, who gave us a brisk smile as we entered. The young man fetched us glasses of water in preference to coffee and then André called the meeting to order.

'Gentlemen, I have no need to introduce Juliette as her reputation precedes her. Similarly, Marianne is well known for her bravery in fighting for our freedom.'

I smiled at the assembly. 'Thank you, André. That's quite an introduction.'

'So,' André went on, 'we all know why we are here and that is to plan an ambush of the convoy bringing three captured agents to Gestapo headquarters from Digne prison. Marianne will now give you the details.'

André nodded at our host, who pressed gently on one of his bookshelves. They swung open, revealing a map of Lyon and its traboules.

I swallowed as I remembered a similar map at Bernard's house and then got to my feet. Every face was turned in my direction. I pointed to the centre of the map, indicating the route we'd earmarked.

'The convoy will have to approach Place Bellecour along this street here,' I said, 'close to the marketplace. We'll set up a distraction here, a farm cart that has seemingly tipped over, spilling its melons. Those melons will contain explosives that we detonate at the appropriate moment, at the same time using smoke and live grenades to cause chaos and block the exit from the street. We'll have a couple of minutes and that is all to extract the prisoners and escape with them through the traboules. We'll sabotage communication lines, vehicles and equipment beforehand to delay the Germans sending in rein-forcements. Any questions?'

Our host, a man with a swathe of white hair to match his clipped goatee, spoke up. His voice was low and cultured. 'Who is in charge of this operation?'

'I am.'

'You?'

'Yes. I am the new leader of the Lyon network. I understand

some of you may have known the former leader, my brother Edward.'

It was a calculated risk. Ordinarily I wouldn't reveal our connection, but time was short and loyalty needed to be cultivated fast. Suzanne had told me how highly they held Edward in their esteem. I needed to play on that to bring these men onside in what could turn out to be a massacre. I'd made it sound so simple; we all knew it was anything but.

'We only have a couple of days to get everything in place. You think you can do that?' he pressed.

'Yes I do.'

'And the explosives. Where do you intend to get those?'

'I believe you have a more than adequate supply.'

'I think we can sort you out, but our numbers are depleted,' said the doctor. 'We need more men as backup if we are to carry this off. Klaus Barbie will not take kindly to an attack in what he considers his city.'

'We have men we can bring in from the countryside,' I said. 'Loyal Maquis fighters as well as trained soldiers.'

'There are thousands of them,' added Juliette. 'Just waiting for their chance to fight.'

'We won't need thousands,' said André. 'But it's good to know they're there.'

'I have a courier who can liaise between us and them,' I said. 'She'll advise them of the plan immediately after this meeting. We need them in place along the entire route from Digne to Lyon to ensure nothing goes wrong. I'll bring in our best men to help us carry out the ambush and the escape. Now, if there are no more questions, I'll delegate tasks.'

I caught the look that passed between André and the doctor.

'Is there a problem?' I asked, frosting my words with sufficient ice to command respect.

'None at all,' said André.

'We are here to do whatever we can to help,' added the doctor.

'Good. Then let's get to it. We have a long evening ahead.'

'Bravo,' I heard Suzanne murmur as I turned away from the map. 'Edward would be proud of you.'

There it was again, that stab to my heart. Perhaps a little less painful this time, cushioned as it was by the kindness of her words.

'He would be proud of you too,' I said.

Her eyes shone a little brighter. Then she got to her feet. 'We have work to do.'

THIRTY-SEVEN

It was dark by the time we left the doctor's surgery and made our way back to the apartment. The streets were empty, the good citizens of Lyon once more at their dinner tables or settling their children into bed, only the odd bistro spilling light and sound across our otherwise silent route. The silence wasn't uncomfortable. Far from it. We'd settled into a new understanding that evening, a sense that we truly were fighting on the same side. At least, that was how I felt.

We rounded a corner yards from the apartment and out of the corner of my eye I saw a flicker of movement, a street cat slinking in search of food. All of a sudden, I felt Juliette slip her arm through mine and tug me down a side street.

'In here,' she said, pulling me after her as we turned and began to march back the way we'd come.

As soon as we hit the relative safety of the backstreets, Juliette broke into a run. I had no choice but to keep pace. We kept twisting and turning, choosing our direction at random until, at last, we stopped in an alleyway, gasping for breath.

'What on earth...?' I gulped in another lungful of air.

'I saw them outside the apartment,' said Juliette. 'A couple of men in the coats and hats those bastards love to wear, standing by a black Citroën.'

'Gestapo?'

'Yes.'

'How can you be sure they were there for us?'

'How can we not? It was too much of a risk.'

'Did they see us?'

Juliette shook her head. 'I am sure they didn't, otherwise they would have come after us. They were looking the other way, down the main road, obviously waiting for someone. I really do think that was us.'

I took in another gulp of air, my heart rate almost back to normal. 'They can't have followed us from the meeting. We would have spotted them.'

'They don't need to follow us. All it takes is a word in the right ear.'

I looked at her. 'You think someone informed on us? Again?'

'It is always a possibility. The Gestapo pay well.'

Another betrayal. One as swift as the other. If someone was informing on us, they seemed to know our movements almost before we did.

'First Bernard and Mathilde's house. Now this.' Juliette's eyes were as luminous as those of the cat I'd spied earlier. If it hadn't been for her, that distraction could have cost us our lives. 'But who knew where we were staying both times?'

'André? There's no way he betrayed us. He needs us as much as we need him, if not more. Another local *résistant*?'

'I do not think an ordinary *résistant* would know that kind of thing. The Resistance might not be as organised as SOE, but in some respects, such as information, they operate even better.'

Her words weren't lost on me. It had, after all, been an SOE agent who betrayed his own here. Apparently. That shadow of doubt that had descended refused to disappear. Or maybe it was wishful thinking.

'You think it could be someone in our network then?'

'As I said, anything is possible. They knew where we were going when we first arrived in Lyon.'

'And I sent them that message to say we were with Suzanne. She was right. Perhaps it was a foolish thing to do after all.'

Juliette touched my arm, a brush of reassurance. 'Not at all. You thought you could trust them. But it seems we cannot.'

Faces flashed before me: Henri. Marcus. Maggie. Impossible for it to be one of them. As for Antoine and the Americans, doubtful.

'So what do we do now?'

I looked around, sizing up the narrow alley ahead that led to a street beyond. We listened for a moment, but there was no sound save that of a lone nightbird singing and chattering in a nearby tree.

'The only thing we can do is go to Suzanne's establishment. Which means going back the way we came, although we need to avoid the apartment. Do you know the address of the brothel?'

'I believe it is on Rue Garibaldi.'

'Any idea where that is from here?'

Juliette frowned. 'I did my best to memorise the route André took us but we cannot see any landmarks. We need to get out of here and have a look around to orient ourselves.'

'Let's go.'

We emerged cautiously from the alley into the empty street beyond and then to its junction with a larger thoroughfare. From there, the road curved round until it met an even wider road which led us down to the river Saône.

'I recognise it now,' I said.

'Yes. It's this way.'

We finally hit the wide boulevard that was Rue Garibaldi.

It was so long it extended through three arrondissements, but fortunately Suzanne's establishment was close to the centre, conveniently located for her customers taking a diversion on their way home or to their quarters. André had led us there through the backstreets, but we approached from the main road, the rear one being blocked off to us by the barricade of buildings that lined the boulevard.

From the outside, her brothel was as unimposing as the building in which the apartment was located, the townhouse no different from the others it abutted. Discretion was still a byword in her business – marriages and reputations depended upon it. A small brass sign by the street door directed visitors to the first-floor reception where we were greeted by a woman who looked more like a governess than a brothel receptionist. *Damn.* She wasn't the same one as before.

'Can I help you?'

Her smile was cool, her eyes assessing. She even wore a dress reminiscent of a governess with a high neck in spite of the summer heat.

'We are here to see Madame Suzanne,' said Juliette.

'Is she expecting you?'

'No. But she knows us. We have a mutual friend.'

'This friend's name?'

'André.'

Safe enough. It was his nom de guerre after all. But the receptionist remained unimpressed.

'And we are at present staying on the Rue Boileau. In an apartment with two exits.'

'I see.'

The woman's eyes flicked over us once more. All at once, she stiffened and then rose to her feet.

'Follow me,' she said. 'Quickly.'

We could hear footsteps approaching up the stairs as she shooed us into a side room off the reception area, pulling a curtain across to hide us from view. There was a clothes rail against one wall with hangers swinging from it. As we huddled on the banquette that lined the ante room, we listened to her greeting this new visitor in rather more honeyed tones.

'How wonderful to see you again, *monsieur*,' she cooed. 'May I take your bags?'

We shrank back further into our corner as she slipped through the curtain to prop a couple of bags against the wall by the clothes rail, flashing us a warning look as she did so. We stayed completely still, not daring to move, listening to her lead this customer up a further flight of stairs to what was presumably the brothel itself, footsteps and voices fading into the distance. His responses to her polite chit-chat were monosyllabic, but I thought I detected a French rather than German accent. A Vichy government official perhaps.

The minutes ticked past and then the curtain was pulled aside once more.

'Come with me,' she whispered, picking up the man's briefcase as she led us up the stairs to the next floor. I recognised the door on which she tapped. From the corridor along to the right came the clink of wine glasses and the sounds of feminine laughter.

She hustled us into Suzanne's office, where she was once more seated at her desk with what looked like invoices piled in front of her. The receptionist deposited the man's briefcase on the desk before withdrawing, leaving us to sit in the chairs she indicated.

'This is a surprise,' said Suzanne. 'What happened?'

She listened as we filled her in, all the while expertly rifling through the man's briefcase, scrutinising papers she removed from it before replacing them exactly as they had been.

'You are sure they were Gestapo?'

'Absolutely sure.'

'Thank God you saw them in time.'

'That was thanks to Juliette,' I said, glancing at her. 'But this means we have a bigger problem. It's too much of a coincidence that our safe house is raided so soon after we arrive and now this. Someone is evidently informing on us.'

'You suspect someone in particular?'

'It could be any of a number of people,' I said. 'Some I refuse to believe. But then, I could be wrong. I was before.'

'I see,' said Suzanne. 'It is always wise to keep an open mind. Let me think for a moment. In the meantime, have you eaten?'

Without waiting for an answer, she pressed the bell on her desk and, when the receptionist reappeared, instructed her to fetch us some food.

'We keep the kitchens open all the time,' she explained. 'In case our customers work up an appetite. We like to keep them occupied as long as possible.'

She indicated the bag through which she was rifling.

'The owner of this is a prominent official in the department of transport. I am looking to see what, if any, transportations they are planning. There have been rumours that Barbie intends to step them up before he is forced into retreat.'

'Is there anything in there?' I asked.

She held up a piece of paper. 'This is a stamped order. They are planning one for Friday at noon, a train from Lyon to Auschwitz.'

'My God.'

I'd heard the whispers and seen the reports from London. The exterminations in the camps were accelerating, especially at Auschwitz.

'We can't let that happen,' I said.

'We will think of something. First we must ambush that convoy and stop Barbie getting his hands on our men. As for you, it is too dangerous for you to go anywhere right now. They will be out looking for you, especially when you don't return to the apartment. You must stay here.'

I glanced at Juliette, then at her. 'Here? In this building?'

She laughed. 'It's all right. I have another floor above what we might call the working one. The doorway to it is hidden and any, shall we say, visitors would assume it is an attic. But no one will come looking here. That is the beauty of running an establishment like this.'

Juliette leaned across the desk and took Suzanne's hand in hers. 'Thank you,' she said. 'You are a true patriot.'

Unexpected tears sprang to my eyes. The last time I'd seen Suzanne, we'd both been in England. Now I was so far from home. Hundreds of miles from the country house where I'd lived my entire life. I could see it in my mind's eye, gables rising above leaded windows that were generally shut to keep out the chill but only succeeded in trapping it within its walls, even when the fires were lit. It was a home that had once contained three of us, running amok in the orchard, Edward always the fastest, or creeping along dim corridors inside the house, careful not to disturb Mother with her near permanent headaches.

Edward had been the most solicitous of us, bringing her flowers from the walled garden while Marcus and I hid from her outbursts in the orchard. I could hear her voice in my head, instructing him to take them away. He was never deterred, returning again and again with his colourful posies, determined to bring beauty to her bedside or the chaise longue where she occasionally lay. He had the gift of always seeing the best in people. It was probably that gift which had killed him. And yet I was alive, we were alive, and we all lived to keep on fighting. That had to mean something in this world gone mad. I would make it mean something. For Edward, for Marcus. For us all. And yes, even for Jack.

Another memory in the summerhouse by the orchard. His arms around me. Our breath intermingling, eyes meeting in the mirror. His gaze then had been true. Guileless. I'd thought then he would never lie to me and now I realised that something deep within me still believed that. Or maybe it was what I wanted to believe. I had no idea anymore. What I did know was that love really did never die. I loved Edward still. I would always love my brother. The same way a part of me would always love Jack, even when I hated him.

THIRTY-EIGHT

Barbie appeared agitated beneath his thin veneer of charm. If you could call dropping her a perfunctory nod of greeting charm.

'How are you, my dear?' Christine cooed. 'You seem a little distracted.'

Something had evidently happened in the few hours since their lunch. His eyes were darting, suspicious. They settled on her as if she were a particularly annoying mosquito.

'Not at all. Whatever gave you that idea?'

'Well for one thing, you haven't noticed that I'm wearing your gorgeous gift.'

The necklace burned into her flesh, its diamanté art deco pendant glittering against her skin. She wondered if it had been stolen from the neck of one of his victims. The box had been delivered to her room late that afternoon along with two notes. The first had offered Barbie's admiration, the second informed her that the dressmaker looked forward to her attending her appointment the next day at 9 a.m. sharp, 55 Rue St Jean. The ambush was on. Which meant she had to play her part to perfection tonight.

'It looks good on you.'

'Thank you.' She smiled up at the sommelier. 'I think a glass of champagne.'

'Make that a bottle.'

'We have something to celebrate?'

His face was unreadable. 'I hope so.'

Steady, Christine, don't overplay this.

'I found a divine little bookshop after our lunch,' she said. 'I bought you this.'

She withdrew a slim volume from the evening bag she'd placed at her feet. It contained precisely three items: the book, a lipstick and a tiny pistol wrapped in an embroidered hand-kerchief.

'For you,' she said, placing it in front of him.

Barbie's face lit up when he saw what it was. *'The Song of the Faithful,'* he said.

'You probably already have a copy,' she said, 'but I didn't know if you had one translated into French.'

He turned it over in his hands, admiring the tooling on the spine. The twenty-nine poems inside extolled the virtues of Hitler in a stomach-churning outpouring of sentiment, all of them written by members of the Austrian Hitler Youth. She had barely managed to read a quarter of them, all the while wondering which craven member of the Vichy regime had commissioned this translation. Barbie was leafing through it, his lips moving as he murmured some of the lines.

'Something to remember me by,' she said.

'I could never forget you,' he said, raising his glass to her, mollified by her gift. 'But why are we talking of remembering? You are here – now. Or are you planning on going somewhere?'

'Of course not,' she said. 'I just meant that, well, this war is long and who knows what might happen? You'll probably be posted somewhere even more fitting for your talents or given an important ministerial appointment once the Fatherland declares victory.'

His eyes now were inscrutable, unblinking as they swept across her face, finally settling on the spot just between her brows.

'Perhaps,' he said. 'Although you may find this war is over sooner than you think.'

'Oh really?'

She affected indifference as she addressed herself to the menu, all too aware that the waiting staff couldn't hope to obtain, never mind eat, the luxury food items listed. Poulet de Bresse. Quenelles. Coq au vin. Obscene when local people struggled to buy fresh vegetables, never mind meat.

It was why she barely pecked at her plate, making sure to send back most of it untouched so that they could at least feast upon her uneaten dinner. This evening, she would treat them to a fine *salade de foies de volailles* followed by pike quenelles, courtesy of the Gestapo. If Barbie noticed she hardly consumed a morsel of the expensive food he ordered, he would no doubt assume it was to maintain her figure for his anticipated pleasures.

She had to make sure to maintain that anticipation even as she accelerated the game. While Barbie still danced on the end of her piece of string, she held most of the cards. Once he'd tasted what lay beneath her array of tastefully alluring outfits, the balance of power irrevocably shifted. She had no intention of that happening, not least because the very thought of Barbie touching her made her flesh crawl. She had to force herself not to flinch when he laid a hand on her arm, as he did more and more, or undressed her with his eyes, as he also increasingly did. She wasn't even sure he was aware that he did it – not that he would have cared one way or another. Barbie was used to getting what he wanted whether it was freely given or torn from someone's grasp as they cried out in agony.

'I was thinking,' she said, 'that we might have breakfast together tomorrow.'

'Breakfast?'

She hated his knowing smile and that new gleam in his eye.

'Yes. The owner of the bookshop was telling me that there is a famous café near the Place St Jean where they make the best brioches. It's also close to something I want to show you.'

'What is that?'

She pouted. 'Silly. It's a surprise.'

Barbie smiled that knife-edge smile of his, thin lips extending while his eyes remained as watchful as ever.

'All right. You keep it a surprise. But I cannot come tomorrow morning.'

'Oh? Why?'

'I'm busy.'

'Ah. That is too bad.'

Damn it, he wasn't giving anything away. But nor was he being lured into her trap. *Deep breath, Christine. Don't blow it now.*

There was only one thing for it.

'You know,' she said as if she'd only just thought of it, 'we could always have breakfast earlier.'

She could hear the blood rushing in her ears.

'I have to be at my office by 9 a.m. That does not leave much time for breakfast.'

He sounded wary, as if he was wondering why she was suddenly so amenable. *Play to his ego, Christine. Make him think he's irresistible.*

She threw him a look from under her lashes. 'Room service is available at any time.'

He broke a breadstick in two with an audible snap. 'Is it now?'

That smile spread wider, exposing his teeth.

Fighting back a surge of nausea, Christine smiled back into his eyes. 'I believe so.'

She wouldn't think about it. Wouldn't think about anything except saving Jack and the other men by any means possible.

'Well then,' he said, raising his glass in a toast to her, 'tonight is a very special night indeed.'

'I'm sure it will be,' she purred. 'In so many ways.'

Of course, if she failed then there was no going back. She would be tortured alongside Jack and his men before Barbie put a merciful bullet through her brain. But she couldn't think like that, not if she were to have any hope of succeeding. The only way through was forward, through a hell she didn't even want to imagine. She could feel her mind shutting off, as it had back then, alone in that stinking East End alleyway. *Detach. Cut yourself loose, Christine. Float somewhere far away, where no one can hurt you.*

She was doing that right now, retreating, looking down at herself and Barbie at their table from a safe distance. Except there was no such thing as safe. Only pain and brutality and abuse. Her mouth was working, stretching in its lovely smile, soft words spilling out of it. But Christine, the real Christine, was no longer there. It might all be for the best. Maybe this time she really would be cut free at last. Maybe, finally, she would find peace.

THIRTY-NINE

I jumped as the telephone on Suzanne's desk rang. It had been a long time since I'd heard one and they almost never signalled good news.

''*Allo?*'

She said little but listened hard to whoever was on the other end. Then she replaced the receiver in its cradle and looked at us.

'That was the manager at the Grand Hotel,' she said. 'He is concerned about his stray cat. Apparently it is being a little too affectionate, and he wonders if I know of a vet who can neuter it.'

I gaped at her for a second and then gathered myself. 'The stray cat is our agent?'

'Yes.'

'And she's being a little too affectionate with Barbie?'

'The sommelier overheard her inviting him to have breakfast with her in her room.'

'My God... she's going to try and do it tonight.'

I was only half-aware I'd spoken aloud.

Suzanne fixed me with a sharp stare. 'Do what?'

'I can't tell you.'

'Yes you can. You have to. Or she might die when there is a chance we could do something to stop her.'

I took a breath. 'All right. My guess is she's going to try and assassinate Barbie tonight. She knows they're bringing the men to Lyon tomorrow. She probably thinks it would help.'

'It would be a grave mistake.' Suzanne's voice was flat but her eyes were alive with concern.

'How so? Surely we want Barbie dead.'

'We do but not like this. Not by putting her life at risk too. Barbie may not be the biggest man but he is strong. Ask anyone he has strung up by the wrists with his own hands and beaten senseless. He is also suspicious of everyone and everything, so he keeps his guards close at all times. Even if she succeeds, which is highly unlikely, his men will kill her on the spot.'

'Christine would take that risk,' I said. 'She doesn't seem to fear death at all. But I fear her sacrifice would be wasted.'

'Absolutely,' said Suzanne. 'It would do more harm than good. The reprisals would be swift and merciless. Not just that, it could compromise the entire operation. There is time enough to kill Klaus Barbie. That time is not now.'

'I agree,' I said. 'But how can we stop her without alerting Barbie?'

'Unless we do not try to stop her but rather to aid her in her efforts.'

'What do you mean?'

Suzanne pulled a packet from a drawer and placed it on her desk. It looked ordinary enough, a folded square of brown paper.

'You know that we are proficient here in the art of slipping substances into drinks. Our customers never suspect they have been drugged. Rather, they think they have simply fallen asleep and are embarrassed by their lack of stamina.'

'You're suggesting Christine does that to Barbie?'

'Why not? It could even work to everyone's advantage. Christine will be safer, Barbie will be out of action until tomorrow morning and his men will simply assume he has spent a night of passion with her. He will not contradict them. He is a man after all.'

I looked at Juliette and saw the same glint in her eyes that must have been shining from mine.

'It's worth a shot,' I said. 'We need to know the correct dose and then get that to Christine along with instructions.'

'Not a problem.'

Suzanne smiled, unfolding the packet to reveal an innocuous-looking white powder.

'I measure the doses myself. This is a particularly potent sleeping concoction that lasts at least twelve hours. It is odourless and tasteless. My own recipe, if you like.'

'It sounds perfect. You're a woman of many talents, Madame,' said Juliette.

'I studied chemistry in Paris, a long time ago. And please, it is just Suzanne. We are friends in this fight.'

'I hope we are friends long after this fight,' said Juliette.

Her face softened for a second. 'I hope so too. Now, to business. I will make up the mixture and ensure it is delivered to the manager at the hotel. He will then find a way to get it to Christine and instruct her on its use.'

'Can he also let her know that we're here as backup should she need it?'

'Of course. But he cannot tell her where you are or with whom. That way, they cannot torture the information out of her if it comes to that.'

'Of course,' I echoed, slamming down the gates in my mind to that possibility. Christine was brave and resourceful. Beyond that, she was cool and cunning. If anyone could carry this off, it was her.

'And when Barbie wakes, what then?' Juliette asked.

'Then she will sweetly reassure him that no one need ever know he fell asleep rather than rise to the occasion.' Suzanne's smile was impish but her eyes were serious. 'If I get the dosage right, he should sleep late. That will put him out of action or at least throw him off balance as we enact our plans tomorrow morning.'

'How difficult is it to determine the dosage?'

'To be absolutely accurate I would need to know his weight and also have some idea of his metabolism. We observe our clients closely before we start to spike their drinks. Some can handle their alcohol with ease. Others are tipsy after a few sips. These are all good indicators of how much to give them.'

'From what we saw in the hotel dining room, Barbie seems to be able to handle his drink.'

'Indeed,' said Suzanne.

'You're quite sure he'll suspect nothing?'

'I cannot guarantee anything, but we have never had a client yet who claimed to be drugged. I am careful to use substances that do not produce the hangover effect you get with some sleeping potions. He will merely feel very tired as the potion starts to take effect and then as if he has had a long sleep when he awakes.'

'And even Barbie won't want to admit he fell asleep rather than act the great lover.'

'There is a danger that might make him vicious towards Christine,' said Juliette. 'Some men get nasty when they cannot or have not performed.'

'Not if she plays it right. Don't forget that he'll also be embarrassed and in a hurry to get to his men. This is a big deal for Barbie, the capture of three agents. He'll be focused on taking out his frustrations on them.'

I suppressed a shudder. 'Which is why we have to make sure that our other plans work. When you send the message to the hotel manager, we must also alert Maggie. We need to coordinate with our men in the countryside.'

'Leave it with me,' said Suzanne.

She rose from her desk, every inch of her exuding calm determination. Then her face broke once more into that mischievous smile and she dropped us a wink.

'This will be fun,' she said. 'Thinking of Barbie desperately trying to remember what did or did not happen as he scrambles into his clothes.'

I couldn't help but smile too at the image she conjured up.

'We women,' added Suzanne, 'we are the ones who will really win this war.'

I thought for a long time afterwards of her words. They didn't so much haunt me as prove again and again to be true.

FORTY

The road looked different in the dark. It took Maggie some time to locate the correct turning and then navigate blind up the rutted track to a derelict farm building, the waning moon no help as it was obscured by a layer of cloud. When she finally got there, she let out the long, low whistle that was their agreed signal, but there was no response.

She propped her bicycle against a half-collapsed wall, her senses alive to the night sounds all around. There may not have been any humans present, but there were certainly birds and small creatures, scurrying through the undergrowth and occasionally letting out a snatch of song from a nearby branch. Overhead, bats swooped, searching out the night insects they would hunt until dawn. She watched as the clouds parted and a sliver of the moon shone through, blurred by a halo of curiously orange light.

Her grandmother would have looked upon that as an omen or, at the very least, as a portent of a storm approaching. But Maggie wasn't her grandmother. She was a scientist by instinct and by training. So when she heard the snap of a twig breaking as a foot landed upon it, she reached immediately for her gun.

'For Christ's sake, it's me,' hissed Henri.

'You're late.'

'There are Germans everywhere. I had to get past three roadblocks.'

'So they know something is up.'

'They suspect it for sure. But we do have a plan that we think will work well with yours.'

'Tell me.'

'The Germans will be looking out for an attack while they are en route. So we plan to attack them from within.'

'You mean you're going to infiltrate the convoy?'

'Yes.'

'But how?'

'Our contact within Digne prison is going to get a couple of our men inside tonight, after the guard changes. Those men will take the place of the French guards who are supposed to accompany the prisoners but have unfortunately been detained.'

'Won't they realise they're not the right guards?'

'The Germans are sending a special prison lorry from Valréas in the mistaken belief that will be more secure for what are very valuable prisoners. The drivers of that lorry do not know the guards from Digne. Similarly, the guards at Digne do not know the guards from Valréas. They will simply assume they are the correct ones as long as they are wearing the right uniform and behaving appropriately, which they will be.'

Maggie sucked in her cheeks. 'I like it. But two men alone can't do much. Surely the Germans will send a lot of men to accompany the prison guards? And probably outriders?'

'They will. That's why we are arming our men with stun and smoke grenades, along with a special explosive to stick to the interior walls of the lorry. It will blow from the inside at precisely the right place and moment, which is where your plan comes in.'

'How do you know your special explosive will be enough to blow the lorry open without killing all those inside?'

'It's something called Explosive 808. A plastic explosive. They have used it in anti-tank shells and on many sabotage missions.'

'I've heard of it but I've never seen it.'

'It's good stuff. You can bend it and mould it so it will stick easily to the inside of the rear doors. We have calculated that it should be more than sufficient to blow them outwards. Our men will instruct the prisoners to crouch at the front of the lorry by the driver's cab.'

'What if there are other guards besides your men inside the lorry?'

'There probably will be. At an opportune moment, our men are instructed to overpower and, if necessary, shoot them. We are relying on the element of surprise there too.'

'It could work but, if it doesn't, everything will be blown. Literally.'

'I know.'

She looked up at the night sky, the stars floating in their indigo sea. So much was at stake. In the end, it was the throw of a dice into the lap of the fates. As a scientist, she hated that. As a *résistant*, she couldn't wait.

FORTY-ONE

The attic room felt even smaller with the five of us crowded into it. I glanced around our small group, wondering. We had pulled this inner circle as tight as we could but, even so, there was always a chance it was one of them who was the informer. A slim chance. But one I had to take.

A sudden noise. I could feel my heart trying to burst from my chest.

Four taps on the door. A pause. Then four more taps.

Suzanne moved to open it, admitting the slight figure who stood there, a wide smile belying the shadows under her eyes.

'Maggie. It's so good to see you.'

I enfolded her in a brief hug. She smelled of fresh air, the countryside. Of sweat. She had pedalled far and fast to get here on time.

'You got in all right? No one saw you?'

'Only some German soldier who was leaving. He looked a bit drunk. I'm sure he thought I was here to work.'

'Excellent.'

'That's what makes this a good place to meet,' said André. 'People assume that we are customers when we come here.'

'I would give you a discount,' said Suzanne. 'But I know you're not interested in our services.'

'Indeed,' said André. 'My wife would take a knife to my private parts if she ever found out I had visited one of your beautiful young ladies.'

'Very wise,' said Suzanne. 'Especially as we do our best to infect our customers with anything we can. That soldier you saw leaving was probably drugged rather than drunk, my dear.'

I could see Maggie assessing our small group, that analytical brain of hers working.

'First,' I said, 'tell us what you got from Henri. Then we can update you on what's happening.'

'They're planning to get two of our men dressed as guards inside a special prison lorry they're sending from Valréas. They'll then use plastic explosive to blow it from the inside to coincide with the explosions you have planned.'

'Sounds promising,' I said. 'As long as we get the timing absolutely right. But I think we need to throw in some more distractions beyond cutting communications and sabotaging their vehicles. Get the Germans running off in different directions so they can't muster a huge counter-offensive.'

I looked at Suzanne. 'We know they're planning a final transportation. Let's blow the line early in the morning, before the convoy gets here. Kill two birds with one stone. Stop the train going through and, at the same time, send the Boches off to deal with that as well.'

I turned to Maggie. 'I want you to send another message. The next three lines of the poem.'

'Understood.'

'Send it from south of the city this time.'

'No problem. But once I've done so, I'd like to help lay the explosives on the railway line. For Antoine.'

Antoine, who I had wrongly suspected. Whose entire family had been taken to those camps.

'Of course.'

'And what of Barbie?' asked André.

'Christine's handling him,' I said. 'She'll get him to her room and then slip him one of Suzanne's concoctions that should knock him out for at least twelve hours. So just as the Gestapo need their leader tomorrow morning, he'll be nowhere to be found.'

'But won't they come looking for him in Christine's suite?'

'Yes, but before that they have to deal with this cascade of crises and then they have to pluck up the courage to disturb him. It takes a brave man to distract Klaus Barbie when he's apparently focused on another objective.'

'Surely he'll know he's been drugged?' said Maggie. 'Most sedatives or sleeping pills have some kind of lasting effect.'

'Not with what we use, I assure you,' said Suzanne. 'We've had a lot of practice.'

'I'll go back to the Grand Hotel and make sure things are going to plan,' I said.

'That's far too dangerous,' said Suzanne.

'Why? They don't know what I look like, especially now that I've changed my appearance. I'm going alone. They're looking for two women. Besides, I have to go back. I have no choice. And right now, we need to focus on the ambush.'

André pulled out a map, unfolded it and laid it out on the floor.

'The convoy will have to approach Place Bellecour along this street here,' he said, 'close to this marketplace. We will set up the distraction here, a farm cart that has seemingly tipped over, spilling its melons. Those melons are primed with explosives that we detonate at your signal, at the same time deploying our grenades. We will have a couple of minutes and that is all to extract the prisoners and escape with them through the traboules.'

'We must make sure the others know the exact timing so

they can coordinate the detonations inside the prison lorry,' I said.

'Exactly. The Germans are nothing if not efficient, and the convoy is due to arrive at Place Bellecour at 9 a.m. precisely. We need to liaise with your men in the countryside and also work with our *résistants* here to lay those explosives in time.'

'Do you think we can do it before dawn?' asked Juliette.

I looked at our small group, at the exhausted but eager faces staring back at me. There was a silence just like the one you hear before dawn, before the birds start to sing and the world springs back to life. It was a silence of hope and anticipation. Of not knowing what the day might bring.

I squared my shoulders. 'Of course.'

FORTY-TWO

I could see the faint sheen of sweat on Christine's chest, moistening it and making the fabric of her gown cling to it all the more. Barbie was mesmerised. She played on it, licking her lips in that alluring way of hers. He was looking at her as a beast does when it knows it has cornered its prey. Now all he had to do was savour her at leisure, at least in his mind. *Not so fast*, I thought. *You're not the one calling the shots yet.*

There was every chance she could deal with him before he so much as laid a finger on her. The only question was how and where. Her suite was the obvious place but fraught with so many difficulties. I could see his men at the next table, keeping a covert eye. There were more in the bar, the lobby and stationed outside the hotel. Her one advantage lay in the fact he didn't suspect a thing. At least, that was what we hoped. Through all her years of training agents, Christine had learned to read people fast and accurately. Her instincts were good. But even the best could get it wrong.

'Is everything satisfactory?' I asked, bending to apparently retrieve her napkin, standing back up with the lipstick in my hand. Chanel. Nice touch. Those backroom boffins knew their stuff.

'Yours, madame?'

She looked at it.

'Thank you,' she murmured, 'It must have fallen out of my bag. Everything is wonderful, as usual.'

She tucked the lipstick into her purse and smiled across the table.

'More champagne,' said Barbie.

'Of course, sir. At once.'

Christine pushed her chair back. I retrieved her napkin once more.

'Would you excuse me?' she said, flashing Barbie another smile full of promise.

Barbie grunted in response.

Before she was even through the door, Barbie moved to talk to his men at the neighbouring table. Something was afoot, that was for sure. Possibly something to do with the convoy that was heading their way in around twelve hours. By now, Christine should be reading the tiny piece of paper tucked inside the lipstick case along with a small packet.

For the treatment of anxiety and insomnia, it said. *To be administered in liquid five minutes before bedtime. On no account should an overdose occur.*

She was back, gliding to the table, throwing me a glance to show she understood. Barbie was still conferring with his men. I signalled to the sommelier who appeared bearing an ice bucket and a bottle of champagne. Barbie finished off his conversation before joining her.

'Bollinger Grand Cru,' said the sommelier. 'Compliments of the Grand Hotel.'

Barbie nodded, his gaze fixed on Christine. I could almost feel the cross hairs meeting as he trained his sights.

I moved to her side and dropped a fresh napkin on her lap.

'Why don't we drink it somewhere more private?' said Christine, glancing meaningfully at his men.

Barbie caught her look. The triumph in his eyes almost made me gag.

'What a good idea, my dear. Shall we have it sent to your suite?'

Christine inclined her head.

The sommelier bowed.

'I will arrange that at once.'

My stomach turned somersaults as they headed for the lift. So many things could go wrong. I forced myself not to think of those things. Christine had done this before, many times, leading a man to a suite or a hotel room only to outwit him. This time would be no different. Except that it would. Because this was no ordinary man. This was Klaus Barbie, a man with more blood on his hands than Herod and a heart that simply didn't exist, although it apparently kept beating.

Which meant he was still a man and not some kind of untouchable immortal. She could slow that heart with what she had tucked in her lipstick case. Knock him out for twelve hours, although I had no doubt she would rather do that on a permanent basis. We all would. But she had her orders. No overdose. A clear warning. So she would administer whatever lay in that packet and then let events play out as they must. Today wasn't the day we killed Klaus Barbie. But that day would come.

FORTY-THREE

From the other end of the corridor, I could see her fumbling in her purse for the key, Barbie's impatience evident. Good. Make him wait. She smiled coyly at him as I pushed the trolley forward, laden with the ice bucket and champagne.

'Silly me,' she said, flourishing her key. 'It was here all the time.'

She unlocked the door and murmured, 'I'll just go and freshen up,' before disappearing into the bathroom, no doubt to apply a swift slick of lipstick as she palmed the packet, returning to the room with a newly rouged smile.

I fussed over the placement of the trolley and the uncorking of the champagne, playing for time. Finally Barbie had had enough.

'Yes, yes,' he said. 'You can go now.'

I executed a tiny curtsey, hesitating by the door a fraction too long.

'Ah yes.'

Barbie fumbled in his pocket before handing over a couple of coins. It was all the time Christine needed to slip the powder into his glass. As he practically shoved me out the door and turned towards her, she held it out to him. I pulled the door to, not quite closing it so that I could peer through the tiny crack. Luckily, Barbie was too hell-bent on his conquest to notice.

'To us,' Christine cooed, clinking her glass against his.

She kept her eyes on his, inviting him in. It was too much, even for Barbie.

'To us,' he muttered thickly, greedily knocking back his glass before reaching for her, grabbing at her breasts and squeezing so hard she gasped. Pleasure flickered across his face. He was enjoying her pain, the shit. He moved his hand, this time grabbing at her groin. She didn't give him the satisfaction of crying out a second time.

'Not so fast,' she said. 'Come, sit here with me.'

She patted the bedcover beside her, and Barbie eagerly stumbled towards it. I noted that stumble. Then he was reaching for her throat, pushing her back down on the bed, his fingers tightening again, his eyes fixed on hers as he squeezed, the gleam in them one of pure lust. She was helpless as he reached down, unzipped himself and, with a triumphant grunt, thrust into her, his fingers clinging to her throat all the while.

I could see his eyes bulge, his teeth bared in a rictus grin, as he stared down into her face, squeezing harder at her throat, thrusting faster and faster. Then he threw back his head and came with an animal howl. The saliva slid from the corner of his mouth as he panted, landing on Christine's cheek. I held my breath, my fingers itching for my gun, unable to tear my eyes away.

Just as I thought she might lose consciousness, his grip slackened and he slumped beside her. Christine sat up, sucking air into her lungs, rubbing at her neck. She looked at Barbie lying face down on the bed and smiled.

'Gotcha, you pig,' she whispered.

Barbie muttered something unintelligible.

I pushed the door open a fraction, hesitant after what I'd

just witnessed. It felt indecent to intrude when the air was still filled with the smell of sex. Christine, cool as ever, gave me a thumbs up. I slid into the room, pulling the door to behind me and then locking it from the inside.

'Help me,' whispered Christine as she began to undress him. I reached for his trousers as she deftly unbuttoned his shirt.

Barbie stirred, throwing out an arm and mumbling something in German. I froze, my hands clamped on his waistband, my heart thudding a staccato tattoo as I watched him sigh and relax once more. The drugs were supposed to knock him out for twelve hours. We would have to trust they worked as instructed. Even so, it was no easy feat to strip Barbie. He was heavier than he looked.

He might not be especially tall or well built, but his muscles were honed, presumably by hours of vicious torture. By all accounts, he liked to swing a heavy spiked ball down on his victims' backs, breaking their spines, or to hang them up in a harness and then take out his rage on their defenceless bodies. It was always simmering, his anger. I had seen it bubble up at times when he was talking to Christine over dinner, provoked by the thought she might not be as subservient as he wished or as loyal to the Führer. It would be hard to be as loyal as Barbie, who was an out-and-out fanatic. Like all fanatics, he held everyone to his own impossible standards.

I eased his trousers over his feet and then steeled myself for the rest. He had to be naked so that he would believe they'd spent a passionate night together rather than an unimpressive few moments. And he had to believe that to keep his pride intact.

A wounded Barbie would be a dangerous animal indeed, and there was no greater wound to a man than the thought he wasn't a great lover.

'He's just a man after all,' I murmured.

'Makes him seem even more of a monster,' muttered Christine. 'I need to have a wash. Thank God for my diaphragm, that's all I can say.'

I stared at her.

'Aren't you afraid of catching something?'

'Luckily, he's absolutely paranoid. Gets tested every week. Although you can be sure I'll be paying the doctor a visit as well.'

I wanted to hug her, she looked so wan and fragile at that moment. But I knew it might be the thing that broke her so, instead, I gave her a brisk smile. 'Good.'

We scattered his clothes beside the bed as if he had ripped them off with abandon. Then Christine slipped out of her dress and into a negligee, making sure that her sleeve gun was tucked in place. She might have no intention of using it but you never knew. Barbie could wake and realise what had happened or, worse, guess what was about to happen.

Looking down at his sleeping form, the temptation to finish him off was once more overwhelming. He was as helpless as the children he'd tortured and killed, as all the other women and men he'd defiled and destroyed. His mouth was slack, slightly open. I could hold the muzzle of my gun to it and one shot would send him to damnation forever.

'I can't bear to lie beside him,' whispered Christine, settling herself in the armchair by the window.

I took a step towards her but she curled into herself, tucking her knees up much as a child would in a foetal position, staring through the glass as if lost in thought. It was time for me to leave if I was to have any rest at all before the ambush. He was gone, out cold, for at least twelve hours. Now all Christine had to do was wait and watch to make sure he didn't come round too soon. The game was on. One we fully intended to win, come what may.

FORTY-FOUR

The Gestapo's trucks were parked not too far from Place Bellecour, in a yard guarded by a solitary soldier. In a further stroke of luck, the solitary soldier was easily distracted. I watched as Juliette sauntered along the darkened street, stopped and lit up a cigarette a few metres from his guard post, apparently oblivious to his presence. I reached for my pistol, as much for reassurance as to be ready. Shooting the guard would seriously scupper our plans, but needs must.

'Halt!' he called out to her. 'What are you doing there?'

She turned, her face illuminated by his torch, and smiled, holding up her cigarette.

'You caught me,' she said. 'I was just taking a break from work. It's hard, isn't it, working when others are sleeping? Want one?'

She shook the cigarette packet, offering it to him. He hesitated and then took a couple of steps towards her, pocketing his flashlight once more.

'Thank you,' he said. 'Why are you working at this time of night?'

'I work at the hospital. Ward assistant.'

'Oh right.'

His face in the light from her match was so young. He appeared to be barely out of his teens. He looked at Juliette in the drab outfit which matched her story and visibly relaxed.

I left them to their chit-chat and began to work on the fence with my wire cutters, making sharp, precise snips as we'd been taught. When I'd made sufficient inroads, I peeled it back with one hand to allow myself to slip through. A row of trucks concealed me from the guard, who was still deep in conversation with Juliette.

Staying low, I crept from truck to truck, slashing just one tyre on each with my jack knife.

The cuts were tiny but the extra blade on the dagger was especially designed to slash irreparably deep. The tyres would slowly deflate, rendering each truck undriveable. For good measure, I removed the plug in the back-axle housings, shoving in carborundum grease so that the gears would seize as it mixed with the oil, working as fast as my fingers would allow. Juliette could only sustain conversation with the guard for so long before he grew suspicious.

As soon as I was done, I crawled back under the fence, pulling it back together as best I could, then hurled the tin can I'd tucked in my pocket along the street. It landed with a clatter in the opposite direction to where I was hiding in the shadows. Instantly, the guard was on the alert, spinning away from Juliette with his sub-machine gun raised.

'It's just a tin can,' she said. 'Probably that cat did it.'

'What cat?'

'Big old alley cat. Didn't you see it? Anyway, I must be getting back to work. Nice talking to you.'

He continued scanning the street for a couple for minutes before returning to his post and taking up his bored posture once more.

'Nice talking to you,' he called after Juliette as she strolled away, raising a hand in acknowledgement. They weren't all bad, the Nazis. As with our boys, many were scarcely out of school. But that didn't stop us doing everything possible to sabotage and kill as many as we could. All really was fair in love and war. And this operation was definitely both.

I met up with Juliette in the nearby churchyard, as we'd planned. We waited there, crouched behind an especially impressive tomb, until I noticed a shadow separating from the others.

'Mission accomplished,' I whispered to André.

'Us too,' he said. 'We have laid explosives along the railway line about a mile out of town. They are set to detonate at around 9 a.m. which should stop them sending that train through and keep our friends busy.'

'Where's Maggie?' I asked.

'She has gone with two of my men to lay more explosives on the signal box. They will detonate those manually in case the others fail to go off and to cause more chaos.'

'Excellent,' I said. 'Any news from the hotel?'

'Barbie is still in your friend's suite, apparently out cold. His men are currently stationed downstairs, waiting for him. According to the manager, they seem resigned to being there all night.'

'Probably seen it all before.'

'Indeed.'

'I'll go back and check on things once we're done here,' I said.

'Where to now?' asked Juliette.

'The marketplace, to help prepare the ambush.'

'I will take you there,' said André.

I looked up at the clocktower that loomed above us, then checked it against my watch. Almost 1 a.m. We had about seven hours to get everything in place, less if we were to get any rest. And we needed to rest if we were to be sharp for the following day. So much depended on timing if everything were to go according to plan.

We followed André out of the churchyard and into the increasingly familiar traboules, taking the twists and turns that led us to the marketplace where the cart was already waiting in a side yard, hidden from view. *Résistants* were working in stoic silence, packing explosives into melons before stacking them tightly on the cart. Others were concealing yet more explosives in pats of what looked to be horse dung that were to be strategically scattered along the street. I recognised the young man who'd let us into Dr Gaspard's surgery, along with Paul, one of Suzanne's men, who was directing a couple of other men who had been present at that meeting.

I stroked the nose of the donkey hitched to the cart. 'We must make sure this one isn't harmed.'

'Don't worry. We will release him when we turn the cart over,' said Paul.

'You seem to have it all under control,' I said. 'So why don't Juliette and I throw another spanner in the works? We could cut the phone lines from Place Bellecour. That will delay them even further.'

'An excellent idea,' said André.

'I disagree,' growled Paul. 'You'll get yourselves killed.'

'If that thought stopped me, I would have done nothing throughout this war,' I retorted. 'You with me, Juliette?'

'You bet.'

'I will come too,' offered André.

'No need. Between us, I'm sure Juliette and I have cut hundreds of phone lines.'

'Hundreds,' echoed Juliette.

I glanced at my watch again – 1.29 a.m. I still had to get back to the hotel.

'We'll rendezvous with you all back here at 0700 hours,' I said. That would give us enough time to cut the phone wires and for me to check on Christine before our operation got underway. I might even fit in a quick rest if I was lucky.

'*Putain*,' Paul muttered under his breath. *Fuck.*

I smiled. 'You want to keep an eye on those fuses. After all, size matters.'

He shot me a look but wisely said nothing. Juliette managed to contain her laughter until we were out of earshot.

'Size matters,' she spluttered. 'You said that to a Frenchman.'

I grinned. 'I'd say it to any man.'

Except maybe one.

FORTY-FIVE

1943, FRANCE

My instructions were clear. I was to arrive at the safe house with a suitcase, apparently to stay the night with a distant cousin while I visited a sick relative nearby. If anyone asked, the old lady in question wasn't receiving any other visitors, being close to death. It was unlikely the Gestapo would want to drop in on a dying crone, but it was always wise to ensure your cover story held and so we'd primed my fake cousin's mother just in case.

I recited the address in my head as I walked up from the station carrying my suitcase. The safe house was situated on the outskirts of town, conveniently located next to a school from where the children would call out warnings if the Germans approached. I knocked three times and then once more, as arranged. The door opened a crack and a blowsy woman squinted at me, her face wreathed in smoke from the cigarette she was holding.

'Yes?'

'Cousin, how good to see you. You won't remember me. I've grown since we last saw one another at Uncle's house.'

She stood back, ushering me in with her cigarette. 'Ah yes. Poor Uncle is no more. Come on in.'

I followed her up the stairs and to a room with a hatch that led to an attic. She grabbed a hooked stick and rapped on the hatch twice and then twice again before inserting the hook into it and pulling it open.

A face appeared in the open hatch, looking down at us. I just managed to stifle my cry of surprise.

'Someone to see you,' said the woman, 'I'll leave you to it.'

The swirl of cigarette smoke she left in her wake pricked my eyes. Or maybe it was the sight of Jack.

It took him seconds after she left to push down a set of steps and descend them. Even less time to enfold me in his arms and plant an endless kiss on my lips.

When we finally drew breath, I gazed at him in wonder. 'What are you doing here?'

'I could ask you the same thing. Except we both know.'

His face hadn't changed and yet it was different, his eyes older with knowledge of things neither of us should have ever seen but still so alive. They had a familiar glint in them now.

'How long are you here?'

'Just tonight. I'm to deliver this to you and return on the morning train.'

He glanced at the suitcase by my feet. It contained a radio set under a layer of clothing into which new crystals were sewn, to be inserted before use.

'We don't have much time then.'

'For what?'

'For this.'

He half-dragged me, laughing, to the stairs and practically pushed me up them. Once in the attic, I scarcely had time to take in the table covered in papers and the bed beside it before I was tumbling on to that same bed, smothered in Jack's kisses once more.

Hours later, I sat up, pushing the hair back from my face, replete with happiness and Jack, all of a sudden remembering that we'd forgotten something. Or rather, someone.

'Madame will be wondering where I am.'

'No she won't.' Jack was lazily tracing my spine with a finger, stroking the base of it, sending thrills right through me. 'Come back here.'

'Jack, I'm serious. I'm also hungry.'

'Me too,' he murmured.

'No, not for that. Well, yes for that. But I'm starving. I haven't eaten all day.'

'I haven't eaten all year.'

'Jack, be serious.'

'I am serious. Seriously in love with you.'

After that, dinner, Madame and the rest was forgotten. We had one night together in the middle of this inhuman war. A night to feel flesh upon flesh, hearts beating together, souls touching as one. That was all the nourishment I needed. The fuel that would enable me to carry on. I had no idea when I might see him again. If I might see him again. So for tonight I would feast on Jack and carry the crumbs of him with me to sustain me through what was to come.

FORTY-SIX

AUGUST 1944, FRANCE

She must have dozed off because it was the dawn that woke her, the first fingers of hazy light tickling her eyelids. Instantly, Christine snapped her eyes open and looked at the bed. He was still asleep, his chest rising and falling, now and then emitting a guttural snore.

She stayed as still as she could, watching him, hoping and praying that he would sleep on for many hours yet. His face was half-turned to her and she studied it as she would a particularly interesting specimen. She had loved to collect insects and spiders when she was a child, holding them quite happily. Here was a creature that actually made her flesh crawl.

From a distant church tower, a bell tolled the hour. Six o'clock. The convoy was due to arrive at around 9 a.m. Her task was to keep Barbie out of action until well past then. If he awoke then she would have to use other means to distract him. Whatever it took. Whatever the cost to her. Although she had long ago learned that the price she paid for simply being herself was extraordinarily high.

She heard a tap on the door, so discreet it might almost have been the wind. Barbie's men? Possibly. Although they were prone to rapping on a door as hard as they could. There was nothing for it. She would have to open it or risk them doing just that and waking him.

She braced herself, turning the handle and then stifling a sharp intake of breath.

'May I come in?'

Suzanne didn't wait for an answer, striding to the bed to inspect Barbie's sleeping form before turning to smile at Christine.

'You've done well,' she said.

'You taught me well. But should you be here? His men are all over the place.'

'I had to make sure you were all right. He'll sleep for a few more hours yet. I saw his men downstairs. They're snoring their heads off too.'

'Really?'

'It's when he wakes that you need to be careful. Remember, stroke his ego. Make him feel the most special man on earth.'

She was back there, in Paris, hearing Suzanne say exactly the same thing, her kneejerk reaction the same then too.

'I hate men,' she said, as much to herself as Suzanne. 'They always think I owe them something. Apparently they can't help themselves when they see me smile or even just out for a walk.'

The memory that was always there was swimming to the surface. A walk that had ended in a cold, dark alleyway back in London.

She was aware that Suzanne was looking at her closely. It had been a long night. She was overwrought. Or perhaps just over it. She could feel the cool metal of the Welrod against the warmth of her arm. Sometimes she couldn't help herself either. She remembered each and every one of her targets' faces. It was almost fun to see their expressions when they realised the game was up. Too bad she couldn't end Barbie's game here and now, but she was prepared to play a long one.

'I'll make him pay for what he's done,' she said. 'One way or another. All those thousands of innocent people, dead because of him.'

'I know you will,' said Suzanne, moving closer to lay a cool hand on her arm. 'Go carefully, Christine. You were always my best girl. I would hate to see anything happen to you.'

'I'll be fine,' she replied. 'I always am.'

She drew herself up, standing tall and proud – something Suzanne had taught her, among many other things. One day Klaus Barbie would answer for his actions, just as the man in the alleyway had. She remembered his face too. And the expression on it as he died. It still brought a smile to her lips. She was smiling now, but instead of lighting up the room, Christine's smile threw a cloak of darkness across it that mirrored the one in her heart.

FORTY-SEVEN

'Time to go.'

The guard who entered the cell was unfamiliar but his manner was not. His voice was brusque, his eyes disinterested. Jack stood up from the bunk where he'd been sitting, as did Guy, and together they followed him out of the cell, along the grimy corridors they'd traversed so many times before. There had been no beating last night, just the same questions thrown at him in bored tones. It didn't bode well.

No doubt Barbie wanted them in good enough shape so that he could work them over thoroughly. Well, they would give him a run for his money, just as they had the others.

Outside, in the prison courtyard, a truck was waiting. As Jack climbed inside, he saw that Charles was already there, handcuffed, slumped on the bench that ran along one side of the vehicle interior.

'All right, old chap?'

He looked anything but all right.

The guard shoved him in the small of his back. 'Sit there.'

While one guard kept his gun trained on them, the other handcuffed each of them in turn, attaching the cuffs to the rail that ran just below head height behind them. It was excruciatingly uncomfortable. Two more guards were posted by the doors of the truck while four motorcycle outriders sat waiting alongside an armoured car and a jeep laden with Waffen-SS. They were taking no chances.

The doors of the truck slammed shut and the engine thundered into life. Jack risked another look at Charles, who was half-hanging from his cuffs, his head dangling. The bruises on his face and neck were fresh, as were the cuts still suppurating at the edges. His lips were crusted, and he didn't look as if he'd had anything to eat or drink in days.

'This man needs water,' said Jack. 'Or he'll die before we get there.'

The rifle butt to his face was swift. His arms jerked involuntarily. Defenceless, his cheekbone took the full force, and there was an audible crack. Jack ground his teeth together, determined not to cry out.

He heard another crack, jerked reflexively again, and then realised it was the sound of a rifle butt connecting with the skull of the guard who'd just attacked him. The man fell, sprawled out at Jack's feet, a booted foot kicking at his torso and face. Jack looked up at the guard delivering those blows and then at the other guard also laid out cold. As he watched, the two were bound and gagged.

'Here.'

One of the guards who'd doled out the beatings unlocked Jack's handcuffs and then those of his compatriots, offering Charles water from a bottle he held to his lips.

'Who are you?' Charles croaked.

'Yes, who are you?' demanded Jack.

The guard smiled and pulled off his prison warder's cap, putting a finger to his lips as he nodded towards the lorry cab where the driver and two more guards sat beyond a thin wall of steel. The rumble of the engine was loud but not loud enough to cover any sudden shouts or bangs.

'The Maquis at your service. My name is Michel.'

'And I am Henri,' said the other. 'I believe you know the leader of our network, Marianne.'

A broad grin broke across Jack's face. 'Well I'll be damned. What's the plan?'

Michel was busy handcuffing the two real guards to the rail.

'Are you any good with explosives?'

'I am.'

'Excellent.'

Jack looked at the two real guards still slumped uncon-scious, now hanging by their wrists from the rail.

'Aren't you going to kill them?' he asked. 'They've seen your faces and they know who you are.'

'Why waste a bullet?' said Henri, extracting slim packages from his pockets. 'I need you to prime and attach the time pencils. We will then stick the plastique to the inside of the wall here.'

He indicated a spot at head height on the steel surface that divided the lorry from the cab. 'It's important that you are abso-lutely precise and set them for 9 a.m. No sooner and no later.'

'You realise there is a margin for error on these time pencils?' said Jack. 'A small one but they could still detonate up to five minutes ether side.'

'Do your best,' said Henri. 'Michel and I will set the explo-sives at this end of the lorry. We will detonate those ourselves and brace by the cab before we jump out of the lorry at this end. There will be covering fire as well as smoke grenades, but we will only have a few seconds to run to safety once we have jumped.'

'Right,' said Jack. 'And where will we be at 9 a.m.?'

'The centre of Lyon,' said Henri. 'Travelling along the road that leads to the marketplace just before we reach the Gestapo headquarters at Place Bellecour. We have to take that route. It's the only one open to vehicles this size. Thank goodness for German punctuality. They won't want to be late for Klaus Barbie. Which is unfortunate because the convoy is going to be held up by an upturned cart blocking the road. A cart also packed with explosives timed to coincide with ours.'

'Out from under their noses. I like it,' said Jack. 'And once we hit the ground?'

'Our people will take you to safety.'

It was obvious from his tone that Henri had given all the information he cared to at that point. He moved to the rear doors of the lorry and began to mould the plastic explosive in his hand while Michel extracted fuses from his pockets and started to carefully attach them to the explosive once it was in place.

The men worked in silence, bracing themselves against the lurches of the lorry as it took corners and bumped over rutted roads. Every time it slowed to a halt they froze, listening hard for the slightest indication that someone might come and check on them. During what felt like a particularly interminable stop, one of the guards stirred and groaned. Jack was the closest and dealt him a swift and satisfying kick to the head, knocking him out cold again. Some of the prison guards at Digne were all right, but this one had been especially vicious, taking obvious pleasure in the beatings he doled out. Revenge felt particularly good in his case.

All at once the sound of the lorry engine changed as it slowed and began to climb a hill.

Henri held up a hand, listening hard. 'We're coming into Lyon. This is the hill that leads up into the city.'

Michel checked his watch. 'It's 0834.'

'*Putain.* We're early.'

The men looked at one another. The explosives were in place, primers set and fuses attached.

'There is nothing for it,' said Henri. 'We follow the plan. Our colleagues on the ground can deal with them.' His eyes flicked to the cab. 'Agreed?'

'Agreed.'

Although the others were technically his superior officers, it was evident Henri was in charge. And Jack was glad of it. He knew the lay of the land and had reinforcements on the ground. More than that, he had a plan. As with every plan in this war, they would have to trust to luck and the fates as much as anything.

Jack shut his eyes for a moment, conjuring her up. Marianne, his lucky charm. His reason to go on. His guardian angel.

He snapped them open again. caught Henri's stare and smiled. 'Let's do it.'

'*Allons-y,*' said Henri.

FORTY-EIGHT

From the cover of the doorway, I watched as the cart was tipped over, melons scattering across the ground, rolling through the boobytrapped dung which was liberally dotted up and down the street. There was enough explosive here to blow several convoys. The trick was to detonate it sequentially so that Jack and the others could get to safety before they blew the Germans and their vehicles to smithereens.

Working through the night, the Resistance had quietly evacuated the street, posing as officials and leading the occupants to a nearby hall until they could return on the pretext of a gas leak.

'I smell no gas,' one belligerent old lady insisted as she was ushered from the vicinity.

'Trust me, madame,' said André, 'it is underground and therefore you cannot smell it, but it is most definitely dangerous. It could blow you sky high.'

She glared at him, unconvinced, but said nothing more, wrapping her shawl around her ever tighter to conceal her nightgown as if potential indecency was an even bigger problem.

As the sun rose and stroked our faces with light, we

retreated into our positions, with André in charge of detonation while Juliette and I each took charge of a small group armed with Sten guns, pistols and grenades. A hush hung over the street like a pall. It felt as if all the air had been sucked from my lungs and replaced with lead.

I took a slow, deliberate breath and then another, trying to relax my shoulders and arms as I did so. It would help me shoot all the straighter. I hated these moments just before an operation, when the wait felt interminable and yet anything could happen. Electricity ran up and down my nerves, every one of them alive to the possibilities of what could go wrong.

Don't think like that. Focus on what could go right. On getting Jack and the others out alive. On Jack.

The church clock chimed the half hour – 8.30 a.m. They were due at the Place Bellecour at 9 a.m. That meant they should be here at 8.56 a.m., if efficiency ran true to form.

I risked a look down the street to the strategically parked car behind which Juliette and her men were concealed, ready to attack, then across to where another group was hidden behind a half-open door. I let out the long, low whistle that was our signal and heard one echoing back at me, then another. We were as ready as we would ever be. Now all we had to do was sit tight.

All at once, I heard a sound which was out of place. The unmistakable clatter of a bicycle approaching along the cobbles, its chain rattling as its rider pedalled furiously towards us. Whoever was coming was in a hurry, and that was never a good sign.

I raised my pistol, my eyes fixed on the bend which the bicycle would have to round to reach us. I caught a glimpse of a figure bent low over the handlebars, slender legs pumping as hard as they could, then stepped out, tucking my pistol back in my waistband, and held out my arms to steady Maggie as she flung herself from the saddle.

'They're early,' she gasped. 'The convoy is entering Lyon now.'

'Damn it. How far away are they?'

'I left them near l'Hôpital Sainte-Eugénie. I took the back roads as a shortcut but I reckon they'll be here in around ten minutes.'

I grabbed Antoine. 'Go tell the others. The convoy will be here in ten minutes maximum. Ten minutes. You got that?'

He nodded and sped off, zigzagging up and down the street to deliver his message.

'I must go,' said Maggie. 'I was about to blow the signal box when I saw them.'

'Good luck.'

She smiled. 'And you.'

With a toss of her curls she was gone, pedalling back the way she'd come. That was our Maggie. Straight into the line of fire with no qualms.

'Godspeed,' I whispered. Then I checked my Sten gun and pistol before indicating the pile of grenades we'd set ready.

'When I give the signal, we fire while you two throw grenades. Under no circumstances does anyone do anything before that signal.'

The *résistants* looked at me solemnly and nodded.

Antoine skidded back into place and gave me the thumbs up. 'All is OK.'

I looked at my watch – 8.43 a.m. They would be here any minute.

My stomach gurgled and I pressed my hand against my belly as if to quiet it. And then I felt it – the shudder up the street, a rumble of heavy vehicles approaching, ripples growing into waves and then drumbeats of sound as the convoy came closer and closer. We held what felt like a collective breath as it paused before taking the bend, the accompanying snarl of motorbikes reaching a crescendo as they revved in readiness.

In the event, the donkey played its part to perfection. As the convoy turned up the narrow street, he brayed and bucked for all he was worth, clearly the cause of the unfortunate accident.

The lead car drew to a halt and an infuriated German officer emerged from it. 'What is going on here?' he demanded. 'Clear this road at once.'

'I-I am so sorry, sir,' stammered Antoine, hauling the donkey away by its rope. 'Of course. Right away.'

He pretended to fumble with and then drop the rope, all the while using up more precious minutes. The German officer kicked a melon in frustration. I held my breath. But we'd used plastique, which was stable until detonated. The skin split and pink flesh spilled out but nothing else. The German spat into it.

'Hurry up,' he said, drawing his revolver and pointing it at the retreating Antoine with his donkey.

'Of course, of course,' called out Antoine. 'Let me just tie up this stupid animal.'

The officer turned and barked an order. More soldiers spilled from the cars and began to pick up the melons while the prison lorry stayed stationary.

8.58 a.m. Two minutes until the primed explosives were due to go off. I forced myself not to stare at them, for fear of jinxing what would happen next.

8.59 a.m.

Right on time, the cart blew. A wall of smoke and flame shot up the street, shattering glass in windows, sending melon flesh everywhere, spattering the street with oozing lumps of pink and red. Or maybe that was what was left of the Nazis caught in the blast.

Amid screams and shouts, more ran forward only to be caught in the second blast as the lorry cab erupted in a ball of flame, the driver spilling from it with his hair and most of his upper body on fire.

I lobbed a grenade, dropping my other hand to signal to my

men to do the same. It landed by the first motorcycle, which hit the ground, its mangled frame skidding along until it came to rest metres from where I crouched, its rider already dead.

The other leaped from his machine only to be mown down in a hail of machine-gun fire. Among the billowing smoke and *ratatatat* of the Sten guns, I could sense a vacuum like the eye of a storm. Then a roar as the rear doors of the lorry exploded. The armoured car at the rear of the convoy was trying to ram its way forward, accelerating through the carnage. More explosions as André and Antoine hit their detonators, keeping the oncoming foot soldiers at bay.

We kept firing, aiming at the armoured car and its occupants, my eyes smarting and streaming from the grenade smoke. Where the hell were they? Had they got out? *Oh please God, let them have got out alive.*

That's when I saw them running towards us through the smoke and flames surging from the lorry cab, keeping as low as they could, Jack and Guy half-dragging, half-carrying a limp figure as they ran.

'Hold your fire,' I shouted as I lobbed another smoke grenade to give them more cover. Behind them, Michel and Henri blasted back at the Germans as they too ran, only stopping when they reached the safety of our outpost. There was no time for greetings. We hadn't made it yet. I needed to get us all out.

'Cover us,' I yelled to my men. Then, to the others: 'Follow me.'

Keeping low and tight to the buildings that lined our side of the street, I raced towards André, who was standing by the entrance to the traboules. Out of the corner of my eye, I saw Juliette converging on us with her men, pistols at the ready, zigzagging under the hail of bullets that kept coming as the Nazis returned fire. The man Jack and Guy half-carried was slowing us down. This operation was timed to the minute. And yet we couldn't abandon him. There was nothing for it but to keep going.

We were almost at the entrance to the traboules when I saw him. I had to blink and blink again before I believed what I saw. Marcus. My baby brother. Bringing up the rear, beckoning and pointing. Not to our men but a German officer who was hard on our heels. The world slowed and then speeded up, my thoughts slamming around my head like bullets. Marcus. It couldn't be. He was in Paris, not here. This wasn't happening.

It was.

No time to hesitate. I fired, blasting the German in the chest. Marcus whirled, saw me. Our eyes met and I saw it there. The truth. I shook my head, my mouth forming one word.

'No.'

His gaze fell away, just as it used to when we were children and he'd been caught out. Then it was trained on me once more and so was the gun in his hand.

'No, Marcus. Don't. Don't do this.' My voice came out as a croak. This couldn't be happening.

'Come with me,' he shouted. 'Surrender. I'll make sure you're not harmed.'

I could see it on his face. The blind fanaticism. He really believed what he was saying. This wasn't the Marcus I knew and loved. Someone, or rather something, else had taken over his form.

'Never.'

'Then I have no choice.'

'Nor do I.'

I didn't think twice, pulling the trigger at the same time as he did. I felt a hot flash of pain in my shoulder. Then Marcus hit the ground, rolled over and was still.

'No.'

A cry of agony echoing from somewhere deep inside me.

'Marianne, come on.'

Henri was shouting at me from the entrance to the traboules. The smoke from the grenades was clearing. Any moment now the rest of the soldiers would see us.

But I couldn't move. I could feel my body turning to stone, crushing the air in my lungs.

My name. I heard someone shouting my name again.

'Marianne.'

Jack's voice, bringing me back from the brink. Jack. What was his part in all of this? Things were happening too fast, so many questions exploding in my head.

I turned my back on my brother lying in a pool of his own blood and raced after the others into the safety of the hidden labyrinth.

Our footsteps seemed to echo more loudly than ever as we pounded through the traboules, not knowing if the Germans were at our heels, praying all the while that our men had held them off.

Deeper and deeper we went, taking twists and turns that I'd never seen before, the pain in my shoulder stabbing with every step I took. Now and then a flash of the sky above before we once more plunged into the half-light of the passageways that seemed to close in around us, offering a promise of safety even as they appeared menacing. Finally, a bigger patch of light that expanded as we emerged into another narrow street where a wine delivery van waited, its engine idling.

Suzanne stepped smartly out from the passenger seat. 'Get in,' she said. 'Hurry.'

Henri and Michel levered the injured man into the back of the van and we all scrambled in beside him, perching on the wooden crates of wine that were Suzanne's daily supply for the brothel.

'I will see you there,' said Suzanne. 'My man will drive you.'

The van doors slammed shut and darkness descended.

I started to shake with pain and shock. My brother. Marcus.

A traitor. Our mole. I couldn't believe it. I had to believe it. I'd seen the way he'd beckoned to that Nazi officer, leading him after us into the traboules. Then the gun in his hand. So Paris had been a lie. It had all been a lie.

A searing ache tearing through me, becoming more agonising with every bump and lurch of the van.

I could feel eyes upon me and took a breath, trying to pull myself together, to stop the tell-tale tremors. As my own eyes adjusted to the darkness, I could see who was staring at me.

Jack. Of course.

I turned my head away. Treachery lay everywhere I looked. I had no idea who to trust anymore. But then, I never had.

I could feel Henri pressed up against me, the warmth of the others all around. We were in this together, yet I had never felt so alone.

FORTY-NINE

We slowed to a crawl and then stopped. I held my breath. Sunlight streamed in as the doors were flung open once more.

'Up the back stairs. Hurry.'

I recognised the receptionist standing by the fire escape at the rear of the brothel. I led the way up to the top-floor apartment where Henri and Michel deposited the injured man on one of the beds.

'What happened to him?' I asked.

'They beat him half to death at Digne,' said Jack. 'Bastards gave him a particularly hard time because they suspected Charles is Resistance.'

'This is my fault,' said Juliette. 'Charles is one of my men. I sent him to that meeting to collect our share of the money. We need to get him to a hospital now.'

I looked at André. 'Is that possible?'

He shook his head. 'Not here in Lyon. It is far too dangerous. If a stranger appears in this state, the Germans will be on to it straight away. By now, they will be starting to realise the full extent of what we have done. They will want revenge.'

'Then we have to get him out of here as soon as we can. Juliette, is there a hospital near the chateau that would be safe?'

'There is a small cottage hospital run by nuns. They would take care of him. Reverend Mother has sheltered many people for me.'

'How do we get him there?'

'I'll go find Madame Suzanne,' said André.

'As quick as you can.'

'You're injured too.' Jack was staring at the growing patch of blood on my shoulder where I'd been hit.

'Just a graze,' I said. 'Bullet nicked the flesh, that's all.'

'Let me see.'

Before I could stop him, Jack was peeling my shirt from my shoulder, sticky with coagulating blood, stopping as I winced and bit back a cry of pain.

'I need scissors,' he said.

The receptionist hurried off, returning with a first aid box.

I looked at the scissors in Jack's hand. 'It's fine. Leave it.'

'It's not fine. We have to make sure there's no bullet in there and clean you up.'

He didn't wait for my response, just began slicing through my shirt.

I closed my eyes. Bastard. How dare he?

I could hear a buzzing in my ears, felt the floor lurch under my feet. My own brother. I had killed him. I started to shake as much with grief as with shock. Then Jack's hand was at my waist, steadying me. I knew it was his hand – I would know his touch anywhere.

'I'm all right,' I said, although nothing more than a gasp emerged from my lips.

'You're lucky,' said Jack. 'No bullet and it didn't hit muscle or bone, but you really need stitches.'

'No stitches,' I said. 'We can bind it up.'

'What if it gets infected?'

'No stitches. You heard. It's too dangerous. Just clean it up.'

I clocked the hurt and surprise on his face. Too bad.

'I'll do my best,' he muttered. 'Sit here.'

As Jack dabbed at the wound with antiseptic, I bit down hard on my lower lip, determined not to cry out. By the time André reappeared with Suzanne, my arm was clean and bound. She soon found me another shirt.

'We always have them,' said Suzanne. 'In case our clients need to replace one before they go home.'

I could only imagine.

'Here.' She held out a glass full of amber liquid. 'Drink this. It will help with the pain.'

She must have seen the look on my face because she added, 'It's not doctored, I promise.'

I took a healthy slug and felt the fire rake the back of my throat. Cognac. Another gulp and I could feel myself steadying.

Suzanne looked at Charles, still unconscious. 'I will drive him part of the way,' she said. 'I can get him to the outskirts of the city. The Germans will not stop me and, if they do, I can talk my way out of it. André can send word for one of your men to meet me there and take him the rest of the way.'

'I will take Henri with me,' said André. 'We need to rendezvous with Antoine and prepare for tomorrow's extraction.'

'Antoine is safe?' I asked. 'What about the others?'

'Everyone is safe. Everyone except Maggie.'

I felt as if someone had punched me in the stomach. 'What do you mean?'

'She was arrested trying to blow up the signal box.'

I stared at him, then at Suzanne.

'We only just heard. Someone must have spotted her and alerted the police.'

Maggie. No. Not our Maggie. I could see her now, bent low over her handlebars as she pedalled like the wind, coming to warn us. If she hadn't done that she might never have been spotted. She would have blown the signal box and got away.

'No.'

I heard myself wailing, the room spinning once more, the anguish cutting right through me, splitting apart my heart. Why couldn't it have been me? Me instead of Maggie. Anyone but Maggie.

I started to shake. Took a breath to steady myself and shook all the harder.

'Marianne.'

Jack's voice from somewhere far off.

'I'm all right.'

I shrugged off his hand.

Another breath or two and the world stopped whirling. I opened my eyes and looked at André, this decent man who laid his life on the line day after day.

'We will find her,' he said.

I so wanted to believe him.

FIFTY

The tentative tap at the door turned into a demanding rap and then an unrelenting pounding. Christine glanced at Barbie. He hadn't stirred for hours but surely this would wake him.

She slid from the bed and padded across to the door.

'Who is it?' she asked as softly as she could.

'Gestapo. Open up.'

Christine obliged. Three men stood there, two of whom she recognised from his protection detail.

'You realise Hauptsturmführer Barbie is asleep? You will disturb him. I'm sure he will not be pleased.'

'Wake him. Now. This is urgent.'

Christine stared at the man in front of her, his face red with anger, his eyes full of fear.

'He will not be pleased,' she repeated, stalling as long as she could.

'He will be very displeased if you do not wake him. We have an emergency situation.'

'Very well.'

She shut the door on the officers once more and padded to the bedside. Barbie's mouth was open and he was snoring softly, as he had been for hours. One arm dangled down the side of the bed while the other was flung wide. She had studied that arm during the many hours she'd sat awake, making sure Barbie didn't suddenly regain consciousness. She felt lightheaded now with lack of sleep and an exultant rush. If there was an emergency, it meant their plan had succeeded. Or at least, she hoped it had. There were so many things that could go wrong. She was going to make sure this wasn't one of them.

'Klaus... Klaus, wake up, my love...'

She shook him by the shoulder, laying her hand on him as lightly as she could. Even so, the feel of his flesh under her fingertips made her want to recoil.

'Klaus...'

He moved his head, his eyelids twitching as he came back to consciousness. He yawned, exposing curiously pointed canines, and then those strange pale eyes snapped open, blinking as he took in his surroundings before his gaze came to rest on Christine. Immediately, she smiled.

'Hello, sleepyhead,' she cooed. 'You must have been exhausted.'

There was just enough suggestion in her voice to keep him guessing.

Another loud rap on the door. He sat up, alert now. 'What's that?'

'Oh yes... some of your men are here. They want to talk to you.'

He was out of bed in one bound, Christine averting her eyes as he pulled on a bathrobe to cover his pale, flaccid buttocks.

He strode to the door and flung it open. 'Yes?'

'Sir, my apologies but we have an urgent situation on our hands.'

Barbie glanced over his shoulder and then slipped into the corridor, shutting the door behind him.

With her ear pressed against it, Christine could only make

out the odd word, although Barbie's tone of voice was all too detectable, growing harder and more demanding as he took in the gravity of what had occurred and began shouting, issuing orders.

She leaped back as he marched back into the room and began to dress, his lips compressed.

'Is something wrong?' she asked, her tone soft and sorrowful. 'You're leaving already?'

'It is ten o'clock,' he snapped. 'I should have been at my desk hours ago.'

Christine dropped her chin, staring at her hands resting in her lap, her legs curled under her on the bed where she had quite deliberately sat.

'I see,' she said. 'Then I'm sorry to have kept you.'

Her voice was cool, her posture unyielding. She was an aristocrat, after all. He was lucky to have even entered her bedchamber. Never mind that he had no recollection of the rest. She had to leave him thinking she was the one in control here or all was lost.

He must have heard the note in her voice because he hesitated in tugging on his socks. When he spoke again, his tone was more conciliatory.

'I apologise,' he said. 'It's not your fault. I am sure it was I who wanted to stay.'

She smiled. 'I think we both wanted you to stay.'

His eyes met hers. She held steady, widening hers a fraction.

'I will send a message when I am done,' he said.

Christine tilted her chin to look up at him. 'I will wait to hear from you,' she said, only exhaling when he'd finally left the room, shutting the door behind him with a decisive, finite click.

She waited, counting the seconds – forty-eight... forty-nine... fifty. Then the minutes.

After six, it was clear he wasn't coming back.

She sprang from the bed and began to throw on her own clothes, pulling the bag from the wardrobe that she'd packed the previous night and concealed under a pile of extra bedding.

All of a sudden, there was another rap at the door. She froze. This knock was different to the others. It had a rhythm.

Pushing the bag back inside the wardrobe, she went to the door once more. 'Who is it?'

'Room service, madame.'

She opened the door to see Henri dressed in a hotel uniform, a cleaning trolley in the corridor alongside him. He pushed the trolley inside the room.

'I've come to get you out,' he said. 'There are Gestapo crawling all over the place. No one is allowed to leave the hotel. You need to get inside here.'

He pulled aside the cloth that covered the trolley, revealing an empty space where normally buckets and cleaning materials would be. She pulled her bag from the wardrobe once more and tucked it in beside her, pulling her legs up so that she just about fitted into the cramped compartment.

Henri pushed the trolley back into the corridor, locking her door behind him. It was only when they were safe in the service elevator that he murmured, 'We are going to the basement. There is a laundry van there waiting to take you.'

Once in the hotel basement, she crawled out from her hiding place and dusted herself down as Henri led the way to the door, outside which a van was parked.

'Hurry,' he whispered, shoving her into the back of the van before throwing bags of dirty laundry in behind her.

He slammed the doors shut, plunging her into darkness. She could smell sweat and dust as well as the faint scent of laundry soap and lavender. The hotel sheets were washed on each change, the towels every day. That smell of lavender had permeated her pillowcases, wafting up her nostrils when she pressed her cheek against them. It was a perfume that had got her through the night, a familiar smell that overlaid the unfamiliar stench of Barbie. Not that he was dirty. Far from it. The man was fastidious. But there were some odours you could never erase, and evil was one of them.

She braced herself as the van shot up the slope from the basement to the street and came to an abrupt halt as the driver slammed on the brakes. She could hear him talking, answering the questions delivered in a far more guttural voice. The Gestapo.

She shrank against the cold metal at her back, trying to make herself as small as possible. Then the van lurched forward again, gathering speed as it drove away from the hotel.

Christine let out the breath she'd been holding. They'd done it. At least, for now. There would no doubt be more checkpoints and roadblocks ahead, but their luck was holding so far.

In the event, there was only one more stop, a brief check as they crossed the bridge into the eastern side of the city. The laundry the hotel used was situated on the edge of the old town, in the heart of Resistance territory.

As they pulled into the laundry yard, the back doors of the van were flung wide and hands hurled the bags of dirty linen aside, reaching for Christine. She wriggled forward, smiling her thanks at the two men who helped her out of the van, following them inside to a room that was filled with steam, women standing over the mechanised vats of boiling hot, soapy water which bashed the contents clean.

Through that room was another mercifully cooler one with rows of clean, folded items stacked high on numbered shelves. Here, a portly man received her, taking her into an office at the far end of the room where he bade her sit while he fetched her a glass of water.

'Drink this up,' he said. 'Another van will be here momentarily to take you to your friends.'

She sipped gratefully, exhausted by her long night watching

over Barbie and already feeling the heat of the day. Perspiration was making the back of her dress stick to her neck. She swiped at it, as much to wipe away any lingering traces of Barbie as anything else. Her hair was clinging to her brow, and she longed for a bath or a shower.

All in good time, Christine, she told herself. First she had to get out of here. They all had to get out of here. She wondered how the others were doing. Were they even alive? She had no idea.

At last, the laundry manager returned and bade her follow him. In the yard, another van was idling, with baskets and bags of clean linen stacked waiting to be loaded.

Christine climbed in and was once more half-buried under the laundry, although now the smell was altogether fresher, heavier with lavender and the reassuringly familiar laundry soap. There was something about the smell of fresh laundry that was immensely reassuring. It signalled that order prevailed and that some things remained the same, no matter the chaos all around.

Christine breathed it in and, as she did so, a memory assailed her. Her mother pegging out the sheets, stretching them so they dried in the breeze, the aroma from them filling Christine's nostrils as they flapped, astonishingly white in the sun.

At least, that was how she remembered it. Their tiny yard at home had scarcely been big enough to stretch a washing line from end to end. As for the breeze, it would struggle to stir anything between the bricks of the backstreets. The East End was full of washhouses, but her mum had preferred to do her laundry at home. She had always had aspirations, her mum. Too bad she hadn't lived to see any of them realised, although, to be frank, her dreams had died the day Christine's dad had succumbed to Spanish flu.

If she could see her now, her mum would be horrified. She had wanted Christine to marry well, to get out and to escape her own fate. Too many nights Christine had pressed the pillows to her ears to drown out the sounds of her mum getting another battering. Until the night she was old enough and bold enough to march out of her bedroom and downstairs to where her stepdad was landing punches on her mum's stomach, careful not to touch her face so none of the neighbours would know.

Of course they knew. Everyone knew. You couldn't hide anything when people lived on top of one another like they did. They knew but did nothing about it, and that was what drove Christine mad. It was also what drove her to lift the heavy iron pan from the stove and bring it down on her stepdad's head that night when she could no longer bear the screams.

Long afterwards, she relished the crack she'd heard as it had made contact with bone. He'd never touched her mum after that. But he'd followed Christine the next night down the alleyway where he'd exacted his revenge. She could never tell her mum. Never tell anyone.

Not long after that, she'd left to make her own way. One that took her to Paris, where she learned her craft, and then to the training camps of SOE. A way that had ended up here, in the back of a van, doing her bit against the Nazis.

There were worse places to be.

FIFTY-ONE

Swimming up to the surface. No. Didn't want to wake up. Wanted to sink back down under the sleepy waters where it was calm and peaceful and none of it had ever happened. My shoulder ached. My heart ached even more.

Loud voices. Men's voices. Guttural accents.

I opened my eyes. Sat up. Took in the attic room, the shape in the bed beside mine, the others slumped on the floor. One of those shapes stirred. Sat up too.

'What's going on?' mumbled Jack.

'Shhh.' I hissed out a warning.

The voices were louder now. They must be right outside the door. Or the curtain that concealed the door, draped to match the other that covered the window so they looked like a pair.

I crept as quietly as I could to the top of the wooden stairs and listened. There was another voice, a female one. Suzanne. She was speaking in low, soothing tones, the way she might to a difficult customer. I couldn't make out a word.

I could feel my ribs pressing in on my heart and realised I was holding my breath. I let it out as quietly as I could, every sinew in me screaming.

At last I heard the other voices receding and Suzanne call out a farewell, perhaps slightly louder than necessary. A few moments later, the door to the attic opened and she stood there, looking slightly paler than usual.

'The Gestapo,' said Suzanne. 'They are going house to house, trying to find anyone connected with the events this morning. They asked if I had seen or heard anything. I told them that I had only seen a couple of their fellow officers leave here in the early hours. I am not sure they believed me.'

'What do we do now?'

'I think they will be back. Their blood is up because we managed to kill so many of them this morning. They don't care that this is considered a protected establishment. They want revenge.'

'Then we must leave at once,' I said. 'Or we will put you in grave danger.'

'That is that last thing you should do,' said Suzanne. 'They will be watching this place, and I have no doubt they will search it from top to bottom. We need to hide you all in plain sight.'

I watched her face as her mind worked. Her eyes cleared as she came to a decision.

'I will put you in the working rooms,' she said. 'The two men can be the clients and you the girls.'

I looked at my watch. Ten to five. I had slept for over six hours.

'What time do you normally open for business?' I asked.

'Five o'clock, in time for *cinq à sept.*'

Of course. The customary two-hour window for liaisons, dangerous and otherwise.

'Then we'd better get ready.'

Juliette was fully awake now, taking in everything we were saying. 'The Germans were here?' she asked.

I nodded.

'*Putain.*'

She brushed a tendril of hair from her face and threw back the thin coverlet, scrambling up fully clothed. Guy, too, was yawning and stumbling to his feet.

Suzanne surveyed our ragged band. 'I will fetch suitable clothing for you ladies. In the meantime, have a wash and neaten yourselves.'

I looked at Jack and then Guy. Black streaks and smudges adorned their cheeks, while their hair stuck up at odd angles from sleep and sweat. Even Juliette's Parisian sangfroid seemed ruffled by the dust and dirt smeared on her face and arms. I had no doubt I was similarly daubed in the tell-tale marks of battle, not to mention the bandage that poked from my borrowed men's shirt. One glance and the Gestapo would realise we were not what we seemed.

One by one, we did our best at the corner washbasin, dragging the combs Suzanne brought through our hair and applying the make-up she supplied. In the tiny mirror set above the basin, my face looked drawn in spite of the quantities of rouge I applied. A slick of lipstick helped.

'Here.'

Juliette ran her fingers through my hair to loosen and tease it out, frowning as she wound strands around to form curls.

'Voilà.'

I looked once more into the mirror to see a more wanton version of me staring back.

'We might just get away with this.'

'You will get away with this,' said Suzanne, handing Juliette a chiffon peignoir, its sleeves edged with ostrich feathers. To go with it, a silken slip of a nightdress that left little to the imagination.

The men turned their backs while she changed into it and I wriggled awkwardly into a scarlet satin number, biting my lip as my shoulder screamed in protest. I caught the look on Jack's face when he saw what I was wearing. Raw desire mixed with something else. Longing, maybe. Let him long. That stable door was now firmly shut. Did he know about Marcus? Were they working together? So many questions. Not enough answers. And no time now to get anywhere near them.

'You men will have to be in your underwear,' said Suzanne. 'Or at least half-dressed, to look convincing. Remember, you are both French and, if they ask, you are a travelling salesman, and you work for the government.'

She handed Guy and Jack papers. 'They are authentic so will pass any check. We obtained them from our customers. Come – we need to get you into place.'

She beckoned to Juliette, returning minutes later for me.

I tried to look as nonchalant as I could as I wove along the corridor, following Suzanne into a room lit only by an orange lamp. I barely had time to take in the crimson walls and black bedspread before Jack was shoved through the door.

He stopped short, looked around him and laughed. 'Your very own dungeon.'

That was when I noticed the whip hanging on the wall and the handcuffs beside the bed.

I did not laugh in return.

My breath was coming in shallow pants, my heart racing. The pain in my shoulder was once more biting. So many questions.

Go for the jugular.

'Did you know about Marcus?'

He looked confused. 'What do you mean?'

'Marcus. I shot him dead. Back there. He was leading the Germans after us. He was going to shoot me.'

I could hear the tears, treacherous, thickening my voice.

Jack was staring at me in apparent shock. 'I had no idea. The smoke was so thick I couldn't see anything. My darling girl, I'm so sorry.'

'Don't touch me,' I hissed. 'Don't come anywhere near me. First Edward and now Marcus. I have no one left.'

'You have me.'

'You?'

I gaped at him, incredulous. 'You're right. It is almost funny. Here we are. You killed one of my brothers, I the other. And now we're stuck in this room together, hiding from those Nazi bastards.'

'What do you mean I killed one of your brothers?' He spoke so quietly but with such vehemence that I almost reeled back. Almost.

'Don't try to lie, Jack,' I said. 'Not to me. At least give me that. It was you who betrayed the Lyon network. Who betrayed Edward. You might as well have put the bullet in his skull yourself.'

He was staring at me, stunned.

'Don't bother to deny it,' I added even as that tiny niggle in my gut started to scratch at me once more.

'I will deny it because it's not true. Why would you even imagine I could do such a thing?'

'They showed me your poem code. They intercepted your messages. The ones you sent from Lyon. It could only have been you.'

'Who showed you?'

'A man named McMahon. Jim McMahon. He's CIC.'

'Marianne, Marcus was the radio operator here, not me. I was nowhere near Lyon when the network was blown, and I haven't used that poem code ever since we suspected I'd been compromised by a double agent. I was arrested along with Guy and sent to an internment camp. We broke out but I was shot during the escape and extracted back to London. I only returned to France with the money for Dragoon. As for McMahon, he's as dirty as they come.'

I looked at him, at his face, sincerity shining from it. Should I believe him? I had no idea what or whom to believe.

'Marianne, I love you. I loved Edward like a brother. I could no more betray him than I could you.'

I wanted to believe him so much. I'd seen Marcus with my own eyes, his gun aimed at me. Leading that German after us. Or had I? It was so confusing. I was so confused. I felt the certainty drain from me.

A commotion from the corridor outside broke through the spell. Shouts and doors slamming. The sound of boots on the wooden floors.

'They're here.'

I plucked the whip from the wall with my good hand and held it by my side as Jack dropped to his knees in front of me.

The Gestapo burst through the door. I could feel the hysteria bubbling in my throat. Feel the tears sting my eyelids. I blinked them back.

'Yes?' I snapped, embracing my role as fully as I could.

There were two SS soldiers accompanying the plainclothes Gestapo officers.

'Papers,' demanded one of the officers, unfazed by the situation.

As Jack scrambled to his feet and produced his papers from his trouser pocket, I pulled mine from the bedside table and held them out. They proclaimed me to be one Marie-France Beaumont from a small village some twenty kilometres from Lyon. The accompanying white certificate declared that I was clean of any venereal disease. I thanked the Lord for the forgery skills of Suzanne's contacts as well as her tame gynae-cologist.

One officer passed my papers to the other, only giving Jack's a perfunctory glance. It might have been male solidarity but they seemed uninterested in a lowly member of the ministry for transport indulging in a little fun before he returned home to his wife with some well-worn excuse. I had no doubt they did the same.

Satisfied, they handed us back our papers.

'Be careful,' said one to Jack. 'She looks fierce, this one.'

He smirked back. 'Oh she is.'

I wanted to shout out with sheer relief, but the game wasn't over by a long chalk. They could come back at any time. One remark out of place, a whiff of suspicion and we were all dead.

The door had barely closed behind them when we heard shouts from the end of the corridor.

Then a yell.

'Halt!'

I was at the door in a flash, easing it open a couple of inches. Guy stood in the corridor, his hands raised above his head as the SS soldiers trained their guns on him. Behind him, Juliette held her robe tight around her, protesting his innocence.

'I know this man,' she said. 'He is a regular.'

The Gestapo ignored her, waving Guy's papers in his face. 'You, what is your name? Your real name?'

'Jean Charlet. My name is Jean Charlet.'

I heard Jack's sharp intake of breath in my ear.

One of the Gestapo officers pulled out his pistol. 'I asked you for your real name.'

'Jean Charlet.'

Crack.

Guy didn't even cry out as the bullet hit him in the thigh. He staggered and swayed but remained on his feet. The officer raised his gun once more.

'Stop. My name is Claude,' said Guy.

That was when Jack stepped out from behind me, hands also raised in surrender.

'It's me you want,' he said. 'I am Claude. Not him.'

'No.'

That single word fell from my gut, from my very soul.

Jack carried on walking towards them. 'I am Claude,' he repeated.

The Gestapo officer hesitated, looking from one to the other. Guy seemed paralysed with shock, his mouth agape as he stared at Jack.

'What did you say?' The officer now had his gun trained on Jack.

'I said I am Claude. And I wish to speak with Klaus Barbie.'

The silence filled my ears, buzzing like a swarm of locusts. I tried to focus, but the corridor swam in front of me. What the hell was Jack doing? What was he saying?

I took a step, opening my mouth to protest, when all of a sudden Jack whipped the gun from the officer's hand, turned and shot Guy at point-blank range in the heart. The scream that emerged from my chest almost ripped it apart, echoing along the corridor, merging with Guy's dying rasps.

'Stay where you are.'

That was when I realised Jack was pointing the gun at me.

'No.'

The word was softer this time, a whisper of disbelief. Our eyes locked, looking beyond what was happening here. I felt as if I was staring down an abyss. My knees swayed at the edge of the precipice. This couldn't be happening.

It was.

Jack's eyes held mine for another fraction of a second and then he turned and handed the pistol back to the German.

'Do you believe me now?' he said.

The Gestapo officer looked him up and down. 'I will let Hauptsturmführer Barbie be the judge of that.'

'Good. I can't wait to see him. We have much to discuss.'

I watched as he fell in with the Germans, his retreating back a blur.

Jack. It couldn't be. It was. Marcus had been right after all.

My eyes sought Juliette's across the corridor. She shook her

THE SILENCE BEFORE DAWN

head in warning and slipped back inside her room. We had to play our parts come what may or risk the lives of everyone who was left.

Dumbly, I listened as their footsteps descended the stairs, dying away a little more with each step. With every beat, a little more of my heart left too.

'Traitor,' I whispered.

There was no response. Of course there wasn't. There was no answer to the question I wanted to throw after him, to scream to the rafters.

Why?

Then the sound of boots running up the stairs once more. An SS soldier pointing his gun at me.

'You. Come with me.'

Had he denounced me too?

Slowly, I raised my hands above my head, the barrel of the gun not more than a foot from it. He nudged me with it to walk ahead of him. I stepped over Guy where he lay. At least in death he was vindicated. The real traitor had ripped off his own mask.

Downstairs, he waited for me, his wrists now cuffed, his eyes averted. Mine bore into his back as they marched us down to the car that was waiting to take us to Place Bellecour and to Klaus Barbie.

FIFTY-TWO

My overwhelming impression was of brown. The room was vast, more of a hall, its panelled walls hung with portraits of Hitler and Himmler, who glared down from within their gilt frames. It was bright after the gloom of my cell, the light flooding in through tall windows that were framed by mushroom-coloured curtains. Brown everywhere I looked. Except the man sitting behind the desk at the far end of the room. He wore grey.

He beckoned to the guard to bring me forward. 'Sit.'

The chair was a good six feet from his desk. He got up, walked round it and slapped me hard across my face. I heard him shouting above the ringing in my ears.

'Whore. Who was the man you were servicing?'

I licked my lip and tasted blood. 'I don't know.'

Keep your head, Marianne. Remember your training.

Another slap, this time from the other side. My head snapped round. I swallowed. More blood.

'Tell me his name.'

'I don't know his name.'

'Liar.'

'He didn't tell me his name. They often don't.'

He took a step back and lit up a cigarette, his eyes darting like a caged animal as he inhaled and blew out the smoke. I kept my eyes on him, damned if I would drop my gaze.

'You sleep with these men and you don't even know their names?'

'Yes.'

In one move he leaned forward, ripped open my gown and ground his lit cigarette into my breast. I gasped, using all of my strength not to scream. The pain was white hot, searing.

He laughed. 'How does that feel, you filthy whore? Worse than his prick inside you?'

'I didn't... We didn't...' I mumbled.

'You didn't what? What did he say to you? Where is he from?'

'I don't know.'

'His name. What is his name?'

'I don't know.'

'Where is he from? Is he French? English? Is he an enemy agent?'

'I don't know.'

'He's a spy, isn't he? Did you suck off a spy?'

'No.'

'What did you say?'

Slap.

'No.'

Slap, slap.

'No.'

My breath rasped in my throat. So dry. I tried to swallow. To breathe. I could taste blood, metallic, in my mouth.

'You look like you need some water,' he said and yanked me by my hair to my feet. Now it was my scalp that was screaming as he dragged me the length of the room, my knees giving way so that he had to haul me the last few feet.

At the end of the room was a door which stood open. In the room beyond I could see harnesses hanging from the ceiling and a bathtub set in one corner, a contraption like a pole above it. Barbie's henchmen stood ready, smirking.

I looked at Barbie through narrowed lids. He was loving this.

'Strip.'

I stood there, mutely defiant.

'Strip her.'

I pushed away their hands, pulling the clothes from my body, gritting my teeth as my shoulder protested, letting the satin gown fall to the ground before I stepped out of my under-wear, keeping my back as straight as I could. As I stood there naked and shivering in spite of the heat, I felt myself detach and float somewhere else. This wasn't happening. I wasn't here. I knew nothing. Remember that.

'What's this?' demanded Barbie, pressing hard on my shoulder dressing.

'I— It's nothing. A customer got rough.'

He tore the bandage away, grunting when he saw the wound. Luckily, it looked like nothing more than a deep graze where the bullet had bitten into my flesh. He grabbed at it again, squeezing until I thought I might faint from the pain.

'Hurts, does it?'

'Not really.'

'Get in the bath.'

I climbed in. Stifled another gasp. It was ice cold.

He laughed again and pushed me down, under the water. Then they were wrenching my legs out of the water, strapping them to the bar above it. My hands, too, were wrenched behind me and tied, sending bolts of agony shooting through me. Barbie yanked on the chain attached to the bar and I was pulled down, under the water, helpless, trying not to panic, to gulp it in.

Just as I thought my lungs would burst, he hauled me up,

water streaming from my hair down my face, numb and frozen to my core.

'What's his name? His real name? Where is he from?'

I tried to form the words. My mouth was too cold to work.

'His name, whore.'

'Don't. Know.'

Plunging under again, ice filling my eyes and ears, water whooshing up my nostrils. I coughed. *No. Don't breathe. Can't.*

I coughed and spluttered once more as I broke the surface, ripped from the water at the end of a chain like an animal.

A clang as the chain dropped.

'Take her back to her cell,' said Barbie.

Rough hands undid the straps. I tried to stand. Couldn't. My limbs no longer belonged to me but someone else, someone far away from here.

Barbie's henchmen hauled me from the tub and threw me on the floor, where I scrabbled for my clothes. The scarlet satin barely covered my modesty but it was better than nothing.

'I will see you later,' said Barbie. His voice had dropped from its screech. He sounded almost conversational. It was schizophrenic the way he could swing from one state to another so fast.

I said nothing but simply stared at my hands as if I'd never seen them before. I had lasted. This time.

Forty-eight hours. That was what they said. Say nothing for forty-eight hours to give your fellow agents time to get away.

But there were no other agents. Just Jack. And I had no idea who or what he was anymore.

FIFTY-THREE

It was dark when they woke me.

'Get up.'

Still fuzzy with sleep, I was marched through the empty building, now eerily quiet. I glimpsed a clock on a wall – 2 a.m. Then they were pushing me through another door into a smaller room this time. It looked like an office with a chaise longue set to one side. Jack was strapped to a chair opposite Barbie's desk.

When he saw me, Barbie smiled, his lips as thin as the blade of the knife set before him. Alongside it, cudgels and clamps. Instruments of torture.

Barbie picked up a riding crop. 'Is this the woman?' he asked.

I could not, would not look at Jack. Instead, I stared at the wall ahead. More pictures. Scenes of rural Germany this time. A half-timbered cottage with a duckpond beside it. Bucolic.

'What woman?' asked Jack.

Crack.

He didn't cry out as the crop caught him round the shoulders, although he swayed in his chair.

'The whore you hired.'

'I don't know. They all look the same.'

Another crack, this time across his cheek. It opened a welt as wide as my thumb. I couldn't help but stare at it in horror.

Barbie grabbed me by the hair once more and yanked me so that my face was inches from Jack's.

'Can you see now? See what you did, whore?'

I could feel Jack's breath on my cheek. Saw his lips move. Heard him murmur.

'Courage.'

Courage. Pronounced the French way. That was when I knew he'd never betrayed me. Never betrayed anyone. It was all there in that one word.

'What was that?' yelled Barbie.

He smashed my head into Jack's. I felt bone meet bone, sending a judder right through me. When I opened my eyes again, I could see blood oozing from Jack's nose. God knows what I looked like.

'Not so pretty now, is she?' sneered Barbie, as if reading my thoughts.

I put a hand up to my face, pulled it away again. That laugh of his rang in my ears. Then he punched me square in the jaw. I felt my brain rattle. Heard a cry. Was it mine or Jack's?

There was something running down my cheek. Blood maybe. Or snot. God forbid it was tears. I wouldn't let this monster see me cry. Wouldn't give him the satisfaction.

'She says she doesn't know your name,' said Barbie. His voice had dropped to normal again. Or as normal as he ever got.

'She doesn't.'

'But you told her, didn't you? My men said she was there when you confessed to being Claude.'

'Was she? I don't remember. For God's sake, she's just some whore.'

'Your friend also claimed to be Claude.'

'What friend?'

'The man you shot dead.'

'He wasn't my friend. I didn't know him.'

'So why did you shoot him?'

Silence.

'Why did you shoot him?' Barbie's voice was rising again to a shriek. 'Tell me why.'

'I thought he must be Resistance.'

Jack raised his chin, looking Barbie full in the face.

'He knew about Claude. Which means he must have been some kind of agent.'

For a second, I thought he'd got away with it. Then Barbie turned to the guard standing by the door.

'Fetch the dogs,' he said.

FIFTY-FOUR

I don't know if I slept. If the dogs were snarling and tearing at Jack in my dreams or in my memories. It was just after dawn when they woke me once more, a grey pall infiltrating the basement where the cells were located.

'You're lucky,' said the guard. 'You have friends in high places.'

I rubbed my wrists where they were chafed and limped after him to a steel door that opened into the street.

I could see a car parked opposite and a woman leaning against it.

'Hurry,' said Suzanne. 'Get in.'

'How...? What...?'

'Save your questions. You'll find fresh clothes on the back seat beside you. Put them on.'

I wriggled out of the satin gown, or what remained of it, the cloth barely intact where Barbie had torn at it, wincing as I eased it over my injured shoulder. The sensible dress Suzanne had brought felt comfortably rough against my skin in contrast, the loose cotton allowing the air to soothe my lacerations and bruises.

She gunned the engine and we shot down the road, Suzanne taking corners at breakneck speed until at last she stopped the car in a side street in what looked to be the suburbs.

'You must go on alone,' she said. 'I will deal with the Gestapo. Take this road until you come to a cemetery. At the southern end of it, there are some tombs that were bombed a couple of months ago by the Americans. Juliette is waiting there for you. Someone will meet you both and take you to the river where there is a barge waiting. His name is Georges.'

'How did you get me out?' I asked.

'Favours. Let's just say I have a client who has a lot of influence. And I know too much about him.'

She gave me a look that warned me not to ask any more.

'Whatever you did, thank you,' I said.

I couldn't bring myself to ask about Jack or to even think of him. It was the only way I could stop my heart from entirely breaking apart.

'Come with us,' I said. 'It's not safe for you either. The Germans will arrest you next.'

'No they won't,' she said. 'I know the right people. Besides, I have to go back. I cannot leave my girls unprotected. It will be all right. I promise. If you need me, call me. My telephone number is Lyon 299. Say there is a problem with a stray cat.'

I looked at her face, alight with determination, slid out of the car, then reached back in and enfolded her in a brief, awkward embrace.

'Be careful,' I said.

'You too. Now go,' she said. 'Hurry.'

It may have been my imagination, but I thought I saw the glisten of unshed tears in her eyes.

I blew her a final kiss and then followed the street as she'd indicated. The cemetery was easy to find, the bomb damage to the southern sector all too visible. Tombs lay smashed open, their contents poking through the ground. Some of the burials were so recent that the mounds of soil on top of the graves had not yet settled and flattened. I didn't want to think too hard about that. Instead, I scanned between the tombstones, searching for Juliette.

The merest flicker of movement caught my eye, a hand reaching from behind a fallen angel, as alabaster white as the marble from which the angel was carved so that, for a second, I thought it was a trick of the light.

The hand beckoned and I slipped behind the angel where Juliette was hiding in its safe embrace, her wings wrapping us in a cloak of concealment as we crouched, alert to the slightest movement or sound.

'*Salut*,' she whispered. 'You look like shit.'

'Thanks. You don't look so good yourself.'

She smiled. Truth be told, she looked as elegant as ever, although the purple crescents beneath her eyes told their own tale. She glanced at her watch, its masculine strap incongruous against her slender wrist.

'Where is this Georges?'

'He'll be here. He's a friend of Suzanne's. Patience.'

I could still see Suzanne's proud profile as she drove away, head erect to face whatever lay ahead.

The minutes ticked past. Still no Georges.

'Anything could have happened,' said Juliette. 'He could have been arrested on his way here. We might even be in the wrong place.'

At that moment, I heard the scrape of a match not ten yards from where we crouched. I saw a man's face briefly illuminated and then a rising spiral of smoke as he took his first drag. It took me a moment to realise he was humming under his breath and another to comprehend that Juliette had joined in, her feminine voice scarcely audible although the tune was unmistakable: 'La Marseillaise'.

There was nothing for it but to chance my arm. I rose from the marble fold of the angel's wing.

'My name is Georges,' the man said.

'Oh thank God.'

Juliette emerged too. He clicked his tongue against his teeth.

'Two of you. I will have to take you one by one.'

'Juliette, you go first,' I said.

Georges hooked his arm through hers before she could protest and they set off towards the river, looking as if they were out for a lovers' stroll.

I studied the face of the fallen angel as I waited for him to return. She looked serene, her marble eyes lifted to some heaven I would never see.

'God help us all,' I whispered. At moments like this, I would believe in anything.

When my turn came, I matched my step to Georges' stride, trying to appear as if it was entirely normal to be strolling the streets with a man who was twice my age and who walked like the boatman he was. Mercifully, we met no one as we made for the river. The Gestapo were probably busy searching the more obvious districts.

Even when Barbie turned the dogs on him, Jack hadn't broken. I'd had to shut my eyes at one point, but I'd still been able to hear his voice above the growls and snarls, the sound of their teeth ripping into his flesh as he kept protesting he knew nothing. I wondered how much longer he could keep that up.

I tried to think through everything Jack had seen and heard since he'd been with us. He knew our codenames. Suzanne's true role. He knew all about the traboules. And he knew every detail of Operation Dragoon.

One more day. That was all he had to hold out. I knew Jack would rather die than tell them anything. Part of me, a tiny part, wished he would and spare himself.

Georges helped me down into the barge. It sat low and dark in the water. Juliette was already inside, perched on one of the wooden barrels that were stacked in front by the galley.

'Follow me.'

Georges led us to the back of the barge, where he prised open a panel. Behind it, there was a concealed crawl space.

'We are going downriver to the rendezvous,' he said. 'You must remain in here until I tap four times. I will do that before I open it again. If you do not hear those taps, you must not move under any circumstances.'

We nodded dumbly at him. Once the panel was back in place, we were plunged into almost complete darkness. The engine started to chug and we were underway, moving down the Rhône and towards safety. Or so we hoped. My nails dug into my palms and my jaw ached with tension. Somewhere downriver we would be reunited with the others, with our network.

The engine slowed, dropping to a gentle putter. We waited, straining to hear, while the barge banged up against what I assumed was the riverbank. Or possibly it was a patrol boat manned by German soldiers.

Then we heard them – four clear, sharp taps on the panel. A moment later it was pulled aside, and Antoine stood there beside Georges. He took my outstretched hands and pulled first me and then Juliette to our feet.

'I am so glad to see you,' he said.

I looked at him, at his thin face, his eyes as intense as ever. It may have been my imagination but I thought I saw a benediction in them.

'And I you.'

The barge engine began to putter, no longer idling. Georges raised a hand as he cast off once more, heading back upriver to Lyon, the barge sluicing through the dark waters like some oversized flotsam.

'How did you know where to meet us?' I asked as we climbed into the waiting car.

Antoine was concentrating on the track ahead, his eyes fixed on every rut and bump.

'Your friend Suzanne,' he said. 'She sent word to the Maquis and they did the rest.'

'Did you hear what happened at the brothel?'

'I did. We'll talk about it later.' His tone was flat and final.

I pressed my forehead against the glass of the window, staring out into the darkness as the road rolled by. With every kilometre that passed, Jack's face grew fainter. I could still hear his voice in my head.

'Courage,' he had said.

'Courage,' I whispered.

FIFTY-FIVE

The road lulled me as the car ate it up, putting distance between us and Lyon. I tried to do that with my thoughts, to pull away and sink into the torpor of complete exhaustion. By the time we reached the chateau, I was in the kind of daze that descends when you've travelled too long in both mind and body.

I looked up at its welcoming walls and felt as if I'd come home. I saw the same thought written on Juliette's face.

Diaz greeted us at the door and led us into the great hall where the others were assembled.

'It is good to be back,' she said. 'It will be even better to sleep.'

'You should both get some sleep,' said Diaz. 'We can debrief later.' His eyes swept over our small group. 'Some of you are missing.'

'Maggie was arrested trying to blow up the railway signal box. Marcus was shot during the ambush. Barbie has Jack. Guy is dead.'

I kept my tone matter of fact. It was that or break down.

'I see. I'm sorry,' said Diaz.

The sympathy in his eyes was too much to bear.

I swallowed. 'What about Christine?' I asked.

'Already here.'

I looked up, my gaze travelling up the staircase just as Christine swept down it.

'Thank God you're safe,' she said.

She was as glorious as ever, but her face was drawn and there were new shadows under her eyes too.

'How did you get here?' I asked.

'Long story.'

Later, as I lay in bed, I heard a gentle tap on my door.

'I couldn't sleep,' said Christine. 'Can I sleep with you?'

'Of course.'

I made room for her under the covers, and she curled up on her side, turned towards me.

'Do you ever see them?' she asked. 'The people who've died? I see them all the time. The ones who've died fighting. The ones they've taken to be tortured and killed. I looked at his hands while he was out cold. Barbie. They were such ordinary hands. The kind of hands you might see on a teacher or a bank clerk. Possibly even a priest. Smooth. No particular marks or scars. And yet those hands have beaten people to death, plunged them into acid baths. Broken backs. Hearts.'

'I know,' I said. My God, did I know. 'Hush now. Try to sleep.'

'He had big hands,' said Christine. 'My stepfather. He wrapped them around my throat so I wouldn't scream. I will never forget his face as he died.'

I wasn't sure if she was lucid now or even what she was saying. All I knew was that it was burning her up inside, as it did so many.

I threw my arm across her, patting and stroking her back as I would a child who'd woken from a nightmare.

'It's all right,' I soothed, 'you're safe now. I'm here. Go to sleep, Christine. It will all be better once you've had some rest.'

'No,' she said, 'it won't. It will never be better. But thank you.'

'One day it will be. I promise. Now sleep. I'll keep watch.'

With that, her eyelids drooped, flitting like a moth's wings as they settled and closed. She began to drift. I watched as the thoughts kept chasing across her face, her brow creasing as she fought them. She muttered in her sleep, words and phrases I couldn't make out. I kept stroking and patting her back until, at last, she let go and sank into a deep slumber. Only then did I allow myself to sleep too.

She was still fast asleep when I awoke, the sun poking around the shutters. I lay and looked at the slices of light for a few minutes, luxuriating in the fact I was here, safe. Then, as I remembered, the day began to darken. My shoulder throbbed, the blood beginning to surge through it, my heart quickening at the memory of his fingers digging in, his face suffused in delight as I fought not to cry out.

I shut my eyes again but it was no use. All I could see was Barbie. And the dogs. And Jack. Marcus lying in a pool of his own blood. Maggie on her bicycle, racing to warn us.

'A penny for them.'

I turned my head and looked at Christine. 'We have to kill him, you know. I don't care what they say.'

'Barbie?'

'Yes. Maybe not now. But soon. Before he gets away.'

She nodded, her face half-pressed into the pillow. 'We will. I promise.'

'It was me who shot Marcus,' I blurted out. 'I had to. He was working for the Nazis. I saw it with my own eyes when we ambushed the convoy. He was leading the Germans towards us, trying to stop us escaping. So I shot one of them and then Marcus. He was our mole all along.'

My words sounded disjointed, unbelievable even to my own ears.

'You did what you had to do,' said Christine.

'I did. But my God, it hurts.'

'I know,' she said, her cool hand a fleeting, featherlight touch on my cheek.

Then she sat up and shook out her platinum hair. 'Don't know about you but I'm starving. Race you to breakfast.'

I got the message. 'You're on.'

I leaped out of bed, splashed some water on my face and flung on the only clean clothes I had left in the wardrobe. It felt good to bound down the stairs knowing that I didn't constantly have to look over my shoulder. The one Barbie had taken so much pleasure from hurting all over again.

Soon the pleasure would be all mine. I was coming for him and, when I did, he would be the one not knowing which corner might be the last one he turned, which word could prove fatal. Two more days until Operation Dragoon was unleashed. Two days to make sure it went ahead, come what may. Then Klaus Barbie was mine, orders or no orders. And so, I prayed, was Jack.

FIFTY-SIX

McMahon was adamant. 'You are not going back to Lyon.'

'You can't tell me what to do. This is my operation,' I said. 'We're working with the Resistance.'

'So are we. Or have you forgotten that?'

I stared at him. 'No.'

'Then understand me when I say that there is nothing we can do right now. The Gestapo haven't arrested anyone in connection with your escape. Not yet, at any rate. They have a man they think is Claude and that's keeping them busy. The reprisals will come but, with any luck, the right people will be spared.'

'What do you mean "a man they think is Claude"? You know who the real Claude is, don't you? Or was?'

McMahon cleared his throat. 'I can't tell you any more at the moment but trust me when I say that I wish I could.'

Everyone jumped, including me, as my fist hit the table.

'No. Not good enough. We've just been through hell back there. You gave me a piece of paper implicating Jack. Now you hint that there's more to this than we know. And it's all about Jack, isn't it? We went there to rescue him from Klaus Barbie only for him to hand himself over quite happily to the Gestapo. None of it makes sense. We could have died. People might still die. Including Maggie. So you'd better start talking and do it fast.'

'She's right,' said Christine.

'Absolutely,' said Juliette. 'My men and the other maquis-ards deserve an explanation too. They risked their lives to stop that convoy. They laid explosives on the railway line to prevent the transportation. Are you telling me that none of us are to be trusted with the truth?'

She glowed with righteous fury, every word enunciated with the utmost scorn. Even McMahon looked taken aback.

'Of course not,' he said. 'You'll get the truth in good time.'

'Now is a good time.'

If he thought Juliette would back down, he was seriously mistaken.

'One thing I can tell you is that the train to Auschwitz got through. With your courier on it.'

'Maggie was on that train? No. That can't be true.'

'I'm afraid it is. They loaded her on it along with prisoners they picked out from Montluc, many of them Resistance. They mended the rails and sent the train through late afternoon. They're nothing if not efficient.'

'My God. Maggie.'

I swallowed back the tears. They wouldn't help Maggie now. What was McMahon even doing here? The man came and went as he pleased, helping only when it suited him. Lying when it suited him even more.

'How many were on that train?'

'We don't know,' said McMahon. 'The Germans always seal them up so no one can say for sure how many are aboard. Hundreds probably.'

I stared at him. 'Don't you care?'

'Of course I care, but there's nothing I can do about it. What

I can do is keep on fighting the Nazis as well as the damn Soviets.'

'What the hell have the Soviets got to do with anything?'

McMahon's colour had risen. Good. I'd obviously hit a nerve. But this thing about the Soviets had come out of nowhere.

'What have the Soviets got to do with it?' I repeated.

'You don't see the danger, do you?' said McMahon. 'You think it's just the Nazis threatening your world. But it's the Soviets too. You wait. They'll try and take over, given half the chance. What would you prefer – living under a fascist regime or a communist one? Trust me, they're equally as bad.'

'I want to live in freedom,' I said. 'As does everyone here, I suspect.'

'If that's what you want then you'll listen to me,' said McMahon. 'The most important thing now is that Operation Dragoon proceeds as planned. The Allies are already pushing down through France. The Germans are on the run. If we squeeze them from the south, this war is as good as done.'

'Oh right. It's that easy.'

He controlled himself with difficulty. I watched the colour seep up his neck again, his Adam's apple rising as he choked back his words. When he spoke, it was with visible effort to remain calm.

'I realise this is especially hard for you. We know that you and Jack were close. But this is war and sometimes things happen that we don't especially like.'

If he'd hoped to mollify me, his words had the opposite effect.

'You patronising shit,' I said. 'You know nothing about Jack and me. As for this war, I think I've seen more of it than you ever will.'

'Who is the real Claude?' Juliette's cool, precise tones cut through the rising tension. 'You more or less told us it isn't Jack.

If he is not Claude, then who is? And why the hell did you tell Marianne that he is Claude if he's not? If the Germans discover that, then his life is in greater danger than ever.'

I felt a trickle of hope begin to rise in me, buoyed up by a wave of relief. She was right. If Jack wasn't Claude then he wasn't our traitor.

But I already knew that. I had seen it with my own eyes. Heard his voice whispering to me to have courage. In truth, I had never really believed it deep in my soul, despite the fury that had engulfed me – the fury I'd needed to avoid falling apart. But that still meant Jack had, for some reason, willingly walked into the mouth of the monster.

'Who are you protecting?' I snarled. 'Tell me or so help me God, I will shoot you here and now.'

McMahon raised his hands, turning away with a shrug. I wanted to slap him and hard.

Diaz spoke up. 'They're right. This isn't fair on anyone. You can't expect people to risk their lives in the field when they don't know half the story.'

'Of course we can,' said McMahon. 'We do it all the time.'

I stared at him. 'We're nothing more than pawns to you,' I said. 'You think you can manipulate us and get away with it.'

'Not at all. You are the people I am trying to protect.'

'Thanks but we don't need your protection.'

'Very well. I'll see myself out.'

'Wait.'

McMahon was already halfway through the door.

'You can't go without at least telling us who the hell is Claude.'

He wheeled round, his face twisted with a fury I never expected to see in him.

'Actually I can. I can and I will. But here's something to think about after I'm gone. Why would Jack shoot one of his best friends dead? You think about that. Now I'm going to go and do what you should be doing – fight the war.'

His words echoed louder than the door he slammed behind him. I looked at Juliette, her frown deepening, and then at Antoine, who was staring after McMahon.

'Follow him,' I said. 'Find out what he's up to.'

I glared at Diaz. 'You're staying right here. I don't want you talking to your friend McMahon until you've told us everything that you know.'

'I have to talk to London before I can say anything.'

I raised an eyebrow. 'Oh really?'

'Yes, really. I know that this is your network, but things are more complicated than that.'

'You didn't show up here just by chance, did you? I mean, specifically here, to assist our network. It was all part of a bigger plan.'

'No, of course not. London sent us as part of Operation Jedburgh, to support you and the final invasion. That's all.'

'What else did they send you to do?'

I stared him down, watching the thoughts chase across his face.

And then he gave me a rueful shrug. 'You're right. There's more to this than you know. More than I can tell you.'

I pulled my pistol from my belt and levelled it at him. 'You'd better start talking and fast.'

He held up his hands in surrender. 'You win. But you may not like what you hear.'

'Try me.'

Diaz cleared his throat. 'You'd better sit down.'

FIFTY-SEVEN

Barbie sat behind a desk that could have done duty in an embassy or, at a pinch, a bank manager's office. Jack tried not to look at the array of coshes, clubs and whips laid neatly next to a couple of files. He was sure he could see his own blood on one of the spikes.

'So... you are Claude.'

'I am.'

'Congratulations. You have done an excellent job, holding out against my dogs. Not many manage that.'

'Thank you.'

'You understand, I have to make sure you are who you say you are. But of course, your work is not finished yet.'

Jack said nothing, waiting him out.

'I believe there is a lot more you need to tell us,' went on Barbie. 'Names, times, dates.'

Jack held his gaze, noting the half-smile on Barbie's face. He was toying with him, playing as a cat would with a canary. Once he'd sung his last song, Barbie would silence him forever.

'Names, times, dates.'

Barbie was leaning forward now, his forearms resting on the

polished wood. Teak maybe. Or mahogany. His hands were inches from his instruments of torture.

Jack returned his smile, playing for time. 'Where would you like to start?'

'You tell me.'

The half-smile was gone. The cat had turned tiger.

'Start with the local Resistance here in Lyon. What do you know about the sabotage of the convoy that brought you from Digne prison?'

'Absolutely nothing, I'm afraid. I was as surprised as you were.'

'But you were helped to escape by these *résistants*. Where did you go?'

'We ran down the backstreets. I couldn't tell you which ones exactly. It all happened so fast.'

'And then?'

'Then we ended up in an apartment somewhere. We were told to stay there and not go out until they came for us. But Jack grew bored. We'd been locked up for so long, without the sniff of a woman you know? So he suggested we go find a brothel. You know the rest.'

'Why did you shoot Jack? He was your friend after all.'

'How else could I prove to you that I'm Claude?'

Barbie studied him for what felt like hours but could have been no longer than a few seconds.

'I see we have things in common,' he said. 'I too like decisive action. That is why I am bringing one of my men from Digne to help refresh your memory. I believe you had a lot to say to him when you were there.'

Jack resisted the urge to touch his jaw. The bruises had faded but the memories were still fresh.

'I look forward to seeing him,' he said.

'In the meantime,' said Barbie, 'you will be our guest.'

He indicated to the two men hovering by the door, who moved forward to stand either side of Jack.

'These men will escort you to your cell. We will talk again later.'

With that, he turned his attention to the files on his desk. Jack was dismissed.

He could see the meatheads at his sides in his peripheral vision, sensing the barely suppressed hostility that they emitted. But they were nothing compared to the guy they were bringing from Digne. The minute that prison guard saw him, the game was up.

It was in Digne, stuck in a cell with him day after day, that Jack had finally begun to think Guy really could be Claude. Until then, he'd been prepared to give him the benefit of the doubt. More accurately, he wanted to, desperate not to believe that a man he'd known for all those years could betray both him and his country, as well as all the brave souls fighting to protect it. But each time Guy returned from his regular interrogations looking scarcely touched, Jack's certainty had hardened a little more. There was just too much evidence that stacked up. Above all he wanted to know why. And now he never would. There had been no choice in that brothel corridor. He'd had to shoot him before he could talk. Before he'd betrayed them all, including Marianne.

The meatheads marched Jack down three flights of stairs to the basement, which was fitted out with makeshift cells. Jack stared at the locks and bolts on the doors. There was nothing makeshift about those, although they looked pretty standard. Not that he had anything with which to pick them.

'In here.'

Jack felt a shove in the middle of his back. He braced himself and took a step, determined to remain upright. As he heard the bolt slide into place, he stayed where he was, shoulders squared, a British officer. It was only as their steps retreated and died away that he sank down onto the bunk and stared at the graffitied walls, seeing nothing on them but Marianne's face. To never see that lovely face again, hold it between his hands, kiss it. He could bear anything but that. Even Barbie's brutality. In comparison, it would be a blessing.

FIFTY-EIGHT

'As you know, Operation Dragoon is a joint op. I can now tell you that the US VI Corps will land first, followed by the French B Army,' said Diaz. 'They'll be backed up by a large naval task force, but we need to prepare the ground for them. Our orders are to cut every possible communication line before then.'

'You have this direct from OSS?'

'Yes, ma'am.'

He clocked my expression. 'Sorry. Marianne.'

I looked at Diaz, immaculate in his uniform. The Yanks might be running Dragoon, but we were still part of it, a vital part.

'What can we do?' I asked. 'What will inflict most damage?'

Diaz unrolled a map that covered the area between the chateau and the coast to the south of us, extending as far north as Lyon. 'Our troops will advance inland from the landing sites on the Riviera, pushing back the Germans. They have three divisions of the 19th Army protecting Provence and one Panzer division. They'll attempt to join up with their armies along the Loire and to the east. We need to make that as difficult as possible for them. Before the landings start, preliminary aerial bombings will be stepped up.'

'Which means we need to sabotage roads and bridges as well as communication systems?'

'Correct.'

'Do we know the time of the first landings?'

'The preliminary operations commence tomorrow night and the landings are at dawn. That means we have around thirty-six hours to do as much damage as possible.'

Thirty-six hours. I could only hope Jack held out that long.

Diaz drew his finger along the road from where we were up the Rhône Valley towards Lyon, tracing the route.

'Our boys will be advancing north, pushing the Germans towards our armies here and here. We must make sure the roads are open for them while making it difficult for the Germans to retreat. The more we weaken them here, the better. Best case scenario, we stop them altogether before they can join up with their divisions in the interior.'

'How do you propose we do that?' asked Juliette.

'We target them on the ground,' I said. 'Attacking them as they march. Blowing up bridges as they approach. We have men camped all over the countryside from here to Lyon. We can communicate with the networks further south so that we coordinate our efforts.'

'We also have to get back to Lyon and stop that bastard Barbie before he escapes,' said Christine.

'Our forces are aiming to proceed up the Rhône Valley and take both Lyon and Dijon. We can make that easier for them and put the squeeze on Barbie and his men at the same time.'

No one mentioned Jack. No one needed to. For the next thirty-six hours, we all knew he was on his own, holding out against Klaus Barbie, giving away tiny morsels of useless information to keep him at bay until the operation commenced.

'We may have to get there sooner.'

I looked up from the map to see Antoine, his expression grave.

'I have just had a message from our contact at Digne prison,' he said. 'Klaus Barbie has demanded that the officer in charge of interrogating Jack and his colleagues be brought to Lyon.'

'Is that a problem?' asked Juliette.

'It could be Jack's death warrant. The officers interrogating them at Digne were aware they had Claude as a captive. They knew him to be the man called Guy. As soon as Barbie asks the officer to identify Jack as Claude, he will tell them that they have the wrong man.'

'When are they bringing this officer from Digne?' I asked.

'He has already left. A black Citroën picked him up an hour ago.'

'Then he'll be there in a couple of hours, maybe less,' I said. 'We need to do something – and now.'

Diaz shook his head. 'Our focus has to be Operation Dragoon.'

'Yes,' I said. 'And Jack is vital to its success. He knows the precise landing times and sites, remember? The Germans may know that the landings are happening any day, but they don't have detailed information. Of course it has to be somewhere on the Riviera, but when and where exactly is still guesswork for them.'

'More than that,' added Juliette, 'he knows enough about the Lyon operation to destroy it once more if he talks under torture. That would mean us losing our network on the ground there just when we need it most, as the Germans retreat and our troops advance.'

'They're right,' said Antoine. 'Once Barbie realises that he is not Claude, he will do whatever it takes to make him talk.'

'He's already done enough,' I said. 'I can't imagine what more he'll do.'

I couldn't bear to. The sound of those dogs ripping at him

would haunt me forever, as would Jack's groans of agony. He had tried so hard not to cry out. It made my heart cry too. *Courage*. He had more than any of us.

'It's a risk we have to take,' said Diaz. 'We mount an operation to help him now and we use up valuable resources.'

'Jack is one of our most valuable resources,' I ground out between clenched teeth. 'He not only knows the Lyon network, he knows the names and details of agents in all the networks for hundreds of miles. Barbie could clean up before our troops even land. There would be no one left to sabotage anything. So no, Jack is not expendable, if that's what you were suggesting.'

'She has a point,' said Antoine. 'Klaus Barbie is clever as well as being a brutal bastard. He knows that going for the Resistance is the best way to fight back. We need Jack alive. For many good reasons.'

I flashed him a look of thanks.

'There is one person who could help,' I said. 'Suzanne. She's right there in Lyon. I have her telephone number. I can call her and tell her what's happening. She'll think of something.'

'For obvious reasons, we have no telephone here,' said Juliette. 'The Germans would spot the cables, and this place is supposed to be uninhabited. But the Archduke has one. His chateau is the other side of the village.'

'Can we risk driving down there? They're on high alert so there are bound to be roadblocks and Germans everywhere.'

A slow smile spread across Juliette's normally grave face. 'I have an idea.'

FIFTY-NINE

Thirty minutes later we were driving down to the village, a pillow lashed in place under my dress so that I appeared to be nine months pregnant.

Sure enough, there was a roadblock on the outskirts of the village manned by three German soldiers, one of whom called out to us to halt.

'Papers,' he said, peering inside the car. 'What is the purpose of your journey?'

Juliette motioned to me, sprawled on the back seat of the old sedan.

'We are on our way to the hospital. My sister-in-law is due to give birth,' she said. 'And the baby is late. Possibly breech. It may have to be turned. You know how it is.'

I let out a groan, one hand laid across my supposed baby bump to underline her words.

The soldier stared at his feet.

'Drive on,' he said, handing back the papers. He waved to his men to stand aside, clearly keen to get rid of us as soon as he could.

'He's probably terrified I'm going to give birth here and now,' I said.

I shifted uncomfortably in my seat, the pillow under my dress an annoying encumbrance. 'I don't know how women do this for nine months.'

'I would be worried if I were him,' said Juliette. 'That groan sounded very real. When I had my babies, I made so much noise.'

I glanced at her. 'You never mentioned you have children.'

'I did not think it relevant. Besides, I never talk about them for their own safety.'

'Of course. Where are they now?'

'Over the border in Switzerland. I sent them there with my mother not long after the Occupation. I have not seen them since.'

'What about their father?'

'What about him?' She threw me a glance that said everything. 'I walked out when my youngest was still a baby. Best thing I ever did. The man was a controlling bastard as well as a Nazi sympathiser. So I left and started working for an underground newspaper while my mother took care of the children.'

'How old are they now?'

'Eight and six.'

'They must have been tiny when you last saw them.'

'Four and just two years old, yes. I do not know if the younger one would even recognise me.'

'That must be so hard for you.'

'It is. But this war is hard for everyone. It was hard for you not seeing Jack for so long, no? We all have to pay the price and make our sacrifices. It will be worth it in the end.'

'I hope so.'

'No, Marianne, not hope. You must know. Here, in your heart.'

Juliette's hands on the wheel were firm. Her words even

more so. She was like high tensile steel, far stronger than she looked.

We were drawing up outside the Archduke's chateau. The heavy front door was flung open and a tall, elegant man sprinted down the steps to greet us.

'Inside,' he said. 'Quickly.'

'We need to use your telephone,' said Juliette, once we were safely in the salon. The Archduke's wife eyed my baby bump.

'It's not real,' I said. 'It's a cushion.'

The Archduke burst out laughing. 'Very clever. I assume it got you past the roadblocks?'

'It did.'

'We need to call Lyon urgently,' said Juliette. 'I will explain later.'

'But of course. Follow me.'

He preceded us into an office adjacent to the salon where the telephone sat on what looked to be a Louis XIV desk. I picked it up and dialled Suzanne's number. It rang and rang.

'Damn,' I said. 'No one's answering.'

'Try again.'

It just kept ringing. I was replacing it in the receiver when I heard a distant voice.

''Allo?'

'Suzanne? Is that you?'

A silence. I collected myself.

'I have a problem with a cat that has strayed from Digne,' I said. 'It has gone missing. I believe it may be somewhere near the Place Bellecour. I think it hopped in a black Citroën.'

'I see.'

Even over the crackling line, I could hear Suzanne thinking. Everyone knew the Gestapo's fondness for black Citroëns. I prayed I hadn't gone too far.

'He's a tom cat,' I added. 'He could be dangerous.'

I was growing desperate but still I tried to choose my words with care. The Gestapo were adept at tapping telephone lines, as Suzanne well knew.

'I am sorry,' she said. 'I cannot look for him as I have to look after a dog. I will try to get some friends to help, although they are otherwise occupied right now. May I call you if we find him?'

'Yes,' I said. 'The usual number.'

As I replaced the receiver in its cradle, I couldn't shake off a nagging sense that something was very wrong.

'Suzanne's in trouble,' I said.

'How do you know?'

'Something she said about a dog and her friends being otherwise occupied. Suzanne refers to the Germans as dogs. And they are the occupiers. I might be wrong but I think that means they've been picked up. We need to get there as fast as possible.'

'Are you sure this is wise?' asked the Archduke.

I looked at him and smiled. 'No. But it's the right thing to do.'

He drew himself erect and saluted, moustache bristling. '*Vive la France*,' he said. 'May God go with you.'

SIXTY

'I'm coming with you to Lyon. I can deal with Barbie,' said Christine.

Antoine glared at her. 'Don't be ridiculous.'

'Seriously, I can get close enough. He has no reason to suspect me. As far as he's concerned, we passed a night of passion and that was the last time he saw me.'

'And then you disappeared,' I said.

We were clustered in the salon once more, the minutes ticking impatiently in my mind.

'That is easily explained. A family emergency. A sudden illness.'

'You're insane.'

The half-smile of approval on Diaz's face told its own tale.

'Maybe,' said Christine. 'But so is Klaus Barbie. No sane person could do what he does. And he's a man, which means he has an Achilles heel. His ego.'

'We're not all egotistical bastards,' protested Diaz.

'No, but Klaus Barbie definitely is, and it is his arrogance which makes him stupid. If I flatter him enough, there's a chance I can get him on his own and then I can make sure he's out of the way. What's the alternative? The prison officer from Digne will be there all too soon. Once he arrives, Jack's as good as dead. But before they kill him, they'll try and get as much out of him as they can. That's my opportunity.'

'Opportunity?'

'To kill Barbie.'

'No. No way. Klaus Barbie stays alive. That's an order.'

First McMahon. Now Diaz.

'Who are you to give orders?' I snapped.

'This comes directly from Washington.'

'We take our orders from Washington now?'

'You do as far as this is concerned. No one is to attempt to kill Klaus Barbie.'

Christine surveyed him coolly. 'Why? What possible reason can you have for keeping that murdering animal alive?'

'Operational reasons.'

'Well, seeing as we're all in this together, perhaps you'd care to share those?'

'I can't. It's top secret.'

'Oh for God's sake. Top secret my arse.'

Christine ripped a cigarette from her packet, stuck it between her lips and inhaled furiously as she lit it.

'Look, all I know is that Barbie could be of use to us at some point so we need to keep him alive for now. Those are my instructions.'

'Of use? How?' I asked.

'I have no idea,' said Diaz.

He was blinking furiously. Always a dead giveaway. He knew that I knew he was lying, but there was nothing more I could say. There was more going on here than I understood, at least for now. Once this was over, I would get to the bottom of it. Right now, we needed to protect Jack as best we could and, in doing so, protect Operation Dragoon.

'Fine,' snarled Christine. 'I can distract Barbie then. At least buy us more time before he gets a chance to parade Jack before this prison guard.'

'How the hell do you propose to do that?'

'Wait and see.'

'I will not damn well wait and see,' said Antoine. 'You're not going anywhere near Barbie. You'll end up in a Gestapo cell too. And worse.'

'It could just work,' I said. 'But we may not get there in time. That car has already left Digne.'

'Then we must leave too.'

Christine's face was set, her eyes on fire.

'Wait,' said Antoine. 'There is a way we can get there ahead of them. The Maquis stationed in the countryside have been supplied with radio sets. We can send them a coded message asking them to hold up any traffic. Especially any black Citroëns. We can't be too explicit but I think they will understand.'

'Good thinking,' I said. 'And I have another idea. Those preliminary bombing raids are already underway, right?'

'Correct,' said Diaz.

'Excellent. In that case, why don't we get them to bomb Barbie's HQ once we're there, on the ground? They bombed his old one after all. If Christine is keeping Barbie busy, we can get Jack and the other prisoners out in the confusion.'

'We can't bomb the building. We'll kill Jack and the other prisoners and probably you too,' said Diaz.

'Not if we're careful. The cells are in the basement, near the front, so we aim for the top and rear of the building. We blast it just enough that the Gestapo have to evacuate.'

'We don't want Barbie dead either.'

'Right,' I said. 'For top-secret reasons.'

He stared me down.

I kept my eyes level with his. 'I assume you can get a message to whoever is coordinating those air raids?'

THE SILENCE BEFORE DAWN

'I can.'

'Then do it. But we need to be in place before they drop those bombs. We have to work out the timing carefully. Christine, this is where you come in, distracting Barbie. That will give me a chance to get into the building and down to the basement just after the first blast. I know the way.'

I would never forget the stairs that led to the basement cells and back up to Barbie's torture salon.

'You'll need these,' said Christine, reaching down and unscrewing the left heel of her shoe. She withdrew a slim metal cylinder from inside the heel, opening it to reveal a set of lock picks.

'Thank you. I left mine behind in Lyon.'

'You know how to use them?'

'Of course. Gentleman Johnny taught me at Beaulieu.'

He'd also given us all a thorough grounding in explosives. A Glaswegian safe cracker and ex-convict turned instructor, he got his nickname because he was unfailingly polite.

'You're even crazier than I thought,' said Diaz, shaking his head in admiration.

'Maybe. Maybe not. We'll soon find out.'

I looked at their radio operator, the quiet Frenchman who'd parachuted in with the Americans. Just for a moment, I saw Maggie's face transposed onto his. I shook my head. Blinked.

'Be on standby,' I said. 'I'll send a message as soon as we know the exact timing.'

'Remember, we have to keep Barbie alive at all costs.'

'Fine. If those are our orders.'

'Those are your orders and mine. Good luck.'

SIXTY-ONE

Suzanne replaced the telephone in its receiver. The fair-haired man opposite regarded her coolly.

'Who was that?' asked Harry Stengritt.

'Someone who needed help with a cat,' said Suzanne. 'People know that I take in stray animals.'

'Animals or people?'

Suzanne studied the handsome man in front of her. His French was immaculate, as was his appearance. He was clearly educated and spoke in a well-modulated voice, unlike some of his more brutal colleagues. She wondered how such a man could act as a lieutenant to someone like Klaus Barbie. But then, war made beasts of the best of men.

'I prefer animals to people,' she said.

'Yes, I would imagine that, in your line of work, you probably do.'

'We have never had the pleasure of your company here before,' said Suzanne. 'To what do I owe the honour of this visit?'

Stengritt smiled, his thin face appearing almost boyish. He must have been in his early thirties, Suzanne guessed. He probably had a nice wife at home. They all did. But in Stengritt's case, he also had a notoriously beautiful French mistress. She could understand why. Stengritt wasn't only handsome, he was persuasive.

'I wanted to talk to you about the unfortunate incident that occurred here three days ago,' said Stengritt.

'What incident would that be?'

Stengritt was no longer smiling. 'A man was shot dead in the corridor out there. You don't forget something like that in a hurry.'

'Ah yes. Horrible.' Suzanne gave a tiny shudder. 'What would you like to know?'

'Had you ever seen this man here before? Or the one who shot him?'

'No. They were new clients. We have so many at the moment, what with things changing all the time. You know how it is. Troops moving across the country. People too.'

This time, she offered him an enigmatic shrug.

His grey eyes didn't waver. 'I don't suppose you keep a record of your clients?'

'We ask them to sign in of course. But I can guarantee you that the vast majority do not sign with their real names. I am sure you understand.'

'Of course.'

She wondered if he was softening her up for Barbie or just making his own enquiries. Stengritt was the brains and Barbie the brute, although he was no intellectual slouch either. What was it that made these men so unquestioningly loyal to Hitler and his vicious diktats? If others in his regime could tear off their blinkers and see what a monster the Führer was then why not them? Already there had been attempts on Hitler's life. There was talk of insurrection. And yet the Germans were still here, in Lyon, wielding their iron fists of power over Pétain's compliant government. It was a travesty.

'Did you manage to find out who he was?' asked Suzanne.

'That is why I am here, Madame. His identity papers turned out to be false. We believe that he might even have been English.'

Suzanne raised her eyebrows in a perfect expression of astonishment. 'An Englishman? But how?'

'You tell me.'

'I'm afraid I did not speak with the man or even see him before the... ah... tragic incident. My receptionist greets our visitors. I am usually in here, taking care of administration.'

'And stray animals.'

'The occasional stray animal, yes. Our clients are not so different to those animals. They too need sanctuary and affection, even the worst of them. If this man was an Englishman then he was far from home and probably lonely. Perhaps he came here for company or for reassurance. It's not just about sex, you know. In fact, it is rarely about sex. What most want is a listening ear and a soothing voice. The physical act, well, as I am sure you know, that is just a brief release.'

This time it was she who held Stengritt's gaze, looking for his reaction. To his credit, he tilted his head in acknowledgement of her words.

'I believe you are correct, madame. But that does not bring me any closer to discovering the true identity of the man who died in your corridor.'

Suzanne sat back in her chair and spread her hands. 'I am so sorry that I cannot help you. It is very sad, especially for his family who will wonder what has happened to him. But there is nothing more I can do. I wish I could.'

Stengritt reached for the hat he'd placed on Suzanne's desk. The gesture wasn't lost on her.

'Well, if you think of anything then please contact me. Or if you hear something. You know where we are.'

'I do indeed.'

She was on her feet before he was, determined not to give an inch.

Harry Stengritt looked up into her face. 'It has been a pleasure making your acquaintance, madame. I have heard much about you.'

'And I you, monsieur.'

She handed him her card. 'Should you need to reach me. Although, of course, you know where I am too.'

'Indeed I do, madame. Indeed I do.'

Suzanne continued to stare at her hands long after Stengritt had left, her fingernails involuntarily tapping out a tattoo that she hated to hear. It wasn't fear for herself but for the others that made her tremble, the men and women who fought day after day in any way they could to defeat the enemy within. The hotel managers and concierges. The restaurant owners and receptionists. Then there were the foreign agents who'd come to help France in her hour of need, brave women like Marianne and Christine, brave Frenchwomen like Juliette. All of them prepared to lay their lives on the line to rid France and Europe of men like Stengritt. If he arrested her, as she was sure he would, then she would have to withstand whatever they did to her to protect them.

She unlocked her desk with the small key that hung from her concealed belt and withdrew a slim journal along with the papers she kept filed in manila folders. The journal was full of her personal notes and observations. Details of agents, operations and members of the Maquis, all meticulously recorded along with her impressions of them. She had been careful to always use codenames and aliases along with false addresses but she couldn't risk it falling into Nazi hands.

The files were the ones she kept on her clients, on their real identities if she discovered them and on what she and her girls had been able to obtain from them by way of information. They were even more dangerous than her journal, stuffed as they

were with the names of SS officers, policemen, leading industri-
alists and members of the Vichy government. She read them
through carefully one last time and then rose from her desk.

She made sure her office door was locked before carrying
her incriminating bundle to the fireplace. As she kneeled and
placed the papers in the grate, she caught sight of a name.

Jack Hamilton.

The first flame ate into his name, turning it to ash along
with all the details of his operation. The real details. She
wondered if Marianne had guessed the truth by now. She
hoped so. Those two belonged together, no matter what Marianne thought. She had loved only twice in her life. Loved the
first man so much she'd married him. But he was far away now,
somewhere in Poland, sent to a labour camp for his part in
publishing what the Germans called subversive material. She
knew in her heart that she would probably never see him again.

Tales of what happened in those camps filtered back via
agents who'd escaped Poland and Germany and made their way
to London. It made her own work all the more important.

Then there was Edward – the other one she'd loved and lost
to the Nazis. The Germans might take her too, but they
wouldn't take anyone else if she could help it.

As she watched the flames rise, licking at the papers,
cremating them, Suzanne smiled. One more victory to SOE and
the Resistance.

Once the ashes were cold, she swept them from the grate,
emptying them out of the window. Below, in the street, she
could hear a cat yowling. She hoped that Marianne had heard
the warning in her words to stay away. She would handle this
on her own.

She sat, perfectly composed, running the names through
her head, committing as much of the information in her papers
as she could to memory.

A tap on her door roused Suzanne from her reverie. The

receptionist stood there, the look on her face telling Suzanne everything she needed to know.

'They're back, madame,' she said. 'I told them to wait but they insisted.'

'I see.' Suzanne rose and smoothed her skirt. 'It's not your fault. Show them in.'

Before the receptionist could do so, a couple of men barged past her and into the room.

'Madame Suzanne Rousseau?'

'Yes.'

'You are under arrest. You must come with us.'

'On what charge?'

Over their shoulders, she glimpsed Stengritt, his hat now firmly in place.

'On charges of spying and consorting with the enemy while aiding the Resistance.'

'Then I would like to call my lawyer.'

'Please do,' said Stengritt. 'I can assure you he will be of no use.'

She straightened her spine while she made the call, turning her back on the Nazis in a show of defiance.

'It is Suzanne. I have been arrested by the Gestapo.'

A silence at the other end. 'I will be there immediately,' said the doctor, safe in his surgery. For now. 'Where are they taking you?'

She repeated the question to Stengritt.

'To the Place Bellecour,' he replied. 'Hauptsturmführer Barbie is looking forward to meeting you.'

They were taking her straight to the Butcher himself.

'I am sure he is,' said Suzanne, reaching for her coat.

She took a last look at her office, nodded to the receptionist hovering anxiously and smiled at Stengritt.

'Lead the way,' she said. 'I am ready.'

SIXTY-TWO

We roared away from the chateau, Juliette at the wheel of the jeep while the rest of us rode shotgun. I could see Antoine's knuckles whitening as he clung to the door handle. Juliette hurled the car at the bends in the road, the tyres screeching as we rounded them, picking up even more speed when we hit a straight run. Mercifully, the road was all but empty, the early morning farm traffic long since gone. I prayed that a certain black Citroën wasn't long gone too. We were at least sixty kilometres closer to Lyon than Digne. We should just about outrun them with any luck.

All of a sudden, Juliette's foot hit the brake even as I shouted, 'Watch out!'

A tree lay across the road ahead, blocking it completely. We skidded to a halt a few feet from its branches and reached for our guns. It could simply be a fallen tree, but it could equally be an ambush. The numbers of maquisards were swelling by the day, with thousands now camped out in the countryside, but among those were some who saw this as an opportunity to rob and plunder.

As Juliette got out of the car, keeping the door between her and the tree, a voice called out, 'Madame, it's you.'

There was the sound of scrambling, stones skittering across the road in front of us and then three men appeared, one of whom I vaguely recognised.

'François, my friend, what are you doing here?' cried Juliette.

He flung his arms around her in a rough embrace. 'I got your message,' he replied. 'I have a radio, see.'

He proudly flourished it.

I remembered now where I'd seen François last – in the great hall of the chateau, busily taking stock of supplies. He was one of Juliette's most stalwart men.

He nodded at Antoine and clasped his hand in a brief embrace.

'Give us a hand,' he said.

He gestured to his men to help, and together they heaved the tree to the side of the road.

'*Voilà*, my friends,' he said, bowing low. 'You may meet more of us on the road ahead, but they all know you. You will be perfectly safe.'

Safer than we would be once we reached Lyon, that was for sure.

'Are we the first car you've stopped today?' I asked.

'There was a farmer's van about an hour ago. We let him through. Apart from that, yes.'

'So no black Citroën?'

'Assuredly not. I would remember that.'

'You are all in place along this route?' said Antoine.

'All present and correct. We are ready for those Nazi pigs.'

'I'm sure you are,' said Antoine. He was one of them, a maquisard too. He understood these men and women and their burning hatred for the Boches. 'It may help if you know who you are looking out for and why.'

François' eyes gleamed. 'Tell me.'

'There is a prison officer being brought right now from Digne to Lyon in a black Citroën. If he gets there, it will be very bad for us and for one of our men they have taken prisoner. I cannot explain further, but if you could make sure you delay him permanently then that would be helpful. But you need to proceed with the utmost caution. We cannot risk alarming the Germans or they may harm this prisoner.'

'Just the one black Citroën?'

'As far as we know, yes,' I said.

'In that case, I have an idea,' said François. 'In fact, you could help. They are more likely to believe you than one of us.'

He gestured to the same three men who were standing with him, grubby and worn after days camping out in the countryside.

'You are, shall we say, a little more presentable than us.'

'I don't understand,' I said.

'It is easy,' said François. 'We can kidnap this prison officer and those with him. We then substitute our men, taking their uniforms. This way, the Gestapo will not become suspicious when the car does not arrive. You would be perfect to take the place of this officer, Antoine. They will not look too closely at the other occupants of the car.'

'A brilliant plan.'

'I agree,' said Antoine. 'It means I will be right there to help you.'

'Indeed.'

'Come. We must prepare.' François nodded towards the tree-lined verge. '*Au revoir, mes amis.*'

'We'll see you in Lyon, Antoine.'

He was already heading into the trees with the maquisards, but he turned and raised a hand. I ran over to him and grabbed it.

'Thank you,' I said. 'For everything.'

'I do what I have to do,' he said. 'The same as the rest of us. The same as you, Marianne.'

His eyes were bleak, his expression the same. I wondered if he would ever forgive me for doubting him. If I would ever forgive myself.

'Marianne, come on.'

I climbed back in the car.

'To Lyon,' I said. 'Let's go get the Butcher.'

'I vote we ignore what that stupid Yank said.' Christine blew smoke from the back seat, her legs sprawled across it. 'We should kill that bastard while we have the chance. Claim it was an accident.'

'I second that,' I said.

'That makes three of us,' said Juliette.

A road sign flashed past. *Lyon 5 kilometres.*

Not long now. Not too far until we were back in the beast's lair. Or at least, that was what it felt like.

'I'm going to enter the city from the east,' said Juliette. 'Through the suburbs. We can leave the car somewhere quiet and proceed on foot. I suggest we go to that restaurant you mentioned, Christine. Restaurant Daniel. The proprietor is part of the local Resistance, no? Hopefully he can make contact with André for us.'

'Perfect.'

Everything in me was screaming to drive straight to the Place Bellecour and stage a daring rescue, but there would be time enough for that. Right now, caution was our watchword. We had less than thirty-six hours until Dragoon was launched. We couldn't afford to blow it now, not even if lives were at stake.

If Jack died, part of me would die too. I knew that and I accepted it. Far better to live with that kind of love than die having never experienced it. So yes, I would sacrifice him if necessary. If it meant many more lives could be saved. But in doing so, I would sacrifice myself as well. It was, as Juliette said, the price of war. A price I was prepared to pay.

SIXTY-THREE

We peered through the restaurant windows. The door was locked and the sign proclaimed it closed, but there were coffee cups strewn on several of the tables and a newspaper laid out on one, open at the page where someone had abandoned it. Either Monsieur Daniel's housekeeping was slipping or he'd closed his restaurant in a hurry. My money was on the latter.

I knocked again and thought I saw a movement at the back of the restaurant. Then a head appeared around a door at the back. I glanced over my shoulder. There was no one else in the street. I waved and beckoned to the man.

After another minute's hesitation, he moved across the restaurant and unlocked the door.

'Monsieur Daniel? Do you remember me?' asked Christine. 'These are my friends.'

He looked at Christine. He was hardly likely to forget her. But we had no code words set up, and the last time he'd seen her, she was with the Gestapo. I watched his face as he came to a decision. He stood aside.

'But of course, madame. Please come in.'

He looked up and down the street before locking the door

once more and leading us through the door at the back into the kitchen.

'The Gestapo are rounding people up,' he said. 'I fear they are getting information out of some poor soul they are torturing. At least, that is what I heard.'

I glanced at the others.

'We need your help,' I said. 'Klaus Barbie is holding one of our agents. A man called Jack. He's already tortured him for a couple of days. We have to get him out of there before he reveals vital information. Plans that are top secret but could end this war in France once and for all.'

Monsieur Daniel hadn't survived the Occupation this far by being slow to grasp a situation.

'I see,' he said. 'In that case, I will send for André.'

Twenty minutes later, André was standing in the restaurant kitchen along with two other men.

'André, it's so good to see you. I'm worried about Suzanne. Has something happened?'

His lugubrious face sank deeper into its own creases. 'She was arrested earlier today and taken to Place Bellecour.'

'I knew it,' I said. 'I spoke to her on the telephone. She sounded odd, like she was trying to warn me or tell me something.'

'They were probably already there. Harry Stengritt himself came for her. I believe they are keeping her there, in the cells, along with your agent.'

'We have a plan to get them out,' I said. 'But first we have to stop a certain prison officer from reaching Lyon. Then we rescue Jack and Suzanne.'

'A prison officer?'

'From Digne. If he gets here, he'll be able to tell Barbie that he has the wrong man. There are maquisards out on the road between Digne and Lyon who will attempt to kidnap the prison officer and his companions. They will then take their place. Christine here will distract Barbie long enough to stop him torturing Jack any further until these men arrive. She'll also keep him occupied until the Allies bomb the Gestapo HQ this evening at 1800 hours. I'll extract Jack and the other prisoners from the building. To make all this happen, we need your help.'

André's gaze swivelled from me to Christine and back again.

'You're crazy,' he said. 'Barbie is busy interrogating this agent of yours. He won't allow you to interrupt.'

'Too bad,' I said. 'It's all we've got.'

'I have no doubt that Barbie will see me,' added Christine.

'How can you be so sure?'

'Last time he saw me, he woke up in a bed we had evidently shared. A bed in which he'd passed out rather than perform. He won't want anyone else hearing what really happened in that hotel room. Klaus Barbie is a monster, but he's an intelligent one. He knows he cannot lose face in front of his subordinates.'

'You really think he will care?'

'Yes, I do. Because like most monsters, he has a fragile ego. I spent enough time with him to know that his family background has left him deeply insecure. It's my job to get these things out of people. Barbie is no different to any of the others. He has his Achilles heel.'

André sighed. 'I know there is no changing your mind, but you must proceed with the utmost caution. We cannot afford to lose people like you.'

He included us all in his shrug.

I smiled. 'You won't.'

'Do we know anything about those cells? The layout and how they are constructed?' asked Monsieur Daniel.

'There are four of them,' I said. 'All in one row. Barbie kept me there before Suzanne got me out.'

I instinctively touched my shoulder, feeling his fingers digging into it.

Monsieur Daniel looked at my hand, then at me. 'I am sorry to hear that.'

One of the men with André spoke up. 'The cells were meant as a temporary solution when the Gestapo moved from the École de Sante Militaire. As such, their construction is not that solid. The doors are ordinary doors rather than the steel they used at the École and the locks on them standard along with bolts. The Gestapo rely on their prisoners being too beaten to be able to try to escape.'

The man turned towards me as he spoke. That was when I saw his left eye. It was half-closed, the socket deformed and the eyeball within it milkily sightless.

'Thank you,' I said. 'That's extremely useful to know.'

I didn't need to ask how he came by his information – I remembered only too well.

'Once the bombs have dropped, we'll use the chaos to get the prisoners out, but we need your help to provide covering fire,' I said. 'And to keep the Gestapo at bay after they've evacuated the building. Give them a taste of their own medicine.'

André's eyes gleamed. 'It will be a pleasure. We can station as many *résistants* as possible on rooftops around the Place Bellecour. Then when the Germans come running, we start firing.'

'Snipers? That will get them hopping.'

'It's easier for our people to escape across the rooftops and back through the traboules. The Boches won't know what has hit them.'

'Monsieur Daniel,' I said. 'May we use this as our operational base? You're so close to the Place Bellecour. It's ideal.'

'But of course,' he said. 'My restaurant is at your disposal. I will put a note on the door to say that, owing to a family emergency, we are closed for today. In any case, the Gestapo should be too busy to come for dinner tonight.'

'Thank you. We'll bring the prisoners here once we've got them out of the building.'

'I will need a couple of hours,' said André. 'To gather my people and get everything in place.'

'And I want to stake out the building. Make sure that Antoine and the others arrive in place of that prison guard. Let's rendezvous here at 1700 hours.'

'I'll set off now then,' said Christine. 'I can keep Barbie busy that long.'

She smoothed down her dress and patted her hair.

'Don't worry,' she added. 'I still have my spike in the other heel. I wish I'd used it when he was lying there out cold.'

'If you had, you would be dead by now, along with the rest of us. Their reprisals for the ambush have been bad enough. Imagine what they would have done had you killed Klaus Barbie.'

'We may yet find out.'

SIXTY-FOUR

The guard on the front desk was adamant.

'You cannot see anyone without an appointment,' he sniffed.

'I have already told you, this is an emergency,' snarled Christine, equally intransigent. It was the only way to handle them – be twice as arrogant. 'Hauptsturmführer Barbie will be extremely upset when he finds out that you wouldn't even tell him I was here,' she added. 'When I have dinner with him at the Grand Hotel tonight, I will be sure to describe you very clearly to him.'

The soldier blinked at the mention of the Grand Hotel. Doubtless, gossip had filtered down the ranks.

'Wait here one moment,' he said before disappearing into a back office.

Christine took the opportunity to look around the foyer. The stairs that led down from it must go to the basement. There was no door closing them off from the foyer, a relic no doubt of the haste with which the Gestapo had requisitioned what had once been an ordinary office building. Or perhaps they didn't care that their prisoners were so accessible. People were far too afraid to challenge their authority even now, when rumours of an imminent Allied victory swirled.

The guard returned and looked her up and down. She didn't like the knowing sneer that had taken up residence on his already smug face.

'Hauptsturmführer Barbie will see you,' he said. 'Go up those stairs to the second floor and someone will meet you there.'

She looked at the staircase that ascended to the left of the reception desk. There appeared to be no one guarding it save this odious individual. All the better for Marianne when she slipped into the building. Every organisation had its weakness, just as every man did. And complacency filled the corridors of the Gestapo headquarters. They simply didn't expect anyone to challenge them.

That was what happened when you ruled by fear. You grew lazy in your arrogance. Take the man who met her on the second floor and directed her to follow him to Barbie's office. He didn't even bother to check her identity, so sure was he that she posed no threat.

'Sit here.'

He pointed to a hard-backed chair beside a desk where a hatchet-faced secretary pointedly ignored her. He evidently liked to keep business and pleasure strictly separate.

Christine bestowed her most charming smile upon the woman. 'Lovely afternoon, isn't it?'

The woman looked at her as if she'd suggested something obscene, muttered under her breath and carried on bashing at her typewriter. Christine would have given anything to peek over her shoulder and see what was causing her to concentrate so fiercely, but she knew better than to break out of character. Instead, she carried on smiling regally even when Barbie's lackey reappeared.

'You may enter,' he said.

She felt like clicking her heels and saluting but instead marched into the lion's den, making sure to keep her shoulders back and her head high as she stalked.

'Countess, this is a surprise.'

Barbie's tone was dry, his expression inscrutable. His smile, if you could call it that, barely exercised the muscles on either side of his mouth.

Christine took a breath.

'A pleasant one I hope,' she said as she ignored the seat in front of his desk and sashayed over to the sofa set in front of a low coffee table.

He looked at her for a moment, then stood and moved to sit in the armchair beside it, just as she'd known he would. It was higher and so gave him the illusion of an advantage.

'I'm parched,' she said. 'I've just this moment returned to Lyon. I don't suppose I could have some water?'

'Certainly.' He turned to his lackey, still hovering by the door. 'Water for my guest and perhaps some coffee as well?'

'That would be wonderful,' murmured Christine.

The moment they were alone, she seemed to melt into the sofa.

'I'm sorry,' she said. 'It's been quite a time. My poor mother was taken ill. Appendicitis. Happily, she is recovering well from the operation.'

'I see,' he said. 'When did this happen?'

'Not long after you – we – were disturbed at the hotel. I received a message that Maman was in the hospital and to come at once. There was no time to do anything but rush to her side.'

'Of course,' he said, nodding to his secretary, who had appeared with a tray. 'Leave that there, Hilde.'

'You don't want me to pour?'

'No thank you.'

Hilde retreated to her typewriter, no doubt to ruminate over her master and this interloper.

'So,' said Christine, 'here we are.'

'Yes, indeed. Here we are.'

He regarded her, unblinking, and her heart stilled in her chest. Then he leaned forward and placed his hand on her knee.

'It's good to see you,' he said. 'I was worried about you.'

Christine was so taken aback she was lost for words for a second. She hadn't bargained for any show of softness or affection from Barbie. Quite the reverse.

'You were?'

'Yes. I wondered if something had happened. I couldn't imagine why you would suddenly disappear like that.'

A thought flashed across her mind, a memory of Barbie picking up the stray cat in the Place Bellecour only metres from this very room. He had stroked that cat lovingly, yet she had found the display repulsive. Maybe it was because he could turn so fast.

Barbie glanced at his watch, and she caught sight of the dark hairs against the pale skin of his wrists. They were nearly as coarse as the hair on his torso, which covered his chest, spreading down in a V towards his belly button and then fanning out once more to curl around his genitals. It took all her willpower to push the thought of his penis from her head, lying limp and useless among those strands. Or maybe she should think about it to give herself strength. Lord knows, she needed it right now.

She itched to look at her watch too, but that would be a mistake. The aerial bombardment was planned for 6 p.m., at the end of the working day. It was also the time when the guards in the basement changed their shift. She guessed it was around 4 p.m. now. Perhaps a few minutes earlier. Barbie was probably starting to wonder where his man from Digne had got to by now.

She picked up the coffee pot. 'Would you like some more, my dear?'

She was affecting a cosiness she didn't feel, hoping it would transpose itself to Barbie.

It appeared her efforts were in vain.

'No. Thank you.'

A slight correction as he remembered his manners. At least he was still making the effort. That stood in her favour.

He looked at his watch again, his irritation visible. She noticed a cut on one of his knuckles that was starting to bruise.

'You've hurt yourself,' she said.

'What? Oh this. It's nothing.'

'Let me see.' She took the opportunity to cradle his hand in hers even as her stomach lurched.

He snatched it back. 'I said it's nothing.'

She drew herself up, pointedly sipping her coffee.

'I apologise,' he said. 'It has been a difficult day.'

She instantly recognised the note in his voice. There was an immense loneliness in so many men and especially a man like Barbie, who had to run an operation like this on foreign soil. Not that she felt sorry for him. Not in the slightest. But it gave her another point of leverage and she leaped to use it.

'Tell me,' she said. 'I'm a good listener.'

'You are, aren't you?' he said, his eyes assessing.

'You know, Hans used to say I was his sounding board. He said it helped that, as a woman, I could never quite understand the weight on his shoulders. It meant I could listen without judgement – that's what he used to say.'

If any man, never mind a general, had ever said such a thing to Christine, she would have shot him down on the spot, but it struck the right chord with Barbie.

'It is a huge burden,' he said. 'I have so many decisions to make every day. If I don't make the right ones, I dishonour the

Führer and the Fatherland. It is always, you understand, for the glory of both.'

She watched the red seep up his neck, hearing his voice rise and rasp.

'I understand,' she murmured.

'Take this man today,' he went on. 'He refuses to talk to me. I know that what he can tell me will help prevent so many deaths of German soldiers. And yet he will not speak. He will not tell me what I need to know. Of course I have to do anything I can to make him do that.'

'Of course you do.'

'They call me the Butcher. I know they do. But that's not what I am. I save lives. I don't take them. These people, they don't understand that it's the vermin who are killing the rest of us. We must purify so we can multiply. There need to be more people like you and I.'

He reached out and took a strand of her platinum hair, stroking it between his fingers.

'Lovely,' he muttered. 'Perfect. As it should be.'

Christine kept her sympathetic smile in place. So she fitted his Aryan ideal. No surprise there. But it was the depths of his delusion that shook her to the core. He sincerely believed he was doing the right thing. He probably believed that even as he tortured people beyond endurance, burning the breasts of agents like her with lit cigarettes, hanging people by their wrists and flailing the flesh from their bones, all in the name of what he deemed purification.

'I enjoyed our night together,' she murmured.

He stopped. Dropped the lock of hair. Had she gone too far?

'So did I,' he said, his eyes averted.

'It was special.'

'You think so?'

There it was, the knell of insecurity beneath the veneer. She pressed home her advantage.

'I know so. Very special. I hope we can do it again.'

'But of course,' he said. 'We will. Very soon.'

'Good.'

She sat back, a kitten inviting a petting. At that moment, there was a discreet knock on his office door, and Hilde entered.

'You asked me to let you know immediately your visitor from Digne arrived,' she said. 'He is here.'

'Thank you.'

Excellent. So far it was running to plan.

'I should go,' murmured Christine, giving him her most coquettish look. She reached out, stroking the fine material of his trousers along his thigh with a featherlight touch. He responded, just as she'd known he would. She held his gaze with one full of promise.

He reached out and stroked her hair again then tightened his grip, twisting it until she felt it begin to tear from her skull.

'Klaus, you're hurting me,' she said.

'You think that's hurting you?'

He slapped her hard across her face. Then did it again.

Tears sprang from Christine's eyes, but she bit her lip and said nothing. He had turned. Why had he turned? She needed to keep calm.

'Get up, bitch,' he snarled. 'You think I believe your stupid story about your mother? I'll get the truth out of you later, but for now you can wait in here.'

He flung open a door from his office that led into a larger salon, bare apart from a single chair and a cabinet, and shoved her through it. She looked around and repressed a shudder. She could only imagine what happened in there. What might happen to her unless she thought fast.

As the door closed behind her, she waited, listening. The cabinet door was slightly ajar. She padded over to it and prised it open. Inside, there were more whips like the one she'd glimpsed on Barbie's desk, a spiked cudgel on a chain and various tools that looked as if they belonged in a dentist's surgery. Barbie's personal torture collection.

Fighting back her rising panic, she retreated to the door, pressing her ear against it.

She could hear his visitor being ushered in. Words exchanged in greeting. She tried to detect if it was Antoine's voice speaking. Surely it was. The maquisards were a ruthless bunch. They would have made short work of kidnapping a prison officer and whoever was with him. Truth be told, they'd probably not stopped at kidnapping, but that was for them to decide.

Their voices rumbled on. It felt like forever. At least in here she could check the time – 4.30 p.m. Right on target.

All at once, more voices. A silence and then one that was raised, shouting. Barbie no doubt. She froze, listening even harder.

Another shout and then a howl of pure agony. Something had gone horribly wrong. Maybe it wasn't Antoine out there after all but the real prison officer and he'd just denounced Jack. There was only one way to find out.

Christine stepped out from her hiding place. 'I'm so sorry,' she said. 'But I need to visit the ladies' room.'

The tableau that greeted her would have sent anyone else screaming. Antoine, dressed in a prison officer's uniform, stood to one side, his arms folded. Another man in an SS uniform stood by the door. On his knees in front of Barbie, a man who had his head bowed but exuded defiance from every pore, even as blood dripped from his chin. Barbie's face was suffused with rage that seemed to explode when he saw her.

'Get out,' he shouted. 'Get out of here, woman.'

She gasped and stepped back inside the side room but not before she'd seen the face of the kneeling man, navy blue eyes meeting hers in what felt like solidarity. She registered it all in the split second before she shut the door once more, hearing Barbie scream at him over and over again, determined to break him one way or another. Barbie trusted no one, believed nothing except the power of his own cruelty. Jack would have to hold fast to his story that he was Claude to make it through alive. Even then, Barbie might consider him expendable, just as he now considered her to be surplus to requirements.

She stared once more at the cabinet in the corner, picturing the whips and cudgels it contained, imagining them slicing through her own flesh, piercing her to the bone.

Pull yourself together, Christine. There's work to be done here. Falling apart wouldn't solve anything. If she could survive that alleyway back in the East End, she could survive anything. Yes, even Klaus Barbie. Whatever it took.

SIXTY-FIVE

I glanced through the shop window at the grey stonework of the Gestapo HQ, then picked up a bolt of cloth, pretending to examine it. The shop was almost directly opposite the building, a few doors along on the opposite side of the street. The perfect vantage point. The cotton fabric slipped, silky smooth between my fingers as I caught a blur of movement out of the corner of my eye. At last. A car arriving at the main door. A black Citroën.

'May I assist you, madame?'

I turned, saw the shopkeeper hovering.

'I... No. No, thank you. I'm just looking.'

The shopkeeper sniffed and retreated behind her counter. I could feel her glare as I peered through the window once more. I was just in time to see uniformed figures mount the steps. Three men in total. I thought I recognised Antoine's lope, his way of holding his head beneath his cap. But I couldn't be sure.

'We also have that in blue.'

I looked at the yellow cloth I'd picked up at random.

'I see. Thank you.'

I adjusted my handbag on my arm and drew myself erect.

This was no time to arouse suspicions. Especially not so close to the Gestapo HQ. For all I knew, this woman earned a nice little side living spying for them.

'I'll take two metres of the yellow and two of the blue.'

The shopkeeper seemed visibly relieved. Perhaps I was mistaken. Maybe this woman simply wanted to make a decent living, a difficult task in such chaotic times.

'Of course,' she said, taking the bolts and measuring out the cloth before cutting it and carefully parcelling it up. It gave me a chance to take another look. They'd disappeared inside the building. The car was still there, parked ostentatiously right outside. It might come in handy later. I made a mental note.

'Thank you, madame.' I picked up my package. 'Have a good day.'

Outside the shop, the street was quiet. For now.

I looked at my watch – 4.25 p.m. Perfect.

I glanced up at the rooftops on either side of the street as I walked away, towards the main square. An hour from now those rooftops would be teeming with *résistants* lying low, waiting for the bombs to drop. That was our signal, theirs and mine. So much could go wrong. The plane could be shot down, flying as it was in broad daylight. Or be delayed. Barbie could lose patience. Might already have done so.

No. Don't think like that. Jack's alive. They're alive.

I was going to get them out. One way or another.

SIXTY-SIX

She was sitting, prim and upright on the chair, when Barbie reappeared. It felt as if an age had passed, although it had been less than an hour. An hour she could only imagine for Jack. She had no idea what state he was in or even if he was alive.

She gripped the side of the chair, ready to throw it at him if necessary. Not that it would make much difference, but at least she would feel like she'd fought back. She looked at Barbie, trying to gauge his mood. It could swing from murderous to mellow in minutes.

'My apologies,' Barbie said stiffly. 'But you interrupted a most important meeting.'

She wanted to laugh out loud and simultaneously cry with relief. A meeting. That was what he called it. At least he appeared to have used up all his rage, although what that meant for Jack didn't bear contemplating.

'It is I who should apologise,' she said, watching his face closely for a reaction. 'I shouldn't have come here. You are at work.'

He ran a hand through his hair. She noticed a fresh welt on

his knuckles. Antoine and Jack were gone, the latter presumably returned to the basement cells. Or worse.

'My working day is nearly done,' he said. 'Have dinner with me.'

My God. He really was a monster. In some ways, he reminded her of her stepfather, swinging from insanity to apparent normality as if nothing had ever happened. The only thing to do was play along. It was a lesson she'd learned far too early.

'I was hoping you'd say that.'

His face brightened. 'You were?'

Strange, too, how this brute could appear so childlike at times. It was as if he'd never accused her of lying to him.

'Of course,' she said. 'I've missed you, Klaus.'

She watched the ego return, puffing him up once more. That moment of vulnerability had been an aberration. Here was the real Barbie.

'I will meet you at the Grand Hotel, usual time,' he said. 'I have some paperwork to finish here.'

Christine thought fast. She needed to keep him occupied a while longer.

'Klaus, this may sound ridiculous but I'm afraid. On my way here, people spat at me in the street. They called me a Nazi lover.'

She dabbed at her eyes with her handkerchief.

'I will have some of my men escort you to the hotel.'

'Thank you, but that will only make it worse.'

She made a play of gathering her things, sliding her capacious bag up her shoulder so she could surreptitiously check the time – 5.53 p.m. She had seven minutes to fill.

'They mentioned you by name, Klaus, these people. Somehow they know that we are... spending time together. They said such horrible things.'

Now she had his attention, just as she'd thought she might. Hit him in the ego every time.

'It is no one's business what I do,' he snapped. 'What exactly did they say?'

'I cannot repeat it. All I know is that it isn't true.'

She could hear him thinking, pride overcoming good sense.

'Tell me,' he said again.

She shook her head.

He took a step, shoving his face into hers. 'Tell me,' he roared.

She shrank back, eyes wide, hiding the surge of triumph that rose from her gut. She had really got to him at last. Perhaps some faint shame over their night together still lingered, doubts curdling his mind.

'I – I must go,' she said.

'Not before you tell me.'

She straightened her shoulders and looked him straight in the eye.

'Is this how you treat everyone, Klaus? As if we are all simply here to do your bidding? That man who was here earlier – you hit him, didn't you?'

She was playing a dangerous game and she knew it. She had to goad him just enough to keep him occupied but not so much he flew out of control again. By her calculation, there were still a few more minutes to go before the bomb was due to be dropped, always provided they were on time.

'That is none of your business.'

'Why? Are you ashamed of it?'

'I am ashamed of nothing. Everything I do is for the glory of the Führer and the Fatherland.'

'What about me? How do I fit into that? Am I also for the glory of the Fatherland?'

She could see a tic gathering pace in his cheek, flickering faster as he struggled to control himself.

'You, madame, serve the Führer and the Fatherland just as I do. Your job is to provide pleasure and support to those of us who are fighting to protect and preserve both.'

'In that case,' she said, 'you'd better sack me because I'm obviously not up to the task.'

She would never know his response because, at that moment, there was an ear-shattering explosion from the rear of the building. The blast ripped through the walls and floors, bringing paintings, furniture and even lumps of ceiling crashing to the carpet where they stood.

Even though she knew it was coming, Christine was still stunned by the force of it.

Another whistle of a second bomb falling. Christine braced herself and looked at Barbie, white with shock, unable to believe that someone was attacking him here, in his inner sanctum. For a split second she thought about just leaving him here to his fate, but then she remembered Diaz's words. They wanted Barbie alive. Those were her orders. And no matter what she felt or thought, she had to obey.

'Come on.'

She grabbed him by the wrist, dragging him towards the door. The lintel was swaying, the second blast sending shudders through the already shattered building.

Crawling on hands and knees, she led him through to the corridor beyond his reception area. Dust and screams filled the air, along with the sound of running feet. Coughing and half-blinded by the swirling dust and smoke, Christine tried to make out the stairwell.

'Sir, over here,' shouted someone.

She felt someone push past her. Barbie. Staggering towards the outstretched hands of his officers. Good. Let him run. She would catch up with him later.

She pulled the gas mask from her bag and tugged it on.

Now she could breathe and, even better, get down the stairs in one piece.

People surged past her as she made her way down. No one was the slightest bit interested in a woman in a gas mask. They were all far more concerned with saving their own skins.

She pushed through the crowd surging out of the main door, heading instead for the basement, instinctively freezing at another long, whistling sound as the final bomb fell.

She braced herself as if she were on a boat, letting her knees sag and dropping her weight forward. Bodies cannoned into her, more of the rats leaving the sinking ship.

She was on her hands and knees once more, using a combat crawl to speed as fast as she could to the top of the basement stairs. A crash as the chandelier in the centre of the entrance lobby hit the marble floor, splintering into a thousand pieces. Cries of pain as the flying glass embedded into the flesh of the fleeing Gestapo.

Good, thought Christine, rising to her feet and snatching up a pistol one of the fleeing Germans had dropped in their haste.

She ran down the stairs, holding the gun in front of her, ready to bring down any guards who remained.

Halfway down, the smoke and dust began to clear. By the time she reached basement level, the air was almost clear. She pulled off her gas mask and scoped the corridor, searching for Marianne.

There was no one to be seen.

SIXTY-SEVEN

I scrambled down the stairs, keeping one hand on the wall to guide me, eyes streaming in spite of my gas mask. The cells were to the left, the guardroom to the right. The lights were out, the electricity lines blown.

I pulled out my lockpick as I stumbled towards the cells, my eyes beginning to adjust to the gloom. I could make out four doors, each with a lock and padlock along with a bolt.

I peered through the observation window into the first. Empty.

Through the second, I could see a figure huddled on a bunk. I rapped on the door as hard as I could. The figure stirred. I had no idea if it was Jack or not, but I had to get the door open.

The lockpick rattled in my hand. I tried to take a steadying breath, working as fast as I could, jiggling gently.

'Eureka,' I muttered under my breath as the padlock gave. Now for the door itself. This one was harder, and it took a couple of tries.

'The steadier the hand, the easier it gives.'

I could almost hear Gentleman Johnny in my ear, sorrowful

Glaswegian tones implying that a woman shouldn't be troubling her pretty fingers with such a task.

'Well, bugger me,' I said with satisfaction as the lock gave and I shoved the door open.

'Come on.' I grabbed the figure on the bunk by the arm, shaking it. 'You have to get of here.'

The arm under my fingers was limp. I shook it again. The man lifted his head, and I gasped.

'Edward?'

He stared at me, unseeing.

He's alive. My God. He's alive after all. Have to get him out of here. Get him to safety. Edward. Alive. Get a grip, Marianne.

'Edward, it's me. Marianne. Can you hear me?'

Something flitted across his face, the faintest dawning. 'Marianne?' he croaked.

'Yes. Yes, it's me. Get up. We must hurry.'

That was when I caught sight of his hands, bent and broken, dangling uselessly from wrists that were similarly damaged. His spirit, though, was still intact, shining out from a face that had been beaten almost to a pulp.

I helped him to his feet and hauled him towards the door, still numb with disbelief. He stumbled through, his legs almost giving way beneath him. There was no time to take him all the way. I had to get the others.

'Go on. Up the stairs. Get out of the building as fast as you can.'

I pushed him gently in the direction of the stairs and turned to the other doors.

The second attempt was easier, my fingers faster and more confident. As I worked the lock, I felt eyes upon me and looked up to see a woman staring through the observation window.

'Suzanne?'

I shoved this door open too and she fell upon me.

'Marianne. Oh thank God. What is happening?'

'The Allies have just bombed the building. All part of our plan. Go. You need to get out. Follow Edward. He's just ahead of you.'

'Edward?' She stared at me.

I nodded towards the exit. 'Help him.'

I was already moving to the final door. Jack had to be in here. No time for lengthier explanations.

I worked the rest of the picks, letting out a cry of triumph as the door gave too. Jack was already halfway through as I flung it open.

'Come on,' I said. 'Follow me.'

As we mounted the stairs, I could see Suzanne and Christine shouldering Edward between them, half-dragging him up the stairs to street level. The foyer was empty, shattered glass crunching under our feet as we staggered across it.

'Wait,' I cried. And then: 'Down!'

From outside, I could hear repeated rounds of gunfire and then the unmistakable sound of a bazooka blast as it hit the building.

'They're firing at us,' said Jack.

'They must think we're already out.'

I looked around, searching for another exit, but we were trapped, rubble blocking the way to the rear of the building which, in any case, had been blasted to bits. If we walked outside now, machine-gun fire from either side could mow us down as easily as another blast from the bazooka. I had no way of communicating with the maquisards ranged on the rooftops around the square and on the ground. We had a couple of guns between us and that was it. There was only one way out. I pulled my white handkerchief from my pocket and tied it to my wrist.

'Follow me,' I said.

SIXTY-EIGHT

'Hold your fire!' I shouted.

The cry ran through the ranks on the rooftops, spreading to the groups on the ground below. I caught sight of Juliette on top of the building opposite, gesturing to the men to hold back.

All of a sudden, Christine sent a volley of bullets in the direction of the black Citroën parked a few metres from the building.

'What the hell are you doing?'

That's when I saw the two German soldiers crouched beside the car, their guns aimed at us. I aimed at the soldiers too, letting out a satisfied hiss as one dropped, sprawling across the ground while his companion darted behind the car and began to run. I caught him mid-stride, his arms flinging up in the air, sending his weapon flying.

'Gotcha.'

Figures ran towards us. This time, our men, Antoine and André.

'Get them out of here,' I cried.

'Come with us,' said André, shouldering Edward as Antoine took Jack.

'You go. I'll catch up with you.'

My mind screamed at me to go with them but I had a job to finish.

'The square,' I shouted to Christine. Together, we darted along the street to the junction where it led to the main square, keeping our backs to the wall and our wits on high alert.

As we emerged cautiously into Place Bellecour, we could see the Gestapo trapped by the statue in its centre, holding off the *résistants* as the net tightened around them. We had snipers on all the rooftops around the square and ground forces firing at them from their cover under the trees. I had no idea if Barbie was there or if he'd escaped. It was impossible to see through the melee.

I was just training my gun on the group by the statue when three armoured cars shot into the square, coming to a halt right where I was aiming. They were swiftly followed by the rumble of a tank approaching. Reinforcements were arriving. Soon we would be outnumbered. It was time to retreat. This wasn't the time for a gunfight. We'd achieved what we'd set out to do.

Instead of firing at the Germans, I fired into the air three times, our prearranged signal to withdraw.

'Another time,' I vowed as I watched the Gestapo scramble to safety in their armoured vehicles. 'Come on, Christine.'

We retreated up the street along which we'd come before breaking up and heading separately to the restaurant by roundabout routes. I tugged at my skirt as I strode, trying to appear as if I was merely going about my business. Not that there were too many Gestapo left to care. They were all far too busy having an attack of the vapours. Like all bullies, they were mostly cowards, especially when the tables were turned, and with any luck, Dragoon would turn those tables permanently. Just a few more hours to go. I wanted to punch the air with my fist. We'd done it. Jack was alive. And so, unbelievably, was Edward. Time enough to get to the bottom of it all later. Right now, I had to make our rendezvous.

The restaurant door was still locked, the 'Closed' sign in place. I walked straight past it, slipping into the alleyway that ran behind and through the courtyard, rapping three times on the kitchen door. I waited a second and then knocked just once. This time the door opened and Monsieur Daniel stood there.

'Thank goodness,' he said, locking the door behind me.

On the kitchen worktops, weapons were piled high. The maquisards had clearly been busy gathering them up.

'Where's Jack?' I asked Antoine, who was busy placing ammunition into boxes as fast as Christine could count it.

He nodded towards the restaurant. Edward was slumped on a chair, being tended to by Suzanne. I reached out and stroked his hair, soft beneath my fingers, my heart constricting at the sores I could see on his skull.

Suzanne glanced up at me. 'He'll be OK,' she said, holding a glass to his lips.

I left him in her capable hands, pushing open the door that led to the restaurant. There, splashing water on his face from the tiny basin, was Jack. I picked up a towel and carefully dabbed it dry, trying to avoid the bruises.

'You made it.'

He smiled. 'Of course I did.'

'Oh, Jack. I'm so sorry.'

I could feel his chin graze my cheek, his lips searching for mine.

'Sorry for what?' he murmured.

'For doubting you.'

'You had every right to doubt me. At least it shows I'm good at what I do.'

'That's true. Very good, as it happens.'

'You think so?'

'I do.'

'Break it up, lovebirds. We need you back here.' André's good-humoured tones filtered through from the kitchen. 'You're taking some of the ammunition with you,' he added. 'To give to the maquisards en route back to your chateau. We need the rest to fight the good fight here.'

'We can't leave without Juliette,' I said.

At that moment there were three gentle taps on the door, followed by a single one. My heart rose as I saw Juliette only to sink like a stone when I saw her face.

'What happened?' I asked.

'There are SS troops everywhere. They are blocking both ends of the road outside the restaurant. I got through just in time to see them appear at this end. They must know we are here.'

'Did anyone see you?'

'No.'

'How the hell do they know we're here?'

'They may not,' said Monsieur Daniel. 'They may simply be closing off every street near the Place Bellecour, hoping to trap you.'

'So what do we do now?'

'There is a reason we use this place,' said André. 'Care to show them, Daniel?'

In response, Monsieur Daniel began to push the central kitchen table to one side. Under the table, the tiled floor looked no different until he kneeled and prised up a tiny round lever, painted exactly the same colour as the tiles. He reached behind him for what appeared to be an ordinary broom handle except there was a hook on the end of it, then inserted that hook into the lever and pulled upwards. I stared in fascination as a tiled trapdoor opened, revealing a cellar below.

'I will go first,' said André. 'You all follow. Antoine, I need you to pass down the ammunition.'

One by one we descended the wooden steps that led to the

cellar, Jack helping Edward down, Antoine bringing up the rear.

'This way.'

André flicked on the torch Monsieur Daniel had given him, and I could see a tunnel leading from the cellar, slightly higher than the top of my head.

'The restaurant used to be a silk workshop,' he explained. 'The workers dug this tunnel so they could access the traboules directly. It leads right into them.'

Sure enough, it did.

We followed the tunnel as the floor began to rise, emerging into one that smelled less musty as fresh air flowed through from outside. Thirty or so minutes later, we were once more looking up at the church where Juliette and I had met up with André among the tombs.

'Inside,' said André, leading us through a side door into the church and then to a lady chapel to the right of the main altar. At the back of the lady chapel was an arched wooden door. André reached under the statue of the Virgin and extracted a key before unlocking it.

Through the door was a priest's robing room. André pulled a priest's cloak over his clothes.

'I will take you out in twos,' he said. 'Gentlemen, put on the spare cloaks. We can hide the ammunition under them. Ladies, there are lay sisters' cloaks here for you. There should be enough.'

I pulled one of the white cloaks around me, tying it tight at the top to conceal my clothing beneath and pulling the hood up over my head so it hid my face. I wrapped Edward's around him, the folds concealing his poor hands and face.

'At a distance, you will pass,' said André. 'All we need to do is get you out of the city centre and to where your vehicles are parked.'

'If my clients could see me now,' quipped Suzanne. Out of

all of us, she looked the most at home in her robes.

The sight of Jack in a priest's cloak would have made me laugh at any other time. Right now, I meekly fell in beside him as instructed by André.

'Do as I do,' he said. 'Walk three metres behind me but do not speak or touch. You ladies must keep your heads bowed.'

'For the first and last time,' I said.

André led us back out into the lady chapel.

'You two come first,' he said to Juliette and Christine. 'The rest of you, wait here. Kneel and look as if you're praying.'

'You never know,' said Christine. 'Those prayers might actually work.'

Edward and Antoine were next, Antoine supporting Edward as if he were an elderly colleague.

I held my breath until André reappeared. Thank God or whoever was watching over us. They'd made it. Now it was our turn.

I did my best to glide beside Jack in sisterly fashion, my fingers working the rosary I'd found in the pocket of my robe. I could see little in my peripheral vision thanks to the hood that almost flopped across my face, apart from the pavement only a few steps in front of me.

It was a relief when André stopped and motioned to us to catch up with him. I threw back my hood and looked about. I had no idea where I was.

'Keep going until you reach a bakery at the corner of this street,' he said. 'There you turn left and left again. Juliette's car is parked at the end.'

Sure enough, the others were waiting for us, Edward already hunched inside the car.

'We are missing one,' said Juliette. 'Where's Suzanne?'

We waited, the minutes ticking past, but there was no sign of André and Suzanne.

Realisation hit me like one of those bombs we'd just

dropped.

'I don't think they're coming,' I said, the words choking in my throat.

'We need to go,' said Jack. 'If we don't leave now, we'll be trapped again. The Germans are sure to extend their search beyond the centre once they realise they can't find us. We have to get out while we can.'

'Just one more minute,' I said.

Five minutes later, I conceded defeat.

'Maybe she went to get her own car instead,' I said, disbelieving the words even as they fell from my mouth. Surely she couldn't have been captured?

'Let's hope so.'

We piled into the sedan, stowing our outfits in the boot alongside the ammunition we'd already concealed under the dirty old blankets that were a permanent fixture. Dusk was falling but we couldn't risk turning on the lights. Instead, Juliette drove as cautiously as she could out of the suburbs, picking up speed once we hit the main road that took us south.

Beside me on the back seat, the man we'd risked everything to save. On my other side, the brother I'd thought was dead. Behind us, people I considered friends that we might never see again. Permeating it all was a sense of exultation. In just a few hours, thousands of men would land on the southern beaches of the Riviera. Our men. With any luck, they would be marching up this very valley within weeks. France would be free of her occupiers, and the Germans would be on the run.

Edward was asleep, exhaustion finally overtaking him. I felt Jack take my hand, his fingers wrapping around mine. I stole a look at his profile, its sharp planes highlighted by the moonlight reflected off the road, hearing the hum of the tyres as they ate up the miles. It was the same as it had always been and yet so very different. We'd been apart so long. So much had happened. Was he still my Jack? Only time would tell.

SIXTY-NINE

15 AUGUST 1944, THE CHATEAU

I looked at him, at that face I almost knew better than my own, my eyes adjusting in the dark so I could take in every feature as if I were stroking each one. He was so familiar to me and yet almost a stranger. The Jack I knew was here, at least physically. His face was the same. His voice was the same. The way he looked at me was the same. And yet everything had changed.

'You're different.'

'So are you.'

Our noses were so close they were almost touching. I pulled back, caressing the pink, star-shaped scar below his ribs. Something else that was new.

'I was lucky,' he said. 'Bullet didn't hit any vital organs.'

'Lucky for me too,' I said, reaching for one of those vital organs, smiling as he moaned.

Later, much later, I sank my cheek into the pillow, cool against my skin. The sheet was rucked around my waist, and I kicked it off, feeling the air caress my sweat-soaked limbs. On this night of all nights, I'd left the shutters open to the breeze. In the far distance, I fancied I could hear the sound of gunfire as our boys took back the south. Though it was still early, by all accounts, Dragoon was a sweeping success. They said that Churchill himself had turned up to watch the landings from the deck of a warship.

'I felt it before,' I said. 'Back in Lyon. But it was so good just to see you and to touch you that it didn't matter.'

'And it does now?'

'Of course not. We were bound to change, you and me. We've seen and done things most people could never imagine.'

'Do you want to tell me about them?'

I trailed a finger down his arm, tracing his bicep, the curve of his elbow crease. 'Some things are best left unsaid, don't you agree?'

'I do.'

'Anyway, I think the only thing that matters is that I never stopped loving you. And wanting you. Forever. If you'll have me.'

He looked at me, his gaze caressing my face. I could feel the silence stretching between us. My stomach lurched. Maybe I'd got it wrong after all. Then he reached his hand round the back of my neck, his fingers threading through my hair, pulling me to him for a kiss that seemed endless and still not long enough.

'Convinced?' he murmured.

'Not quite.'

'How about this then?'

One hand untwined itself from my hair and stroked the length of my spine, his fingers sweeping over my buttocks and then reaching further, deep into me, moving in a rhythm I remembered all too well.

'Don't stop,' I gasped.

He flipped me onto my back and took each nipple in turn into his mouth, savouring them before moving on down, pausing just below my belly button to look up at me, tantalisingly close. I arched my back, feeling the scrape of his chin against my skin.

'I need more convincing,' I murmured.

'If that's what it takes.'

It took more than that of course. So much more. And I loved every second. We fit, Jack and me. So easily and so beautifully. There was no need to say anything else, just to sense and to move and to feel everything rippling through me in wave upon wave of more pleasure than I'd ever known. Of course he was different. I was different too. We'd both been through so much in the time we'd been apart and yet we could let all that go as long as we had one another.

Finally, we lay once more, sweat mingling, limbs entangled.

'I have always loved you,' he said. 'I *will* always love you. Nothing and no one will ever change that.'

'No one?' I teased. 'Not even some blonde bombshell?'

'I don't like blondes,' he said. 'I like fiery brunettes who can fight as well as any man but who are all woman when it counts.'

'Does it count now?'

'What do you think?'

The trouble was there was no time to think. Not then and not in the hours that followed.

My mind let go of the weeks and months on the run, soaring above the burning fields beyond the farmhouse, the fear that Jack was already dead, the elongated shadows of the Gestapo that stalked me along the streets of Lyon, to this moment, this here and now. To Jack.

SEVENTY

17 AUGUST 1944

'Take good care of him,' I said.

The young American saluted. 'We will, ma'am. I promise.'

I pressed my hand against the window of the jeep, bending so I was level with Edward's face. 'I'll see you in England.'

I saw the answering smile in his eyes. His broken jaw didn't permit much more but, for me, it was more than enough.

'Don't worry. They'll look after him,' said Diaz. 'There's a plane waiting to fly him out immediately they get to the airfield. He'll be in England by tonight.'

As soon as he landed, they would take him to the military hospital in Kent where he would be treated for his injuries before being sent to convalesce. They could set his bones and stitch his wounds, but it would take a lot longer to mend the damage to his mind. Edward had said nothing about Barbie or the way he'd tortured him, but it was obvious that his hands had been broken again and again and his nails torn off one by one. As for his wrists, the marks there showed where cuffs had been tightened until they too broke. The one thing that hadn't broken was Edward, at least not enough to give any information or satisfaction to Barbie.

In time, I hoped, he would be back to a semblance of the brother I knew of old. It would be foolish to expect anything more. None of us would ever be the same again. You couldn't go through what we'd seen and done and remain unscarred by the experience.

I felt Jack shift closer to me, his presence alone giving me strength. Together, we watched the jeep disappear down the rutted track that led to the road. It was only when it was finally out of sight that Jack and Diaz dropped their salutes.

'There's just one thing I don't understand,' I said. 'Why did Marcus tell me he was dead? That was just so cruel.'

'I think, in his own way, he was trying to protect you,' said Jack. 'He knew that you'd do anything you could to get Edward out of that cell if you knew he was still alive.'

'He also didn't want you anywhere near Lyon,' added Diaz. 'There wasn't just the risk from Barbie but the fact he might be exposed. I made sure he was out of the way when we actually discussed the plans, and then he went and helped with that urgent message to go to Paris.'

'That message wasn't real?'

'It was real enough, but it was Marcus who got his German masters to send it. All he had to do was send a quick message of his own. He was a skilled radio operator in his own right, remember. He and the Germans knew we were planning something. They just didn't know what. So Marcus hitched a ride with the officers accompanying the convoy. You know what happened after that.'

I did, only too well. And it still hurt in spite of what I now knew. He was my brother after all. And I had killed him. I would have to learn to live with that.

'So you knew about Marcus all along?'

'We suspected he was up to something. His story didn't add up, and his behaviour was odd.'

'I didn't see it. Or rather, I saw what I wanted to see. I

should have realised from the beginning when he turned up at the barn. But I loved him, you know. He was my baby brother. And he suffered in his own way. Now I just have the one to love. I couldn't bear it if I lost Edward too. The real Edward. The one I remember.'

'He's a brave man, your brother,' said Jack. 'And a strong one. He'll be OK. I promise.'

Diaz had tactfully withdrawn inside the chateau. It was just us out here, the sun tickling our faces, all of France stretching at our feet. A free France. At least, that was how it felt.

'I have to find the others, Jack. I need to know what's happened to Suzanne and André, but most of all Maggie. I can't just leave them to the mercy of the Germans.'

'You will,' he said. 'You always do what you say you're going to do. It'll be OK, Marianne, it really will. They're strong, all of them. You'll find them.'

'And what about us?' I asked. 'Will we be OK?'

Jack's eyes met mine. This morning they were as clear as the sky above us.

'What do you think?' he asked.

'I think we'll always be OK,' I said. 'One way or another.'

'I think so too.' He smiled. 'In fact, I think we'll be more than that, don't you?'

Below us, the lavender fields rippled like waves, sending answering ripples of hope through my heart.

A LETTER FROM AMANDA

Thank you for reading *The Silence Before Dawn*. I hope you enjoyed it! There are more books to come in the series, following the same brave women who fought so heroically in this one, so if you'd like to keep updated with all my latest releases, you can sign up at the following link. Your email address will never be shared and you can unsubscribe at any time.

www.bookouture.com/amanda-lees

This book is a love story, mostly to the ordinary women and men whose courage in the face of overwhelming odds was extraordinary. They operated undercover, often alone, fighting one of the most ruthless enemies this world has ever seen. They died alone too.

It was that quiet, lonely courage that called out to me across the years. You know some of their names. Others are less familiar. I devoured all their stories, not just those of SOE agents but members of the Resistance and of the American OSS. They had one thing in common – a strength and spirit that was all too human. At a time when we need genuine heroines and heroes more than ever, these people inspired me, as I am sure they'll inspire you.

The idea that sparked this book came to me during the pandemic. I saw similar stories of ordinary people doing extraordinary things. While writing it, I had to overcome odds that, although nothing like those faced by the characters in the story, still felt insuperable. Thinking of them, and drawing on their courage, kept me going, as I hope it will you, if that's what you need.

Many of the events in this book actually happened. Some of the names I've used are those of people who are important to me. Others are nods to some of those who gave so much to free France, and the rest of the world, from the horrors of war. And then there's the real-life love story that lies at the heart of it. I wrote this book for someone in particular, as well as for all of you.

www.amandalees.com

facebook.com/AmandaLeesAuthor
twitter.com/amandalees

ACKNOWLEDGEMENTS

Acknowledgements must be so weird for the reader – an Oscar speech full of names you don't know and quite a lot of author gush. Yes, there will be gush here, but it's more than merited. Some of these people literally saved my life while writing this. Others gave me the will to go on. And still more reminded me of how much I love what I do. So here we go...

First and foremost, to Lisa and Patrick, my agent and her rock star of a husband, who are always there for me. More than that, Lisa makes the magic happen. As does Zoe, who, along with Jamie and Elena, are the wonderful bunch of people who are CMM. Then there's my constant inspiration, my daughter. I love you and I'm proud of you every single day.

Next, the friends and family who, again, went so far above and beyond for me in ways I will never forget – Julia and Phil, Andrew, Josa, Guy, Nina, Barb, Christian, Jackie and Sam, Marianne and Margaret (the inspiration behind the characters), Claire and, finally, John, who rocks a pair of boxers better than any man I know. There are too many others to mention. Suffice to say, I am lucky enough to have amazing people in my life.

I am also fortunate to have new people in my life from my publisher, Bookouture, especially Susannah, my editor, whose love and enthusiasm for this book and the entire series won me over from the start. Peta, Saidah, Kim, Noelle, Sarah, Jess, Jenny, Alexandra... you are all fabulous. As are your colleagues and Laura, my brilliant copy editor. Thank you for having me.

Above all, thanks to the women and men who served – and gave their lives in service for – their countries and our freedom. We will never forget you.

Lightning Source UK Ltd.
Milton Keynes UK
UKHW011818100922
408656UK00001B/4

9 781803 146874